M000248324

Cold Turkey

Roxanne, Stay Power Reader

Kenny Bonner

Cold Turkey

As told to

Larry Buege

Gastropod Publishing

Marquette, Michigan

Published by Gastropod Publishing, Marquette, Michigan
Copyright © 2013 by Larry Buege

Library of Congress Control Number: 2012953236
ISBN: 978-0-615-72472-0

Printed in America by Globe Printing

To my wife, Nancy
For forty wonderful years

Acknowledgments

It is impossible to name all the individuals who made this prophesy possible, but I must thank Drs. Douglas Chepeha and Theodoros Teknos for removing the cancerous growth on my vocal cord and providing me with a voice that sounds like an Amorous Spotted Slug. The nurses and staff of Helen Newberry Joy Hospital (you know who you are) deserve credit for reading my earliest works and providing encouragement. They are a fantastic group to work for. My brother, Jack, proof-read all my novels and corrected copious spelling errors to make my writing readable. Stacey Willey of Globe Printing provided her expertise and guidance throughout the publishing process.

Several years ago I found an eagle in a public domain clip art collection. In this age of intellectual piracy, public domain is meaningless without knowing the author/artist. I scoured the Internet for over four weeks looking for the artist. I was about to admit defeat when I stumbled on Wendy Hogan hiding in Ontario, Canada. She "fessed up" to being the artist in question and has graciously allowed me to add her goofy-looking eagle to the cover art. (Thank you, Wendy.) Anyone with young children will want to check out Wendy's marvelous web site for children at *kidsturncentral.com*.

Other Novels Awaiting a Sympathetic Publisher

Bear Creek
Miracle in Cade County
Super Mensa
Chogan and the Gray Wolf
Chogan and the White Feather
(See *www.LarryBuege.com*)

Prologue

I was driving home on a misty August evening when I saw it. There in the wash of my headlights, oblivious to the rain, sat an Amorous Spotted Slug. Like all Yoopers, I had heard tales of Amorous Spotted Slugs, but logic and common sense had cast doubt upon their existence. I slammed on my breaks and forced my car into a skid, hoping this would generate sufficient time for the A.S.S. to scamper away from my approaching tires, but it held its ground with that classic "slug in the headlights" look. The A.S.S. was waving a small brown object as if to draw my attention and then it disappeared under my chassis before I could discern the nature of its petition.

After my vehicle skidded to a stop I dashed back hoping that somehow the Amorous Spotted Slug had eluded my tires. But all that remained of the Amorous Spotted Slug was a streak of slime next to a small brown parcel. Using tweezers from the glove box, I carefully retrieved the object. It appeared to be a small book—no, a journal. According to local legend A.S.S. are not only preternaturally wise but also clairvoyant, capable of foreseeing events far into the future. Was the Amorous Spotted Slug trying to warn me of some cataclysmic future event? The A.S.S. had given its life while proffering the wisdom of the journal's contents. It was imperative that I continue the Amorous Spotted Slug's mission and convey its knowledge to the world. I returned home and, with the aid of a microscope, painstakingly transcribed the contents of the Amorous Spotted Slug's journal. This is its story:

Sisu:

n. persistence, determination, inner strength.

Finnish/English dictionary

Cold Turkey

Chapter One

The combined voices of twelve hundred and twenty-four emotionally depressed White Holland turkeys reverberated through Walter's limited cranium, reinforcing his notion that it had not been, nor would it become, a good day. His rapidly deteriorating disposition precluded any sympathy for those fatuous fowl, feeling that, in reality, there was little substance to their complaints. In a few hours after their arrival at the processing plant, they would be relieved of further misery. Walter, on the other hand, had to go home to Sheila.

Walter swallowed a couple of aspirin and chased them down with warm water from the loading dock water jug. He was not optimistic about obtaining relief from his excruciating head pain. Sheila was seldom cured by simple aspirin. No, she would require, at minimum, two boxes of chocolates, a bouquet of flowers, and at least one dinner in a fancy restaurant with linen napkins and entrées bearing prices far above his meager financial resources.

Women expected too much from men. Common decency demanded a few subtle hints about their anniversary; but no, she had to spring it upon him first thing in the morning, long before his mind had geared up to full capacity. He might have remembered before the day was out, had he been given sufficient time. Walter sat back in a wicker chair at the rear of the loading dock to nurse his throbbing headache while two men on forklifts loaded crates of unhappy turkeys into the bowels of his eighteen-wheeler. It was amazing how many turkeys actually fit in the trailer. According to his manifest, 1,224 turkeys had signed up for the cramped, three-hour trip to the processing plant.

Today was the beginning of Walter's second week at the Schroeder Turkey Ranch, a job he had quickly learned to despise. The pay was not bad, but turkeys? At 3,000 acres, the ranch was small by West Texas standards. The soil was typical West Texas: dry, dusty, and peppered with scraggly sagebrush. Turn-of-the-century windmills pumped water from wells dug deep into the ground. The water, stored in elevated, five thousand gallon tanks, was judiciously rationed out to a myriad of shallow watering troughs that quenched the thirsts of over 500,000 head of turkey.

The owner of the turkey ranch was also typical West Texas: pompous, rich, and eccentric. Bartholomew Schroeder, having inherited his ranch and his personality from his equally pompous father, expected all of his employees to share his eccentricities. His establishment was a ranch, not a turkey farm. He had a herd of turkeys, not a flock. Fortunately, Bart spent little time on the ranch, except for the occasional media event in which he could be seen majestically astride his favorite horse named LBJ as he herded fifty to a hundred head of turkey into a small corral.

The sudden silence confirmed the closing of the trailer doors. Walter was amazed so much clamor could be hermetically sealed within the confines of the semi-trailer without even a gobble escaping to the outside world. At least the rest of the day would be conducted in peace and quiet. It was still early. Perhaps after dropping off the turkeys there would be time to take Sheila out to a nice, but expensive dinner, do some serious groveling, and patch things up before bedtime. He was not looking forward to sleeping on the couch. He could pick up chocolates and a bouquet of flowers on the way home.

Walter opened the door and climbed into the cab of the tractor-trailer. At five foot two inches, climbing into the cab was problematic, but what Walter lacked in height he made up in girth, sporting generous love handles. Fortunately, the cab's exterior provided multiple hand holds for the vertically challenged. Once firmly entrenched in the seat, Walter pulled the cab door shut to take advantage of the air conditioning. On the outside door panel, as on the door panels of all other vehicles at the Schroeder Ranch, was the Presidential Seal, confirming not only was Walter's boss pompous, rich, and eccentric, he was also moonlighting as President of the United States. Technically, this was a flagrant misuse of the Presidential Seal, at least in the opinion of many outspoken Republicans, but eccentric Presidents do as they please, and this pleased Bart Schroeder.

Walter had met the President the previous week during the unveiling of his new, state-of-the-art, tractor-trailer system for transporting turkeys with its continuous-flow ventilation system and the electronic temperature and humidity controls. The President rode shotgun next to Walter while brandishing a double-barrel, twelve gauge for the benefit of photographers. Walter didn't know why the President needed chaps and spurs to ride in a truck; but then, Walter had never been big on politics. "Heaven help the man or woman who tries to rustle any of his turkeys" was the quote of the day from the front pages of many major newspapers. A picture of gleaming-white teeth protruding from under a ten-gallon hat accompanied the articles.

Walter shifted the truck into gear and headed down the gravel road. It was less than a mile to the perimeter of the ranch, but travel was slow, since the truck had to plow through herds of squawking turkeys. Walter leaned on the horn, but that only increased the confusion, causing the turkeys to scurry in every direction. Patience was wearing thin. Salvaging the day required a quick and uneventful trip to the processing plant. Walter did not have time for birdbrains.

A row of razor-barb concertina wire garnished the top of the large chain-link fence, which surrounded the ranch perimeter, hardly necessary to keep the turkeys in but definitely necessary to keep the political paparazzi out. Well-equipped guardhouses, bristling with satellite dishes and radio antennas, greeted visitors at every entrance. If the President were in residence, each guardhouse would be infested with a covey of Secret Service agents. Today only a lone guard on minimum wage was there to greet Walter.

The guard flagged Walter through without fanfare. A few freelance photographers reclining in lawn chairs under large umbrellas in front of cheap campers gave Walter and his cargo a quick once-over but decided they were hardly worthy of time or film and returned to their *Playboy* magazines and cheap novels. There were always a few such photographers camped at the front gates in hopes of obtaining compromising photographs of the President or his entourage.

Just past the gates, Walter turned north along two parallel ruts that Texans called a road. It was a shortcut to the highway twenty miles away that management insisted he take to save time and money. Today, Walter was only concerned with saving time.

Normally, it would have been a rough, forty-minute drive to the highway. Today, he would do it in thirty minutes. He hoped Sheila would appreciate the sacrifices he was making for her benefit. His hemorrhoids surely didn't. Walter checked his gauges. The trailer temperature was fifty-eight, airflow was adequate. If any parameter were to fall below specifications, alarms would sound. Instruments monitored all conditions within the trailer except the level of motion sickness. In a moment of weakness, Walter felt sympathy for the plight of the turkeys bouncing around in the back, but this quickly passed.

Only locals used the trail and then very rarely. It was, therefore, surprising to see a sports utility vehicle parked diagonally across the trail. A vague image of a person slumped over the steering wheel was visible through the tinted glass.

"This is all I need," Walter muttered to himself as he climbed down from the cab. Visions of squad cars and emergency vehicles and impounded turkey transporters danced through his head.

"HEY THERE, YOU ALL RIGHT?" Walter did not expect an answer. Having the person simply asleep at the wheel was too much to ask, although he could see no obvious damage to the vehicle or evidence that the car had hit any obstacles. Walter opened the door on the driver's side. "Are you..." The driver sprang to life, producing a can of pepper spray. Three more individuals, all wearing black ski masks, materialized from behind the SUV.

"Ahh, my eyes!"

"Don't rub your eyes. It'll only make it worse."

Walter looked at his blurred assailants through watery eyes. "If you're after money, you're wasting your time. I ain't got none. I'm married."

"We're not after your money. Cooperate and we'll have no problems. If not—more pepper spray."

Walter had been a prizefighter in his youth, but this was four against one. If memory served him correctly, he had lost all his fights. His collapsed nose was a constant reminder of his win/loss record. He was also not particularly fond of pepper spray. His eyes were still burning. "What ya want?"

"We need to borrow your truck…"

"No problem."

"…and your clothes."

"My clothes?"

"Yeah, strip!"

"Now wait a minute." A firing squad consisting of four outstretched arms, each holding a can of pepper spray immediately formed. "O.K., O.K. I just needed to clarify a point. I think it's been clarified." Walter began unbuttoning his shirt under the close supervision of the four commandos, each dressed in jeans, black sweater, and ski hood.

"Hey, wait a minute," Walter said after he noticed two significant lumps in the sweater of the person who had been slumped behind the wheel. "You're a girl."

"Very insightful," replied a soprano voice. "Your mother taught you well."

"I ain't undressing in front of no woman."

With military precision, four outstretched arms again pointed at their victim. "Ready…Aim…"

"I don't care what you do. I'm not undressing in front of her."

"For Pete's sake, how old are you?"

"Us crime victims have rights, ya know."

"O.K., O.K., I'll turn my back. But we don't have all day."

"Ya don't have to get crabby about it. What did you say your name was again?"

"Stuff it!"

"Is that Miss or Mrs.?"

"Ms."

"O.K., Ms. Stuffit. I'll strip as long as you promise not to peek."

"Cross my heart."

Walter neatly folded his clothes and laid them on a rock.

"Now place your hands behind your back," Ms. Stuffit said, turning slightly.

"You peeked!"

"Did not."

"Did too."

"Did not."

"Then why you snickering?"

"Am not."

"I know a snicker when I hear one, and that was a snicker."

"Can we get on with this?" one of the men asked as he bound Walter's hands behind his back with duct tape.

"You aren't going to leave me out here naked, are you?"

"Of course not," the man said as he poured a sticky substance over Walter's entire body. "We aren't barbarians."

"What's this stuff?"

"Molasses."

"You goin' stake me to an ant hill?"

"I said we're not barbarians. It'll help keep your new clothes on." The man in black ripped open two pillows and then poured the contents over Walter's sticky body, totally covering him with white feathers. "I told you we wouldn't let you go home naked."

"Well, well," Ms. Stuffit said as she turned to inspect Birdman.

"You promised you wouldn't peek."

"But you're fully clothed now." Ms. Stuffit bent over to inspect the sensitive areas to ensure modesty was secured. "It's really amazing how few feathers were required to cover the little feller."

"You're snickering again."

Ms. Stuffit retrieved a cell phone from her pocket and dialed a number. "We have everything secured and will be moving out in a few minutes. Is everything ready at your end? O.K., see you in a bit." Ms. Stuffit returned the phone to her pocket.

"Ah, Ms. Stuffit, can I ask a personal favor?"

"Yeah, what is it?"

"Can I use your phone to make a phone call?"

"You want to make a phone call?"

"It's not really for me. It's for my wife. Just to let her know that I'll be coming home a little late tonight."

"Now isn't that considerate. Are you guys paying attention?" Ms. Stuffit asked her colleagues. "What's her number?"

"555-9319"

"Let's see. You said 555-93…"

"No, you have to dial the area code first."

"This is long distance?"

"Long distance isn't expensive anymore."

"You want to call long distance? You're goin' owe me big time for this one."

"I'll be happy to pay you back. Just untie me so I can take down your address, and I'll mail you the money."

"We're not going to untie ya."

"I got a good memory. I'm pretty smart. Just give me the address. I'll memorize it."

"O.K., it's sixteen hundred."

"Right, sixteen hundred."

"Pennsylvania Ave."

"Pennsylvania Ave. Gotcha. Is that in Pennsylvania?"

"No, Washington."

"Which one? There's two ya know."

"Washington, D.C."

"Yep, I know where that is."

Ms. Stuffit dialed the number (with area code) and held the phone to Walter's ear.

Sheila: *Hello.*

Walter: *Hi, Honey. Just wanted to let you know I'll be a little late getting home.*

Sheila: *What do you mean you're coming home late tonight?*

Walter: *I got tied up at work.*

Sheila: *When are you getting home?*

"Ms. Stuffit, about what time can I expect to be home?"

"Let's see. You'll probably want to walk back toward the ranch. That's about twelve miles. With your short legs, my best guess would be about daybreak," Ms. Stuffit replied.

Sheila: *I hear a woman's voice. Are you out with another woman?*

Walter: *No, of course not. I'm here at work. Those turkeys have a high-pitched gobble.*

Sheila: *So when you coming home?*

Walter: *About daybreak.*

Sheila: *Daybreak!*

Walter: *When I get home, I'll make up for forgetting our anniversary.*

"You forgot your wife's anniversary?" Ms. Stuffit asked.

Sheila: *That's definitely a woman's voice. You're spending the night with another woman!*

"You should be tarred and feathered."

"Please, Ms. Stuffit, will you stay out of this?"

Walter: *When I explain what's really happening, we'll both have a good laugh.*

Sheila: *I hope you find the living room couch just as funny!*

Walter: *Sheila, really I can...*

Sheila: (Click)

Walter: *Sheila?*

"I think we got disconnected. Maybe the batteries are dead."

"I hate to be a party pooper, but we really need to get going," one of the men informed Ms. Stuffit.

"I suppose you're right," Ms. Stuffit said as she returned the phone to her pocket. "Hang the sign around his neck, and let's get moving." One of the men retrieved a placard from the SUV and hung it around Walter's neck. It read, "Save The Turkeys."

"The sign's not too tight, is it?" asked the man in black. "I wouldn't want to ruffle your feathers, so to speak." The man chuckled at his own humor.

"No, this is fine."

"Well, you better get going. You have a long walk ahead of you."

"I don't suppose you could give me a lift back to the ranch?"

"Sorry, we're going the other direction."

Walter headed down the road. At least he had his boots, and the feathers did provide some warmth. Nights in Texas can get pretty chilly.

Oval Office, 1000 hours

"This better be good. I got a business luncheon at the club around noonish followed by 18 holes of golf." President Schroeder propped his feet on the corner of his disk. Large pockmarks marred the surface, a reminder of earlier days when he insisted on wearing spurs around the White House. Bart looked at his Chief of Staff; he was not smiling.

"Have you seen the morning papers?" asked Al Webber, the President's Chief of Staff. From the President's insouciant demeanor, it was obvious he had not. Al threw a copy of the *New York Times* onto the President's desk. The headlines proclaimed, "Radical Group Gives the President the Bird." A picture of Walter Brainthorpe strutting around in full plumage accompanied a rather lengthy article. "And here is the *Washington Post*." Al held up a copy of the paper, which proclaimed, "President Gets Goosed During Fowl Play." It too had multiple pictures of a well-feathered, presidential employee in various bird-like poses. "The tabloids are even worse."

"Well, I'll be a horned toad." The President studied the photos for a moment. "Who's this guy dressed like Big Bird?"

Al Webber had been a life-long friend of the President, having met the President during undergraduate training at Texas Tech. It, therefore, had come as no surprise to political pundits when the President appointed him Chief of Staff. Al opened a thin folder to retrieve the appropriate papers. "Mr. President." Even though best of friends, Al insisted on addressing the President formally when dealing with sensitive government matters. "It appears a radical group called the Avian Liberation League hijacked one of your trucks filled with turkeys."

"Someone stole my turkeys?"

"The reports are sketchy, but what we do know is one of your employees, by the name of Walter Brainthorpe, stopped to assist a stranded motorist when he was accosted by approximately ten men wearing black ski masks. Although vastly outnumbered, Brainthorpe refused to surrender his turkeys and offered stiff resistance. Apparently, he had been a prizefighter in his youth, with a fairly decent record I might add. He was doing a passable job of holding his own until someone held gas to his nose causing him to pass out. We think it was ether."

"What about my turkeys?"

"By the time Brainthorpe came to, the truck and turkeys were gone, and Brainthorpe was covered with feathers. He ran the entire twelve miles back to the ranch to notify the authorities. He has to be one heck of an athlete."

"I only hire the best." In reality, the President had little impact on the operations at the ranch, preferring to leave most of the day-to-day decisions to his business manager.

"Brainthorpe says he distinctly heard ribs cracking on three of the individuals, and a fourth has a broken nose. We've alerted hospitals in the area to be on the lookout. The FBI is still debriefing Brainthorpe. We should have more information later."

"I should give this guy a medal," the President suggested.

"Where do you think we should go from here?" Al asked. "The news media is having a field day. We don't need this kind of publicity. Not during an election year." As Chief of Staff, voter approval ratings were foremost on Al's agenda. It had been Al who had masterminded the President's election in the first place.

"I could give this guy's wife a call and thank the little lady for her husband's heroism. The media eats that up." The President picked up his phone and dialed his secretary. "Can you send Veronica in for a minute?" President Schroeder set the phone back in its cradle. "Got a good crop of White House interns this year."

Every six months a new set of overly eager interns rotated through the White House, most of whom were political science majors from large universities. They considered an appointment to the White House a major political plum, as it never tarnished the resume of the politically ambitious.

"You need me, Mr. President?" Veronica asked as she entered the Oval Office. She came well prepared with a personal pen and note pad, unaware the only personal equipment needed was a tight sweater and good-looking legs. She had both.

"I sure do, my dear. And the name's Bart. We're very informal around here."

"Yes, Mr. President."

"Can you find the home phone number for Walter Brainthorpe? He works for me at the ranch. I need to talk to his wife."

"I'll call the ranch. They'll have the number."

President Schroeder inspected Veronica's legs as she left the room. "Fine looking filly. With legs like that she could go places in government."

"I think we should play up the fact that Texas now has a Republican governor, and this type of crime never happened when you were governor," Al suggested, trying to redirect the President back to the problem at hand. "We need to put out a press release to that effect."

"Let people know this President is coming down hard on crime," the President added. "We'll show them what we do to turkey rustlers."

"Y'all come on in," the President said in response to the knock on the door.

"Here's that number you requested," Veronica said, passing a note to the President.

"You do right fine work, my dear. And do call me Bart."

"Yes, Mr. President."

"Say, you got any plans for this afternoon? I'm scheduled for 18 holes of golf. Sometimes I get inspired and need someone to take notes. Ya think you could come along?"

"I think I could arrange that," Veronica replied in what she hoped was a calm voice. Inside, her heart was beating a romantic melody, her feet were turning to rubber, and she had a sudden urge to pee. This was her first day on the job, and she was already scheduled to accompany the most powerful person on earth on 18 holes of golf.

"If you can excuse me a moment, I'll give the little lady a call. We can mention that in the press release." President Schroeder punched in the numbers and waited for it to ring. He considered reversing the charges but decided that would be tacky. The taxpayers could afford it.

Sheila: *Hello?*

President Schroeder: *Hello, Sheila? This is Bart Schroeder.*

Sheila: *Who?*

President Schroeder: *Bart Schroeder, like in the President of these United States.*

Sheila: *Yeah, right.*

President Schroeder: *You must be very proud of that husband of yours.*

Sheila: *Brett, did Walter put you up to this?*

President Schroeder: *That's Bart.*

Sheila: *Whatever.*

President Schroeder: *We're very proud of him here in Washington.*

Sheila: *Brett, you got an extra couch there in Washington?*

President Schroeder: *That's Bart. I believe we do. Why do you ask?*

Sheila: *Because you can tell that two-timing, womanizing scoundrel that when he comes home, he'll find his belongings dumped on the front porch. And he'll need your couch to sleep on.* (Click!)

President Schroeder: *Sheila?*

"The phone got disconnected. Must be something wrong with the phone."

White House Press Room, 1400 hours.

Ronald Clark, Press Secretary for the President, stepped up to the microphone. "I have a brief statement to make concerning the cowardly act that occurred yesterday evening. I will entertain no questions.

"Yesterday at approximately 4:30 p.m. central time, ten to twelve heavily armed terrorists hijacked a shipment of turkeys just outside the Western White House. The lone driver put up a valiant fight causing serious injury to several of the assailants before he was overcome by poisonous gas. We are currently testing to determine whether it was a nerve agent or a mustard gas. The driver is in stable condition and is expected to fully recover. We are withholding his name pending notification of all next-of-kin. I believe the President, however, has personally spoken to the driver's wife who expressed appreciation for the swift government response and the excellent medical care he has received. The perpetrators of this heinous crime should be considered armed and dangerous. If anyone has any information about the whereabouts of any of these individuals, we are recommending they immediately notify law enforcement authorities. Please do not try to apprehend them yourselves."

Somewhere in Uniqueastan, 2030 hours

The kerosene lamp setting on a rock ledge provided only minimal illumination, creating grotesque shadows on the far wall of the cave. The cave was not large but did provide modest shelter from the elements. The two men sitting cross-legged on the floor facing each other did not appear concerned about their humble surroundings. Both men wore turbans and robes common to the locale. Between them, a small fire licked the carcass of a large rodent, extracting the natural juices, which dripped down on the fire causing small puffs of yellow flame.

"Ain't that C-4 you're burning?" asked one of the men in a heavy accent, obviously a Uniqueastanian.

"Yep," replied the other in perfect English. A large wart perched on the tip of his nose invited comment, but his menacing eyes dissuaded all but the fool hardy.

"Ain't that a form of plastic explosive?"

"Yep." The man with the wart cut a piece of meat from the rodent with a large knife and then elevated it to his mouth with the blade. "Care for a piece?" the man asked the Uniqueastanian.

"I'll pass." The Uniqueastanian stared at the burning plastic explosive with unconcealed concern. "You sure burning C-4 is safe?"

"Yep." The man with the wart ripped a leg from the carcass and placed the entire leg in his mouth. He skinned all meat from the bone with his teeth and tossed the bone to the side of the cave. A large pile of lizard bones and snake heads confirmed he had resided in the cave for several days. "Do it all the time. Long as there's no blasting cap, it only burns." The Uniqueastanian did not appear convinced.

"I understand your country might be interested in a major purchase." The Uniqueastanian caressed his AK-47 that lay on the ground by his side. He always liked to know where it was during delicate negotiations.

"Depends on what ya got." The man with the wart had a fully loaded Uzi submachine gun resting comfortably in his lap; however, he preferred his knife at such close quarters, should a difference of opinion develop. He tossed the rest of the roasted rodent into the corner. Maggots could have the leftovers. He wiped his greasy mouth on his sleeve and waited for the Uniqueastanian to elaborate.

"How about a twenty-megaton nuclear bomb. Not too big but can still create a mess. Got it from a Soviet army surplus store. Sort of a going out of business sale."

"Does it come with a missile?"

"Short-range, ballistic missile. Range about sixty miles, but that'll cost extra."

"I think my government would be interested in removing some of these toys from the playground. How much you want?"

"One billion Yankee dollars and ten virgins."

"One billion Yankee dollars and ten virgins!" Nostrils began to flare, and the American's eyes became wide as if suddenly infused with drugs. The Uniqueastanian reached for his AK-47 but was too late. A heavy foot came down hard on the weapon, pinning it to the ground. Subtle motions with the large knife discouraged further aggressive behavior, and the Uniqueastanian released his grip on the rifle.

"You people think America has unlimited assets, that all you have to do is ask your exorbitant price and it will automatically flow out of the land of milk and honey. American opulence has boundaries. Our resources are not inexhaustible. We can't always give in to your greed just because you ask.

The American looked over his nose, past the warty protuberance, and into the eyes of the, now quivering, Uniqueastanian. "Would you consider one billion Yankee dollars and five virgins?"

"Deal."

Chapter Two

Washington Suburbs, 1600 hours

It had been a long time since the old neighborhood had seen such excitement. The vacant lot, frequently used for spontaneous softball games and a storage dump for old tires, was now crawling with every form of humanity. An insufficient assortment of police officers was gallantly trying to bring order to the chaos, but they were quick to admit their shortcomings. Flashing lights beamed from their squad cars in a vain attempt to magnify their presence.

In the center of activity, three bulldozers, engines in idle, sat helplessly while their operators and other construction workers conversed in small groups. Their frustration was palpable. Over a hundred highly vociferous protesters waving large posters and chanting a farrago of provocative pabulum surrounded the helpless construction workers. Although unnecessary, two or three provocateurs with megaphones egged on the demonstrators.

Esther, standing at the edge of the protesters, surveyed the chaos with pride. They had stopped them, at least for the moment. It would be sufficient to obtain a court order, and that was what mattered. There would be no further development here. With environmental impact studies and frivolous lawsuits, she could keep them tied up for years. Esther could do that. With a degree from Harvard Law School and unlimited free time, she could do that.

Except for the megaphone in her hand, Esther should have been no different than any other demonstrator. The demonstration should have been no different than the countless other demonstrations occurring daily in the capital of demonstrations. What made this demonstration different was the number of men in blue suits and dark glasses who were mysteriously whispering into watches. Their eyes, under the protection of the dark glasses, darted from side to side, constantly surveying the crowd, looking for unusual behavior. Slinky-style wires dangled from hearing aids, connecting them to power sources tucked away in coat pockets. What made this demonstration different from the rest of the demonstrations was that Esther Schroeder's husband was President of the United States.

It didn't take long for the media to arrive (they had been alerted in advance). Helicopters armed with telephoto lenses circled above as camera crews set up satellite dishes to provide live feed to the eagerly waiting world. They would be just in time for the six o'clock news.

A TV newscaster thrust a microphone into Esther's face. One of the men in dark glasses reached for the Uzi hidden under his trench coat but relaxed when it became apparent the First Lady was in no physical danger. He had become used to the First Lady's penchant for publicity.

"Mrs. Schroeder, I'm Rob Carter from the Channel 7 News. Can you tell us what this protest is about, and what is the White House involvement in this demonstration?"

Esther smiled at the man with the camera on his shoulders. Form is everything, she told herself. "I'm glad you asked, Rob. We are concerned citizens who are fighting to save the Amorous Spotted Slug."

"Did you say a spotted slug?"

"Yes, Rob. But this is not just any slug. The Amorous Spotted Slug is currently on the endangered species list and is normally found only in Michigan's Upper Peninsula. Many felt they could not thrive anywhere else."

"Are you saying they are now propagating in Washington D.C.?"

"That's correct, Rob. Two days ago several of these extremely rare slugs were found right here in this vacant lot. That's why it is so important we leave it in its pristine beauty."

The newscaster looked around at the hubcaps, old tires and other trash. Only in Washington D.C. could such a pigsty be considered pristine beauty. "Amorous Spotted Slug, that's a strange name for a slug. What makes it so important?"

"Most people are unaware of this wonderful creature's natural beauty. I recently talked with Toivo Rantamaki, Professor Emeritus of Finlandia University, on the phone who describes the sex life of the Amorous Spotted Slug as unique within the animal world. Professor Rantamaki says before the Amorous Spotted Slugs copulate they perform this ritualistic mating dance, which is quite intricate. Each subspecies has a slightly different cadence. Professor Rantamaki says the choreography is unbelievable."

"Have you seen this mating dance?"

"No, Rob, I haven't. Unfortunately, the A.S.S. is nocturnal and is seen best with night-vision goggles. The A.S.S. tend to be very slow, which is why they're so rare. The mating dance can take hours, and often one of the A.S.S. will fall asleep before they copulate. The mating dance is quite meaningful when seen in time-lapse photography."

"And these slugs are normally found only in Michigan's Upper Peninsula?"

"That's right, Rob. Professor Rantamaki believes they originated in the Amazon Jungle and migrated to Michigan's Upper Peninsula on drifting coconuts during the Great Biblical Flood. As you know, the unicorns were less fortunate.

"Mrs. Schroeder, you are aware there are plans to build a school for blind paraplegics on this ground?"

"Rob, sometimes we have to make sacrifices for the good of this planet we live on. I'm sure, when all of those blind paraplegic kids see what we've done, they'll leap with joy."

"How did you happen to find these slugs?"

"That's rather weird, Rob. Someone phoned in an anonymous tip, which is strange since no one except a resident of Michigan's Upper Peninsula would recognize an Amorous Spotted Slug."

"One last question and I'll let you go. What's the President's position on the Amorous Spotted Slug?"

"Well, Rob, I haven't discussed it with him yet, but I know we can count on his full support."

"That's the news from here, and now we return you back to the station."

Virginia Foothills, 1632 hours

Willow Creek Country Club, nestled in the Virginia foothills fifty miles west of Washington D.C., offered neither creek nor willow tree, but it did provide one of the finest golf courses money could buy. The membership rolls boasted some of the richest and most influential aristocrats in Washington D.C., many of whom found the club's cocktail lounge and exquisitely manicured greens a welcome relief from the stress of Washington. Only a limited number of token minorities graced this membership list, most of whom were offered reduced fees or complimentary membership. Few of them lived close by, and none of them was encouraged to participate in club activities. An ornate, but formidable, wrought iron fence surrounded the club to keep out the riff-raff.

For the most part, the club as well as its members participated quietly within the local community. The club members preferred not to associate with the lower class, and the lower class preferred to ignore the people from Snob Hill, as the country club was frequently called. Other than the locals and a modest number of Washington's elite, few people knew of the club's sleepy existence.

This changed when the newest club member flew in one afternoon for a round of golf. Marine One landed in a makeshift landing zone on a grassy knoll north of the clubhouse. In the ensuing months a concrete pad, landing lights, and a small shack teeming with an assortment of electronic gear materialized out of nowhere. Normally, only members and a few well-screened guests were allowed onto the grounds, but the club managers made an exception for the news media whenever a Presidential outing was imminent. This was not discouraged by the President who, likewise, knew the value of free publicity. Since the press was not allowed to follow the President on his round of golf, an impressive golf score was always available upon request. A White House photographer, who did accompany the President, released only the best golf shots to be shown on the six o'clock news.

A Presidential outing was not without its complications. Prior to the President's arrival, Secret Service men (or women) cordoned off the helipad and selected areas of the clubhouse. Three well-armed, James Bond style, golf carts sat in waiting: one would transport the President, one would scout ahead looking for land mines, potential assassins, and the occasional skunk, while the last golf cart guarded the rear. An unofficial duty of the agents in the lead cart was to ensure no golf balls reached the sand traps or lily ponds. The agents carried extra balls to drop just shy of such traps if needed.

A growing number of photographers and TV cameramen standing behind a yellow "Police, Do Not Cross" ribbon confirmed that today would be a Presidential golf outing. Agents Max Langston and Connie Rushford didn't need such confirmation. Their orders and information arrived via earplugs attached to small battery packs tucked away in shirt pockets. The little voices in their ears confirmed that Man-of-War would be arriving in twenty minutes. The Secret Service had code names for both the President and the First Lady. The First Lady was Buttercup and the President was Man-of-War, referring to the legendary racehorse. Informally, he was dubbed the Silver Stud due to his graying hair and his penchant for greener pastures.

"Man-of-War is twenty minutes out," Langston informed Rushford, who received identical information from the little man in her ear. Langston's obsessive-compulsive behavior annoyed her, but he was a stickler for details, and that made her life easier. She could finish her half-pint of butter pecan ice cream guilt free (until she stepped on the scales in the morning) knowing Langston would have everything in proper order by the time Man-of-War arrived.

Langston re-checked his equipment for the third time—one can never be too careful. The .38 was still secured to his left leg, as it had been the last time he checked. An eight-inch dagger with both sides honed to a razor's edge was attached to his right leg. Caressing his left shoulder confirmed that under his baggy sport coat a 9 mm semiautomatic was nestled in its holster. All defensive equipment was present and accounted for; and if the need were to arise, an Uzi submachine gun was never far from reach. He would have preferred to have fragment grenades in his arsenal, but the agency was unduly concerned with collateral damage. They worried too much in Langston's opinion. The two canisters of pepper spray in his pocket were hardly an adequate alternative. He could never understand how Rushford could feel secure with the meager firepower of her lone .38 caliber pistol. Both agents wore bulletproof vests under their shirts. If they had to take a bullet for the President, they wanted to be around to accept the accolades.

"Five minutes out," Langston said, repeating the announcement heard in Rushford's ear.

Agent Rushford polished off the last of the ice cream and deposited the container into a trash bin. As senior Secret Service agent, she should appear to be in charge. That was difficult since she was short, female, black, and somewhat stuffy in the middle, hardly what the public expected. They expected someone like Langston: tall, slender with a closely cropped crewcut, and a square jaw that was never burdened with a smile. Give him dark glasses and a wire dangling from his ear, and he could pose for a Secret Service recruitment poster. When she put on dark glasses and wore an earplug, she was mistaken for a housewife with a Walkman.

"O.K. guys, let's look lively." Rushford adjusted her dark glasses, the hallmark of the Secret Service. With dark glasses, agents could scrutinize the crowd more discreetly. Seven other agents donned dark glasses and formed a line between the press corps and the helipad, the sound of helicopter blades now audible in the distance.

Marine One made a short circle around the landing pad to ensure they had covered all bystanders with a patina of dust before coming to a rest on the concrete pad. Once the crew secured the rotor blades, Agents Langston and Rushford approached the craft to assist the President. If this had been a formal trip, two smartly dressed marines would have assisted him, but as a recreational outing, most formalities were suspended. Presidential attire was likewise informal. The President emerged wearing tan shorts, hairy legs, and a flowery shirt even a Hawaiian would be embarrassed to wear. His ubiquitous Marine Corps cap garnished the top of his head. It never hurt politically to flaunt his military veteran status. Bart had faithfully served two full weeks of Marine Corps boot camp prior to his compassionate discharge, when it was determined his father, Bartholomew Schroeder, Sr., had developed a severe feather allergy and was incapable of running the family turkey ranch. The allergy was well documented by two prominent physicians, both golfing buddies of Schroeder, Sr. Bart would have been willing to finish his enlistment had it not been for the personal plea of his congressman who enumerated the many hardships the people of his district would endure if the Schroeder Turkey Ranch did not continue at full capacity. Bart reluctantly accepted the compassionate discharge to serve his country as best he could on the turkey ranch.

Accompanying the President was General George "Bulldog" Brackendorf, Chairman of the Joint Chiefs of Staff as well as the new White House intern, Veronica Doyal. When the President came in range, strobe lights flashed and reporters began competing for the President's attention.

"Mr. President, what is your position on the Amorous Spotted Slug?" one reporter asked. The President skillfully ignored the question.

"Mr. President, are you willing to sacrifice the school for blind paraplegics to save the Amorous Spotted Slug?" another reporter asked. It appeared the question was not about to dissipate.

"That is a very good question," the President replied. "I'm glad you asked. As you know, endangered species fall under the auspices of the Department of Agriculture. I have recently introduced a farm bill that will give the Department of Agriculture more independence and will also increase the wheat subsidy."

"Mr. President, can you comment on the allegations by the animal rights people who claim the political rights of your turkeys at the Schroeder Ranch are being violated?"

"My position is a matter of record. I have always been supportive of the minimum wage and world peace. I support equal opportunity for all. An excellent example is Agent Rushford here." The President gestured toward the black female agent.

"That'll win a lot of black votes," Agent Rushford whispered to Langston.

President Schroeder gave Agent Rushford an almost imperceptible nod.

"That's all, folks," Agent Rushford told the reporters. "This isn't a press conference."

"One last question, Mr. President. Who's the young lady?"

That seems rather harmless, the President thought. "This is Veronica Doyal, our White House intern. She has graciously volunteered to drive us old fogies around the golf course." The President laughed at his own self-deprecation and was joined by the press corps.

"Well, George," the President said as Veronica drove the golf cart away from the press corps. "Care to place a little wager on today's game?"

"What do you want to bet?"

"Ya know that nuclear powered carrier you been wanting for the navy?"

"Yeah."

"If you win, you get the carrier."

"And if I lose?" General Brackendorf asked.

"I get satellite pictures of that California nudist camp"

"Bart, you got yourself a bet."

Veronica drove toward the first hole.

Oval Office, 1000 hours

Al Webber, Chief of Staff to the President sipped at his coffee while he waited for the President to get off the phone. He was obviously talking to an irate senator who represented an even more irate contractor who was losing money because he couldn't build a school for blind paraplegics on top of an Amorous Spotted Slug. Al met daily with the President at 10 a.m. to brief the President on the happenings of the previous twenty-four hours.

The President slammed the receiver down in frustration. "Damn slugs! Sometimes I think people are importing those slimy creatures from Michigan just to make my life miserable. Am I getting paranoid or what? Detroit can keep all of those disgusting little creatures for all

I care." Bart extracted two aspirin tablets from the bottle he kept in the top drawer of his desk for such occasions.

"I don't think they have Amorous Spotted Slugs in Detroit," Al suggested.

"They don't?"

"No, I believe they're only found in the Upper Peninsula." Al took another sip of coffee. He would need the caffeine to make it through the meeting. Briefings with the President were not noted for their mental stimulation.

"Is the Upper Peninsula far from Michigan?"

"Some people feel it's a part of Michigan."

"Well, I'll be hog-tied. Ya learn something new every day." The President mulled over this revelation for a moment or two. "Ya mean there's more to Michigan than just that mitten thing?"

"I believe so, sir."

"I'll be danged. What else ya got for me today?"

Webber opened his folder to review his notes. "Yesterday one of our agents in Uniqueastan was able to purchase a small nuclear device on the black market. That will be one less bomb for terrorists to get a hold of."

"We should put that out in a press release."

"It would be best if we didn't," Webber suggested. "The agent who made the deal is deep undercover, and it's better if the voters didn't know what we paid for it."

"How much did we pay for it?"

"It's better if you didn't know either."

"You know best, Al. I'll trust your judgment." The President flipped through the pages of an old *National Geographic*, pausing at the pictures of the bare-bosomed natives; the First Lady had canceled his *Playboy* subscription. "What else ya got? Anything new on those dastardly turkey rustlers?"

"According to the FBI agents who are debriefing Walter Brainthorpe, Brainthorpe was able to engage the perpetrators in conversation and extract both name and address of the ringleader. Her last name is Stuffit. The address they wanted to send over a secure line. We should be getting that later today."

"Bust my buttons. That's just the kind of lead we need. We'll have 'em all rounded up and hog tied by evening. Too bad we can't lynch rustlers like the good old days. I'll have to give that Brainthorpe guy a raise."

"From my understanding, he doesn't work for you anymore."

"He doesn't?"

"The way I hear it, he's now working for Acme Mutual."

"Isn't that an insurance company?" the President asked.

"I guess he's their answer to the AFLAC duck.

"The AFLAC duck?"

"He's also the official spokesman for the National Audubon Society."

"You can't expect much loyalty from employees these days."

"They did offer him a lot of money. With that and what he's making on the talk shows, he should do pretty well this year."

"Talk shows?"

"He's going be on Piers Morgan tonight, if you want to catch it."

"At least we're closing in on that rustler gang." The President paused when he came to a revealing picture in the *National Geographic*. He dog-eared the page for future retrieval. Several other pages were dog-eared.

"There may be more than one ringleader," Al informed the President. "The Secret Service intercepted a letter from the Avian Liberation League, which claimed responsibility for the heist. They say they'll continue to harass and embarrass you unless you give into their demands. They plan to throw the upcoming election."

"Dag burn it. I will not submit to blackmail! What are their demands? Is it something we could arrange discreetly?"

"The letter didn't say. They'll send a list of demands later. It was signed Abigail Farnsworth."

"Don't know any Farnsworths," the President said.

"Could be a fake name. The FBI is checking on it."

Chapter Three

The Bare Creek Café, 1000 hours

Abigail sipped cautiously at her tea, finding it too hot for her comfort. Moose, Newton, and Sherlock had ordered soft drinks, preferring to imbibe their caffeine cold. As a security precaution, they had commandeered a table in the far corner of the Bare Creek Café, an easy accomplishment since most of the breakfast trade had left for more productive activities. If inquisitive eyes wandered in their direction, they would appear to be college students whiling away time prior to the start of fall classes. They avoided real names for fear of clandestine listening devices.

An assortment of chips, pretzels, and other quick snacks littered the table, typical of a college student's concept of a balanced diet. The menu of the Bare Creek Café now offered a variety of such fast foods, unlike the wholesome meals Abigail's great grandparents had served when they established the Bare Creek Café three-quarters of a century earlier. Little else had changed over the years. The large portrait of the café's founders still adorned the wall above the fireplace, and the original woodwork spoke of times when craftsmen took pride in their work.

Abigail looked up at the portrait of P.C. Taylor and his wife, Maggie. The portrait had been painted at the time of their daughter's wedding. No one knew what P.C. stood for, but it added dignity to her great, grandfather. A black patch over the right eye added further mystique. Abigail would have liked to think he had been a notorious pirate or buccaneer. Instead, he most likely led a boring life as a businessman within the growing community. He did have the distinction of being the town's first mayor. Abigail wondered what they would think if they knew their great granddaughter was about to bring the government to its knees, or at least to its senses.

Abigail took another sip of tea, now at perfect temperature, and turned to her friends. "That spotted slug idea is working like a charm. It could stop that development project indefinitely."

"People will believe anything on the Internet. I got two thousand hits on my *AmorousSpottedSlug.com* website, and the number's been doubling every three days." Sherlock, an English major at Finlandia University and a prolific writer, had been happy to extend his fiction-writing skills to the genesis of the Amorous Spotted Slug. Not only did an official website exist, but various scholarly papers had been written by erudite professors from numerous prestigious universities, all confirming the social value of the Amorous Spotted Slug. If one were to look closely and had more than rudimentary computer savvy, one would have noticed all references originated from the same desktop computer located at Finlandia University in the Upper Peninsula's Keweenaw Peninsula.

"Is Toivo Rantamaki really a Professor at the University?" Abigail asked.

"He is now."

"Real or not, he's making the President squirm." Abigail took another sip of tea. "Moose, you're caring for the turkeys?" Moose nodded in the affirmative. "We'll need them later...and alive, so don't go eating any of them." Moose, a Phys. Ed. Major, was not as well endowed in the frontal lobe as his co-conspirators, but he was reliable, unless it involved guarding edible objects. At six foot four and two hundred and forty pounds, he represented a formidable eating machine. He wasn't called Moose for nothing.

"It's time we twist the screws a bit tighter on our illustrious President," Abigail said. "Newton's synthesized a compound that'll hit him where it hurts."

"What compound is that?" Moose asked. Patience was another one of Moose's limited virtues.

Newton was happy to explain. Of the four, he was the only one not attending Finlandia University. He was a third-year grad student at Michigan Tech, located across the Portage Canal in Houghton, Hancock's sister city. Michigan Tech wasn't noted for producing student radicals (most students had little interest in newspapers), but it did produce an abundance of nerds willing to demonstrate how life can be manipulated, through chemistry, electronics, or computer shenanigans.

"I boiled some horse hooves creating a collagen material, which I treated with a sulfuric acid. Then I centrifuged..."

"Can't you sum up what you got for us non-scientific types?" Abigail asked. She had more patience than Moose, but time did not permit a lengthy scientific oration on a subject none of them would understand.

"I've created gelatin."

"You've created Jell-O?" Sherlock asked, "...and you expect that to bring the President of the United States to his knees?"

"Does it come in different flavors?" Moose could feel his stomach beginning to growl. Jell-O with fresh fruit was his preference.

"This isn't ordinary gelatin." Newton wondered why he bothered with liberal arts majors. "This is weapons-grade gelatin."

"Weapons-grade?"

It was obvious Newton would have to explain it in the simplest terms. "Normal gelatin has to dissolve in boiling water and then cool in a refrigerator to gel, right?" There were nods of approval. "Watch this."

Newton took a glass of cold water and stirred in some white powder. Within minutes the water had turned into a solid gelatinous mass. "It'll stay like that indefinitely."

"I can see some definite possibilities," Abigail said. "How much of that powder can you make?"

"As much as you want, but it'll take a day or two."

"Start making it," Abigail said. "In two days we'll head to Washington...and pack baggy clothes."

Oval Office, 1000 hours

"Well, Al, how's things going today?" the President asked. "Ya look a little down in the chops. Your tail's draggin' lower than a lovesick gelding. Can't be all that bad. Here, have a cookie." Bart offered a chocolate chip cookie from a cookie jar. He got the idea from Ronald Reagan who always had a jar of jellybeans on his desk. The kitchen sent fresh cookies every morning.

Al declined the cookie. Bart grabbed two cookies. If Al wasn't going to eat his cookie, he'd eat it for him.

"I suppose it's not so bad if you ignore the two percent drop in your approval rating," replied the President's Chief of Staff. "Or if you don't care that animal lovers think your position on animal rights is getting soft. They're insinuating your turkeys aren't getting appropriate care at your turkey farm. That Avian Liberation League got'em all stirred up."

"That's turkey ranch."

"Yeah, right. Anyway, they're demanding a complete evaluation of your farm...ah ranch."

"Dang it! I'd rather be seared with a red-hot, branding iron than let those meddling morons snoop around the ranch. What happens if I don't let'em in?"

"They'll say you got something to hide. The media sharks would have a feeding frenzy. They've already received several anonymous letters suggesting your turkeys are suffering from mental anguish."

"Mental anguish?" Bart helped himself to two aspirin from his desk drawer.

"Right. The animal rights people want to have an animal psychiatrist interview a few of your turkeys, totally random interviews of course. It would be turkeys of their choosing. Basically, they'd check the turkey's stress level. If it's not too high, they'd be on their way."

Bart tried to imagine a turkey lying on a couch while an animal psychiatrist took notes. If they were stressed out, would he have to foot the bill for psychotherapy? He hoped not. He had lots of turkeys.

"We have more problems," Al continued. "The tabloids are having a field day with this slug thing. The headline in the *National Inquisition* yesterday was *Saving the President's A.S.S.*, and I don't think they were referring to the Amorous Spotted Slug. Another paper ran the headline *President Slugs It Out With Big Business*. This is not making you look very Presidential."

"Can't I just come out against those lascivious slugs?"

"Only if you wish to offend both the animal rights people and the environmentalists all in one politically suicidal oration. That would be good for another two percent drop in the ratings. I might add that the First Lady would not be pleased, either."

Offending the first two groups could be considered a calculated risk. Offending the First Lady was unthinkable. Sleeping in the Lincoln Bed Room is considered an honor by most people, but not if you happen to be the President of the United States. President Schroeder sank back into his chair. "Don't ya have any good news?"

"Well, Mr. President, next week you're scheduled for a campaign swing through Wisconsin. You always do well on the campaign trail."

The Oprah Winfrey Show, 1630 hours

"Good afternoon everyone and welcome to the show." Oprah smiled with her usual charm as she worked her live audience. "Today we are fortunate to have with us as a special guest, Sheila Brainthorpe. As you all know, Sheila's husband, Walter, single-handedly fought off fifteen, well-trained, ninja-style, para-militants, who were trying to steal turkeys from the President of the United States. Walter was able to inflict significant injuries to the assailants, incapacitating over half of them with little harm to himself. That is when they resorted to chemical weapons. Walter has been quoted as saying he could have successfully defended the turkeys if the assailants hadn't stooped to weapons of mass destruction. That is quite a man you have there, Sheila."

"Yes, Oprah, a lot of people underestimate his abilities, which is their first mistake."

"I understand he is quite the expert in martial arts."

"Walter was hand-picked for this job by the President of the United

States. The Big Guy isn't in the habit of tapping individuals who come in second place."

"You mention the 'Big Guy' like you are close friends with the President."

"Obviously, not as close as Walter is. A lot of people aren't aware of it, but the President flew down to the Western White House a couple of weeks ago to personally discuss security measures with Walter. I'm not at liberty to disclose the nature of the intel they discussed, but it doesn't take a brilliant mind to fill in the gaps. They used the cover story that the President was there to show off his new turkey transporter. The news media picked this up hook, line, and sinker."

"I guess they had me fooled too," Oprah said.

"That picture of the President sitting in the shotgun seat with his twelve-gauge wasn't just for show. The shotgun was loaded!"

"You don't say."

"Walter was in the driver's seat. He purposely kept in the shadows since he didn't want to blow his cover."

"Sheila, did you or Walter suspect this was going to happen?"

"Oprah, you don't hire a man of Walter's caliber just to drive a truck." Sheila waited for the laughter in the audience to subside. "It wasn't a matter of if it would happen, but when."

"Were you surprised it happened when it did?"

"I think Walter knew. When you've been happily married as long as we have, you know what the other person is thinking. Walter never forgets our anniversary."

"He never forgets your anniversary? Now that is quite a man."

Sheila waited for the applause to dissipate. "When he didn't mention it first thing in the morning, I knew he was trying to tell me something. Obviously, he couldn't come right out and tell me, as we were always concerned about listening devices at the house. You can't be too careful. So, yes, I think we both knew it was going down that day."

"Sheila, you have a very brave and talented husband, and I would like to also commend you on your courage. Too often we overlook the courageous woman behind the man. So what is next for you and Walter?"

"Well, Oprah, with his cover blown, he's of no further use at the ranch. Right now we're in a holding pattern. Walter's doing some consulting for the National Audubon Society. He's always had a soft spot for charities. He's also offered to mediate the conflict over the Amorous Spotted Slug. This is a conflict even the President is unable to resolve. Walter feels a solution can be found that will allow the building of the school for blind paraplegics and still preserve the crucial habitat of the Amorous Spotted Slug. He feels they can coexist."

"Now there is a unique concept," Oprah said. "Have the blind paraplegics and the Amorous Spotted Slug live in harmony. We could use Walter's talents at the United Nations."

Sheila was again forced to wait for the applause to subside. "I would like to make it clear that Walter has no political ambition and has no plans to run for public office. He only wants to do his duty as a patriotic American. Of course, if the public were to demand he run, I'm sure he would feel obligated to serve his country the best he can."

"Our guest today has been Sheila Brainthorpe, wife of Walter Brainthorpe who needs no introduction. Before we move on to our next guest, we need to pause for a word from our sponsor."

East Wing of the White House, 0923 hours

"O.K., folks, if you'll just follow me; the White House tour is about to begin. My name is Linda, and I'll be your host this morning. There are a few rules we must cover before the tour starts. First, there are no bathroom facilities open to the public inside the White House, so you are encouraged to use the rest rooms at the Visitor Pavilion over by the Ellipse. Also, no food or beverages are allowed in the White House." Linda paused for a couple of stranglers who were joining the group. "Due to security reasons, everyone must go through a metal detector before entering the secure area of the White House grounds. After 9-11, I am sure you can all understand the rational for this. If there are no questions, we'll head over for the security check."

A small group of tourists followed Linda toward the checkpoint. The tourists were wearing shorts and sandals, all except for four individuals in baggy pants who carried helium balloons tied to their wrists. On the balloons in large print was "Vote for Bart." One of the individuals was in the early stages of pregnancy. Her doting husband stood proudly by her side.

"This isn't going to hurt our baby, is it?" the husband asked.

"Nope, your baby is quite safe," the security guard replied. "The machine only picks up metal. Now if you'll just step through the portal, we'll get on our way. Normally, we wouldn't allow the balloons, but I'm sure the President won't mind." The guard was not above currying a little favor with his boss in the White House.

"If everyone has been cleared, we can head toward the East Wing." Linda herded her charges toward a two-story structure that was connected to the White House proper by a long corridor. "The East Wing houses the offices of the President's military aides. If we were to go to war, the President would conduct most of the military activities from the situation room deep underground."

The pregnant lady and her overprotective husband maneuvered to the front of the group. Both were wearing Bart for President buttons in addition to the "Vote for Bart" helium balloons.

"When is your baby due?" the tour guide asked.

"Not for another six months."

"The time will go fast."

"I sure hope so. I'll be glad when this morning sickness is over."

"Ladies and Gentleman, we're now entering the White House proper. Please stay close by me and don't touch anything. We have priceless art treasures here that can never be replaced."

"My stomach is feeling queasy," the pregnant lady told her husband in a voice loud enough for the tour guide to hear.

"Are you going to be O.K.?" the guide asked.

"I'll be fine. I'm sure it'll pass. It's just one of the pitfalls of motherhood."

"The tour is fairly short," the tour guide assured them. "It shouldn't be too much longer."

The group headed toward the State Dining Room. To the left of the group was a bathroom with a large sign stating "Not for Public Use."

The pregnant lady gave a subtle nod to her friends and grabbed her stomach.

"I think I'm going to vomit," she told her husband (and everyone in the vicinity).

"You can't vomit on the President's carpet!" The tour guide was horrified. No one had ever vomited on the President's carpet before.

"Quick, in here. There's a bathroom," suggested the overprotective husband as he pushed his pregnant wife toward the door that admonished against public use.

"You can't go in there," the tour guide said. But it was too late, the expectant mother and overprotective husband were already inside the bathroom.

"For Pete's sake, lady, the woman's pregnant." The voice came from the rear, possibly one of the individuals with a helium balloon, but the sentiment was shared by all.

"Quick, we don't have much time." Abigail locked the bathroom door. "I'll flush mine down the toilet, and you flush yours down the sink." Large bags of white powder, strapped to abdomens under loose shirts and strapped to legs under baggy pants, were produced and flushed into the sewer system.

"I feel much better." The pregnant lady closed the bathroom door behind her. "I'm really sorry about the inconvenience."

"That's O.K., the tour is about over."

The pregnant lady followed the tourists back to their starting point. No one noticed that her protruding abdomen was no longer protruding. The four individuals with "Vote for Bart" balloons melted into the crowd.

***

Charlie reached for the phone on his desk. He hated phones. Everyone on the phone wanted repairs, like today. No one believed in delayed gratification anymore. Requests for repairs should all come through the mail. The requests could then be sorted into work that had to be done tomorrow, next week, or never.

"Hello, White House maintenance department, Charlie speaking... Toilet's backed up? Can't do anything until we get a work order....

That would be form 1042-B. Don't get that confused with form 1042-A. That form is used to order replacement parts for the elevator.... No, I don't keep those forms down here. They can be ordered using form 1480-C.... No, I don't have that form either. Hello?"

People can be so rude at times. Charlie considered leaving the phone off the hook but someone would just come to check on him. Feeling that people are easier to ignore on the phone, Charlie hung up the phone only to have it ring again.

"Hello, White House maintenance department, Charlie speaking.... Toilet's backing up? We've been getting a lot of that during the last hour. You're going need a work order.... That's form 1042-B.... You don't have that form?... No, we don't have that form down here.... What?... It wouldn't make any difference if you were the President of the United States, if you don't have a work order, it don't get fixed.... Same to you fella!"

***

President Schroeder hung up the phone and reached for his aspirin. How could he survive without a toilet? He couldn't run over to the gas station every time he had to pee, not with his prostate problem. Schroeder crossed his legs hoping that would buy some time, but the pressure was building fast. He looked around the room. A small potted tree sat next to the wall on the far side of the Oval Office.

President Schroeder picked up the phone and dialed his secretary. "Can you have Veronica track down a form 1042-B. Right, form 1042-B, not form 1042-A. Form 1042-A would be for ordering elevator parts."

A moment later, Schroeder heard a seductive knock on the door that could only be his White House intern, Veronica.

"You wanted form 1042-B, Mr. President?" Veronica asked.

"Thanks, you're a life saver, and do call me Bart."

"Yes, Mr. President." Veronica turned to leave. "I hadn't noticed it before, but the tree of yours doesn't look very healthy. I wonder if it needs more water."

"That can't be the case. I just watered it."

Chapter Four

Amazon Jungle, 0330 hours

Only a trickle of moonlight filtered through the triple-canopy jungle to light the way for the man trudging through the backwaters of the Amazon River. He sauntered effortlessly through the chest-deep swamp, dragging a watertight bag behind him. He glanced at the luminescent dial on his waterproof watch: It was oh-three-twenty-two hours. He had been wading through the swamp for three hours, but still miles short of the destination.

The swamp was deceptively quiet; for off to the man's right, two menacing eyes glowed in the darkness, barely protruding above the surface of the water. Like an iceberg, the bulk of the fourteen-foot alligator lay hidden beneath the water. Slowly, the eyes drifted toward the man, now twelve feet away, then six feet. When the gator was less than three feet from its prey, it displayed a large, toothy grin as it prepared for its savage assault. The man, unperturbed by the pending attack, peered down his nose, past the protuberant wart, and into the glaring eyes of the alligator, giving the alligator his best evil eye. The gator, seized by panic, fled in terror.

The man with the wart on the nose continued plodding through the swamp, his movements obscured by darkness. Just before dawn he climbed up a steep bank at the edge of the swamp and crawled through the brush toward the light emanating from a distant hacienda. The vegetation was thick and lush, impeding forward progress. Using his machete, the man hacked a small hole through the jungle.

Two feet in front of him, a tree branch bent downward, suffering under the weight of an eight-foot serpent with a truculent attitude. The brown snake with gray markings uncoiled slightly to lower its arrow-shaped head to eyeball level with the interloper. The snake glared at the intruder, eyeball to eyeball. This was his turf and the snake had no intention of sharing it with anyone flaunting such a grotesque wart on his nose. The snake hissed at the intruder, exposing large fangs, dripping with venom. The snake coiled its body and prepared for a strike. This intruder needed to be taught a lesson.

With lightening speed, the snake lashed out at the offending nose with its tasteless appendage. But the snake's speed was inadequate. A large hand snared the snake behind the head, stopping the snake's fangs two inches shy of the warty nose. The man with the wart deplored his deteriorating skill. In his prime, the snake would never have gotten closer than eight inches. In anger, he ripped off the snake's head with his teeth, swirled the snake's head around in his mouth for a moment or two, and then spit it out in disgust. He had always felt fer-de-lance was lacking in flavor.

The man crawled toward the hacienda until he came to the edge of a clearing. Guards with assault rifles guarded the front and sides of the building, knowing that no sane man would dare attack from rear, where the swamp filled with poisonous snakes and savage alligators provided protection. On the patio beside the hacienda, six men dressed in light-weight, white suits and Panama hats, typical attire of the local gentry, were sipping lemonade and smoking Cuban cigars.

The man opened his backpack, producing an expensive digital camera with a large telephoto lens. The magnification was powerful, and only faces of the men were visible through the lens. But, then, he only needed faces. The camera had memory for thirty pictures. He used them all. Tonight, when he returned to his hooch, he would upload the digital information to a waiting satellite, which would later download the pictures to CIA headquarters in Langley, Virginia.

Oval Office, 0945 hours

Bart's eyes wandered over to Veronica's legs as they were frequently inclined to do. When seated, her short skirt migrated up two inches, a spectacle too enticing to ignore. "Veronica…" The President paused, his train of thought momentarily derailed. Legs like Veronica's can do that to a man.

"Yes, Mr. President?"

"Ah, yes," the President said as his thoughts, if not his eyes, returned to the problem at hand. "I'm goin' need your help. Got myself a little campaign trip lined up for Wisconsin next week, and I'm goin' need background information. You know, names of Wisconsin football teams, governors, senators, things like that." The President tried to visualize Veronica in a bikini. Then he tried to visualize her without it.

"Shouldn't be hard," Veronica replied. "I'm from Madison."

"Isn't that close to Wisconsin?" Bart asked, pleased with his geographical recall. "We could use someone with your background to keep me informed. Maybe we'll have to take you along."

"Yes, Mr. President."

"Y'all can call me Bart."

"We're supposed to call you Mr. President."

"You're old enough to vote, which makes you my boss. A boss ought 'a be able to refer to her employee by his first name."

"O.K., Bart, but only in private."

"Have a chocolate chip cookie." Bart retrieved one for himself.

"No thanks. I've been putting on too much weight lately."

All in the right places, Bart decided.

Bart looked at his watch. "Dang it. It's almost ten o'clock, time for my briefing with my Chief of Staff." He preferred conversing with Veronica. She was better looking and never brought desparaging news. "Well, that's all I need from you today."

"O.K., Bart." Veronica got up to leave. "That tree by the wall is looking worse every day. Sure hope it doesn't die. I like that tree."

"I've developed a strong attachment myself," Bart replied.

Al Webber arrived promptly at ten, his briefing folder thicker than normal, suggesting a prolonged briefing. Bart had hoped for a round of golf.

"Well, what's the scoop for today," Bart asked. "Did we destabilize any governments, assassinate any foreign leaders, or maybe wipe out a couple of drug lords? Surely you gotta have some good news." Al was not smiling. He had been doing a lot of not smiling lately.

"Seen the *Washington Post*?" Al flopped a copy of the paper onto the President's desk and took a seat in one of the Oval Office's over-stuffed chairs. He plopped down into the chair like an old man. Al had aged a lot in the last two weeks. Bart read the paper's headline: *White House Suffers From Constipation*. Bart had no desire to read further.

"Goin' cost us another percentage point," Al said.

"Damn plumbing is old. Hardly our fault," Bart replied. "The whole system's backed up. We gotta get someone down there with one of those Rotor-Rooters to clean out the obstruction."

"Charlie, down in maintenance already did that. He was able to re-trieve a sample of the substance that's causing the obstruction. Ya know what he found?"

Bart mentally listed common solid substances found in sewers. He only came up with one. People can't expect him to be an expert in every field. He would have preferred a multiple choice question.

Al didn't wait for an answer. "Gelatin!"

"Gelatin? I can't pee in the pot because the plumbing's filled with Jell-O?"

"We're not talking ordinary gelatin here, this gelatin's been weap-onized! Bart, we're talking weapons-grade gelatin. This is big. This is really big. It's gotta be the work of terrorists...with some major connec-tions."

"Slow down, Al, you're hyperventilating." Bart extracted a paper bag from his desk drawer reserved for such occasions. "Here, breathe into this."

Al, a decorated Vietnam War veteran, frequently hyperventilated when excited. Doctors diagnosed it as post traumatic stress disorder caused by a traumatic experience in a Saigon brothel. Years later, he was still unable to talk about it. For his injuries, he was given a Purple

Heart and penicillin.

"Just breathe slowly into the bag," Bart advised.

Al's breathing rate began to slow, as he regained his composure. "We can't underestimate the power of weaponized gelatin."

"You can weaponize gelatin?" Bart tried to visualize weapons-grade gelatin, but all he could come up with was a bowl of red Jell-O embedded with sliced bananas or fruit cocktail.

"Weapons-grade gelatin solidifies water at room temperature." The Chief of Staff, slightly more relaxed, paced around the Oval Office, talking mostly to himself. "We've had some of America's top think tanks working on this project, but they're still years away from a workable formula. We've spent billions on it."

"Billions on gelatin?"

"We gotta get that formula. This could tip the balance of power in the free world. Do you realize how serious this is?" Al again did not wait for an answer. "Do you have any idea what would happen if a dump truck dropped a load of weapons-grade gelatin into the sewers of Manhattan? Wall Street would be shut down. Our entire economy would be in shambles. It could be the end of civilization as we know it."

"Let me get this straight," the President said, trying to put it all in perspective. "You're telling me that someone snuck into the White House just to fill my toilet with Jell-O and now the free world is in jeopardy?"

"Not just anybody, the Avian Liberation League!"

"Ya mean those turkey rustlers?"

"We found 'Save the Turkeys' scrawled in lipstick on the mirror in one of the first floor bathrooms. Apparently, weapons-grade gelatin was flushed down the toilet, but it was programmed not to solidify until a minute or two later, after it had entered the main drainage pipe for the White House."

Bart contemplated the complexity of programming gelatin. He couldn't even program his DVD player. "We talking about an inside job?" the President asked. "That area's off limits to non White House staff."

"Secret Service is still interrogating the staff, but one tour guide remembers a pregnant lady and her husband who briefly had access to the bathroom."

"Ya mean they came in with the tourists?"

"It appears so."

"Hot diggity damn. We got them now." The President stood up and banged the desk with his fist.

"We do?"

"Those turkey rustlers aren't half as smart as they think they are. I knew they would slip up sooner or later. Just a matter of time. They actually thought they could get the best of ol' Bart Schroeder."

"What are you talking about, Bart?" Al asked, forgetting his Presidential decorum.

"Those turkey-rustling renegades overlooked one minor flaw in their plan. We got the entire first floor covered with video cameras!" Bart reached for the phone. "I'll have security send up those video tapes. We'll have photos of the entire bunch. I want their mug shots displayed in every post office. I want an APB for every law enforcement agency in the U.S. of A. We'll notify Interpol." The President could not have performed a better victory dance if he had made the winning touchdown in the Super Bowl. "I want them featured on that TV show. What's it called? *America's Most Wanted* or something. There'll be no place for them to hide."

Al was not smiling again. Bart hated it when he didn't smile. "You've seen the tapes?" the President asked, his finger pausing midway through the phone number.

"I checked them before I came up here."

"What did ya see? Did ya see their faces?"

"All I saw was Bart."

"Bart?"

"Yes. All I could see was "Bart for President." They held helium balloons in front of the cameras. There's absolutely nothing of value on the film."

Bart slumped into his chair. He was Commander in Chief of one of the world's mightiest armies, he was head of the world's best intelligence agency, and his White House was monitored by the finest body-guards, but he couldn't secure the toilets. "When do you think we can have the sewer line fixed?"

"I talked to Charlie down in maintenance, and he thinks he could have it opened up in fifteen minutes."

"Let's do it!"

"He can't do it until he gets a work order on form 1042-A."

"Form 1042-A is used for ordering replacement parts for the elevator," Bart said. "We need form 1042-B."

"Anyway, we need a form for each toilet in the White House since they're all plugged. Charlie says it has to be in triplicate, which is more forms than we have in the building."

"We can order more 1042-B's with form 1480-C," the President suggested.

"The big problem isn't the forms."

"It's not?"

"No. Since this was done by terrorists, this is now a crime scene. We can't touch any of the evidence until it's released by the investigative authority."

"Which agency is that?"

"That's the kicker," Al replied. "The Treasury Department thinks they should be in charge since it happened in the White House, but the FBI feels it's domestic terrorism and, therefore, their turf. The CIA is also snooping around in case there is an international connection."

"This could take a long time," the President said, eyeing his favorite tree with his legs crossed. "What we goin' do for toilets?"

"I think I got that covered," Al said. "Got a friend over in Parks and Recreation who owes me a favor."

"The day's not totally devoid of good news," Al said as he flipped to a different page in his folder.

"It's not?" Bart asked, hopefully.

"The FBI has been tracking down individuals with the name of Abigail Farnsworth, using the social security data base. The only likely suspect they found was an eighty-year-old lady from Pasadena. She holds a third-degree black belt in karate and is a known political activist."

"Ya think she's the one?"

"Unfortunately, she has an iron-clad alibi," Al said. "She was at a bingo tournament when the turkeys were stolen. Apparently, she was a semifinalist. Tore up half the church basement when she lost by one number."

"That's the good news?"

"Not really," Al said. "This guy at the Bureau who's been doing the investigation thinks it's a fake name, but not necessarily picked at random. He thinks someone may have taken on the name of a folk-lore heroine who is considered a patron saint by many Yoopers."

"Yoopers?"

"That's how the people in Michigan's Upper Peninsula refer to themselves. They're Yoopers and those who live below the Mackinac Bridge are Trolls."

"Isn't that where those stupid Amorous Spotted Slugs came from." Bart asked.

"Could be a connection there," Al agreed.

"What do we know about this legendary Abigail Farnsworth?" Bart felt like they were finally making progress on the turkey caper.

"I don't know anything except what I read in the agent's report," Al said. "I made a copy for you." Al tossed the report onto the President's desk. "Read page eight."

The President flipped through the folder until he came to page eight.

Farnsworth Report, page 8

According to records taken mostly from the files of the Bare Creek Gazette, Abigail Farnsworth, an eighteen-year-old daughter of Charles Farnsworth, disappeared near a beaver pond just north of the lumber camp she had been visiting during the summer of 1898. Independent records do confirm the existence of such a person. Details of the incident are sketchy. No body was ever found even after draining the beaver pond. The only evidence found at the scene was the footprints of a large grizzly bear and a pile of Farnsworth's clothes. A legend developed among the locals that she was being chased naked through the woods by the bear. Legend further has it that she returns to the beaver pond every summer during a full moon to look for her clothes (she disappeared during a full moon). Natives celebrate this incident by gathering down by the local beaver pond in the summer during the rise of the full moon to hopefully catch a glimpse of the naked Abigail looking for her clothes.

In 1923 (according to the Bare Creek Gazette) a four-year-old girl by the name of Becky Hakanen fell off the back of a wagon on Christmas Eve and became lost in one of the worst snowstorms of the decade. The girl was purportedly found by the legendary Abigail and brought back to life. Because of this "Christmas miracle," locals have promoted her to sainthood (the Catholic Church requires two miracles).

Today, the small town of Bear Creek resides at the location of the old lumber camp. The beaver pond is still in existence. The town, itself, as well as the small creek north of the town are named after the bear, but many local establishments such as the Bare Creek Café, the Bare Creek Gazette, and the Bare Creek United Methodist Church are named after the legendary naked Abigail.

"Kind of thin," Bart said when he had finished reading the article. "This is thinner than hobo stew on a Friday night."

"As you mentioned, those Amorous Spotted Slugs are from the U. P. Could be the connection we're looking for."

"Won't hurt to follow up on it," Bart said. "Anything else today?"

"Saved the best for last. We had a tip that a special meeting was going to take place with all the South American drug lords. Most of them are unknown to us. Yesterday, one of our agents was able to get photographs of all the participants. Once they're identified, we can bug their offices and tap their phones."

"By Jove, that'll put a dent in their dentures."

"That's all I got." Al got up to leave. "That tree of yours isn't looking very healthy. I think I'll have one of the gardeners take a look at it."

Chapter Five

Oval Office, 0945 hours

Placing his cowboy boots on the corner of his desk, Bart leaned back in his chair. It was moments like this that made his job truly enjoyable. The Oval Office was quiet, the phone was not ringing, and Al was not waving newspapers with disparaging headlines in his face. (That could change at ten o'clock). Even the chocolate chip cookies were unusually delectable and still warm from the oven, but the smaller size disappointed him. Esther must have been talking to the kitchen staff again. She seemed to think he was overweight. Bart stood up and looked down at his generous waistline. He couldn't be overweight; he could still see his shoes. He would have to explain to the kitchen staff that, as Commander in Chief, he was head of the White House. Apparently, they were intimidated by the First Lady. That was understandable since he, too, found her intimidating. He would eat two cookies, he decided in a moment of silent defiance. That would show the First Lady.

Bart closed his eyes while his taste buds savored the exquisite flavor of cookie number one. He was about to reach for cookie number two when the phone rang. The phone was not supposed to ring. He had been quite clear to his secretary: no phone calls. They only brought bad news, and bad news can skew the flavor of a chocolate chip cookie.

Bart: *Hello, Bart here.*

Secretary: *I'm sorry, Mr. President, but I have a man out here who is quite persistent. He says he can't leave until he gets your signature.*

Bart: *Might as well send him in.*

No rest for the wicked. If that were truly the case, he should be quite busy, Bart thought as a devilish smile creased his face.

Bart stuffed the rest of the cookie in his mouth, brushed the crumbs from his clothes, and put on his best Presidential look. While he was still in the process of licking the chocolate from his fingers, the Oval Office's double doors opened, revealing a short man in jeans, red flannel shirt, and hardhat. A cell phone embellished his utility belt.

"Just need your signature by the 'X', Mack." Mr. Congeniality thrust a clipboard and pen at Bart with an air of impatience.

"What's this for?" Bart asked.

"Verifies the delivery."

That's simple enough, Bart decided as he signed the invoice. His secretary could have handled this.

"HANK, GO AHEAD AND BRING IT IN," the man with the hardhat said as he stuck his head out the door.

A man, obviously Hank, fired up the motor on his forklift and drove through the double doors of the Oval Office. Balanced on the pallet in front of the forklift was a baby-blue Porta-Potty. Above the outhouse door was the advertisement: *Johnny-on-the-Spot Porta-Potty*. Below, in smaller print, was *Salubrious Sam's Septic Service*.

"Where do you want it?" Mr. Hardhat didn't wait for an answer. "Hank, why don't you park it over there."

"You can't leave that here!"

"Is this Sixteen Hundred Pennsylvania Ave.?" Mr. Hardhat asked.

"Yes, that's the address."

"Is this the Oval Office?"

"Yes, but…"

"Then this is where it goes. Check the invoice you just signed." Mr. Hardhat gave Bart a copy of the invoice.

"Come on, Hank, we're out of here."

"Can't you move it closer to the wall?" Bart asked.

"Sorry, Mack, that's not in the union contract. You'll want a can of air freshener. These babies weren't made for indoor use. Charlie in maintenance has some."

Salubrious Sam stepped on one of the forklift tines, and Hank skill-fully backed out of the Oval Office.

Not a fashion statement, Bart thought. Although the color did match the Oval Office. Bart opened the door and stepped inside. In addition to the toilet seat, it had a small urinal on the wall. A black plastic drainage tube connected the urinal to the septic tank. No toilet paper. That would be too much to expect. The Porta-Potty was obviously used. On the wall, written in lipstick, was "for a good time, call Kim." Bart made a mental note of the phone number.

It had a self-closing door that automatically shut when he made his exit. Best of all it worked. Feeling much relieved, Bart zipped up his pants. If nothing else, it would save wear and tear on the tree, assuming it wasn't too late. Numerous leaves now littered the base of the tree.

He could use that air freshener and some toilet paper. Bart dialed maintenance. He no longer needed to look up the number.

"Hello, is this Charlie? This is Bart... Bart Schroeder... I work up-stairs... Fine, thank you. I could use some supplies...Yes, I'm aware I won't get them today... Next week?... That'll have to do. I need a can of air freshener... Form 1843?... I also need some toilet paper... Form 840-5? Is that for the soft toilet paper?... Yeah, a little problem with hemorrhoids... You too?... I also want my window fixed so I can open it...Yes; I know we have air conditioning. I want fresh air, even if it's warm...Yes, I'll put in a work order...Yep, form 1042-B, I know. About the toilet paper, is there any chance we could make an except... I didn't think so." Bart hung up the phone. He did have a box of carbon paper he could use. No one used carbon paper anymore.

"I see the guy from Parks and Recreation came through for us." Al never bothered to knock before entering. "They ain't much to look at, but they're functional." Al was actually smiling.

"This is just for a short time, isn't it?" Bart had a hard time sharing Al's enthusiasm.

"We need to talk about that," Al said. He was no longer smiling.

"The investigating agency just has to release the evidence," Bart pleaded. "Charlie down in maintenance can open up the sewers in fif-teen..."

"We received another letter from Abigail Farnsworth. She's claiming the gelatin was laced with mercury."

"Could be a hoax," Bart said.

"It was postmarked from Bear Creek, Michigan. We have to assume it's authentic. It fits in with the Yooper conspiracy theory."

"You think it really contains mercury?" Bart asked.

"The small sample Charlie obtained tested negative, but who knows?"

"I think we can safely ignore the mercury. Go ahead and tell Charlie to clean the pipes."

"We can't do that," Al said.

"We can't?"

"The letter wasn't addressed to us." It was obvious Al was holding back more disagreeable information.

"It wasn't?"

"They sent it to the Environmental Protection Agency. They want a full investigation with an environmental impact study. There're afraid it might contaminate vital streams and fisheries."

"That can take months, sometimes years!" Bart reached for his aspirin. The bottle was half empty. It had been a new bottle.

"Fortunately, the guy from Parks and Recreation said we could keep the Porta-Potties as long as we want. Said they were too old to use for the general public since some of them leaked. We'll have them scattered throughout the White House. Even got one for your bedroom. Can't have a master bedroom without a bathroom. Once a week, we'll have them taken out and exchanged. We'll have a fork lift stationed on every floor to move them around. We can use the elevators to transport them to ground level. I'm sure it'll work well once we get the bugs out."

Bart wondered if he should take two aspirin or three. He decided on three.

Bare Creek Café, 2110 hours

"Not bad." Abigail perused the front page of the *Marquette Mining Journal*. A large photograph of a *Johnny-on-the-Spot* Porta-Potty filled a major section of the first page. Trappings of the Oval Office could be seen in the background. "I think we got his attention." Abigail turned to page 13 where the article continued.

"Better living through chemistry," Newton said.

Abigail laid the newspaper down on the table. As usual they had selected a table in the far corner of the café. Remnants of a large pizza dominated the center of the table. After much debate, they had settled on pepperoni and sausage. Abigail wanted mushrooms, but Sherlock refused to eat molds or other fungi. Newton wanted anchovies. They immediately voted that down. Moose? Well, Moose will eat anything. They were all sipping on their favorite soft drinks except for Moose who was guzzling down a large chocolate shake.

"What's our next project?" Sherlock asked.

"We still got the turkeys," Moose said, grabbing another piece of pizza. "If nothing else, we can provide a barbecue for the entire dorm."

"We need those turkeys, Moose. No barbecues. We're saving them for the grand finale," Abigail said.

"Anyone see the President on TV two days ago at the golf club?" Newton asked.

"I saw it," Abigail said. "Didn't say anything profound. He avoided all the tough questions." Abigail sipped on her coke while Moose snort-ed his chocolate shake.

"But did you see who was with him?"

"General Brackendorf?"

"Besides him."

"Ya mean that new White House intern?" Abigail asked.

"Her name's Veronica."

"So?"

"From what I hear, the President has a hard time keeping his pants on," Newton said. "I think we should help those rumors along."

"How's that?" Sherlock asked.

"You familiar with potassium oxide?" Newton waited for the question to fully register; chemistry was not a strong suite for liberal arts majors.

"That's lye," Sherlock said after a moment of thought. "Nasty stuff but I fail to see how that'll help us."

"You're close. Casuistic lye is sodium hydroxide. Potassium oxide is a white solid normally sold in pellet form. It's very similar to lye when it dissolves in water to form potassium hydroxide. It'll eat almost anything." Not wanting to overload non-analytical minds with concrete information, Newton paused for a sip of his coke.

"So?"

"I got a friend at Tech who has converted potassium oxide into an aerosol. It deposits a fine film when the aerosol propellant evaporates. I accidentally got some on my pants. It was OK until I peddled home; then my sweat changed the powder into potassium hydroxide and it ate a hole in my jeans. Ruined the pants."

"A hole doesn't ruin pants," Sherlock said. "It gives them personality. It's about time you nerds got some culture."

"At least I'm an honest nerd. You fiction writers are just a bunch of professional liars."

"At least we can read and write."

"Hold on." Abigail pulled on Sherlock's belt forcing him back into his chair. He had been about to lunge across the table after Newton. Moose used the diversion to abscond with the last piece of pizza. "I think Newton has something there. If it really eats away clothing when wet, we can put it to good use. The President is scheduled to make a speech at the University of Wisconsin next week. That's a day's drive from here. I say we mosey down to Madison, Wisconsin and pay our respects."

First Bedroom, 2310 hours.

Much as he hated to admit it, having a bathroom in their bedroom was a godsend. With his prostate problems, he needed expedient facilities. A light in the Porta-Potty would have been nice. Some light filtered through the air vents at the top, but turning on the bedroom lights at three in the morning would not sit well with his wife. Without light, it was difficult making the appropriate adjustments to hit the urinal. He was hoping the yellow stains on the wall would wash off.

Bart eased the door shut to avoid irritating his already irritated wife.

"It's about time you got out," Esther said with toothbrush in one hand and bowl of water in the other—the First Lady insisted on having a place to spit when she brushed her teeth. Now that he could open the windows, Bart preferred expectorating out the window. Esther declared that beneath the dignity of a First Lady.

Bart had hoped to crawl into bed without a confrontation, but this appeared unlikely. Lying on his side of the bed was a diet plan with his name boldly printed at the top. Walter Reed Army Hospital was on the letterhead.

"Did you see that diet plan I got for you?" Esther asked through the vents of the Porta-Potty. From the gargled speech, it was obvious she was still brushing her teeth.

"Can't hear you," Bart lied. Maybe she would forget if he quickly changed the subject.

"It's right there on the bed," Esther said as she exited the bathroom, her mouth still lined with residuals of white toothpaste.

Bart checked the three pages to see how many chocolate chip cookies he was allotted. It must have been a typo—they weren't listed.

"I talked to that nice Dr. Hartman the other day, and we both agreed you could lose a few pounds."

Maybe he could inadvertently lose the diet plan. It would be no different than Nixon's twenty-minute tape gap. People would understand. As long as the kitchen didn't know about the diet, he was safe.

"That's just a copy. I sent the original to the kitchen."

Bart slumped onto the bed. A couple of aspirin would be nice. He could feel a headache coming on. Bart made a mental note to store aspirin in the bedroom.

"We also need to discuss our strategy to save the Amorous Spotted Slug."

Since when did it become *our* strategy? Bart wondered.

"The Amorous Spotted Slug Society wants you to come out with a strong statement supporting the A.S.S. We can write the statement if you're short on time."

"What about the blind paraplegics? They need that school."

"They aren't endangered," Esther replied. "We have plenty of blind paraplegics. Some people think we have too many."

"I'll bring it up at the next cabinet meeting, but we can't overlook the needs of the blind paraplegics."

"You can be so sentimental at times. If you're really concerned about those blind paraplegics, why don't you have that Walter Brainthorpe mediate the problem? He thinks the Amorous Spotted Slugs and the blind paraplegics can live in harmony."

"He's a truck driver, for Pete's sake."

"He sounded pretty good on the Piers Morgan show."

"Piers Morgan makes all his guests sound good. That's his job."

"If you didn't spend so much time with that young hussy, you might have time to solve these problems yourself."

"Young hussy?"

"It was all over the newscasts."

"You must be referring to that afternoon of golf with General Brackendorf. One of the White House interns wanted to see the personal side of the presidency. I forget her name."

"I trust it didn't get too personal like it did with that blond bomber last year."

"Have you been losing weight?" Bart asked, tactfully changing the subject. "Your face looks so much thinner."

"It must be that new mud facial. One of our constituents from Wyoming sent me some sulfur mud from one of their hot springs. It takes out the wrinkles." Esther opened a jar of foul smelling mud.

"It smells like sulfur."

"That's what makes it therapeutic."

Bart decided to keep his wrinkles.

"I've been putting it on my face twice a day, a half hour prior to bed and a half hour in the afternoon."

Esther began spreading the soft, muddy mixture over her face until only her bluish green eyes were visible through the mud. Bart was tempted to tell her she already looked better but in a rare moment of prudence, decided against it; Esther did not handle sarcasm well. Feeling it was wiser to keep his mouth shut, Bart crawled into bed.

Madison, Wisconsin, 1032 hours

The President wouldn't arrive for another twenty-four hours, but an advance party, led by Agents Connie Rushford and Max Langston, was already setting up housekeeping on the Hilton Hotel's fifth floor. When the President arrived on the following day, they would have to cordon off the entire floor.

Road trips always provided too much to do and too little time to do it. They would have to coordinate activities with local law enforcement agencies, evaluate any route the President might travel and establish threat levels, scrutinize personal files of all hotel employees, and run their names through police data banks seeking individuals with any criminal or mental illness background. A multitude of small, but critical, tasks demanded personal attention.

It was quite understandable, therefore, that no one paid attention to the muscular, young salesman from Duluth in room 519. If the Secret Service had, they might have discovered the young man's company— the Sleepy-Time Casket Company—didn't exist. They also might have noticed he spent most of his time with his door open, inserting magnetic cards into his electronic door lock. Since he would vacate his room prior to the President's arrival, he was no concern to the Secret Service.

The honeymooners in room 623 on the floor above would be there when the President arrived. This was the room the Secret Service should have been concerned about. If they had been observant, the Secret Service would have discovered the honeymooners had a guest—highly unusual for honeymooners. They would also have noticed the honeymooners of Schenectady, New York were receiving frequent visits from the Sleepy-Time Casket Company salesman. If they had looked inside room 623, they would have found a wide assortment of electronic equipment, far more than required by even the kinkiest honeymooners.

But since the room was on the floor above, the Secret Service had no reason to be concerned, nor had they opportunity to peek inside.

"You sure this is going to work?" Abigail asked. "There are so many variables and loose ends."

"You worry too much." Not bothering to look up, Newton continued entering data into his computer. "What specifically bothers you?"

"How about Moose? What'll we do if he can't find the right code for the door?"

"That's the easy part. Each electronic lock responds to two magnetic codes. One is unique to the lock and is used by the hotel guest. The other is the master code used by housekeeping. It'll unlock all the doors on the floor. Since the number of codes is finite, it's only a matter of time before Moose hits the right code. If he runs out of cards, I'll program more code numbers to try."

Moose had a pack of one hundred magnetic keys, which Newton had already reprogrammed twice.

"What about the Secret Service communications? We didn't plan on their communications being encrypted."

"That's a minor setback," Newton admitted. Newton finished entering data into the computer and pressed return. "But hardly the end of the game."

"If we can't hear their communications, our plan won't work." Abigail, normally quite composed, was blatantly agitated. She did not share Newton's faith in science.

"Will you relax?"

"Well, how are you going to decipher it?"

"I'm not going to decipher it."

"You're not?"

"Nope, I'm goin' let the computer do that. Decryption of the radio code is no different than what Moose is doing—trial and error. It just has more combinations. I've got a sample of their communication signal plugged into the computer. The computer tries various codes at the rate of about six hundred a second. If one of the codes produces human voice, the computer stops."

"How long will that take?" Abigail asked.

"Should be easier than hacking into the Pentagon. That took two days."

"You broke into the Pentagon's computer?"

"Twice," Newton confessed. "I needed some information on stealth technology that wasn't in the public domain. Needed it for a term paper."

"That kind of information isn't supposed to be in the public domain."

"It is now," Newton said. "Aced the term paper too."

"Newton, you're scary, you know that."

"You'll have to excuse me," Newton said. "I have to work on the sprinkler system. Let me know if the computer starts flashing 'Eureka.'"

Newton placed a paint-splattered hat on his head, grabbed a ladder he had commandeered from a utility closet, and headed toward the stairwell. An assortment of tools dangled from his utility belt.

Newton set up his ladder in the fifth floor stairwell, just below an overhead sprinkler. Each floor had a sprinkler at the stairwell landing. He propped open the door to prevent anyone from bumping his ladder when opening the door. Then he placed a yellow "men working" sign in the doorway.

Newton climbed the ladder to examine the sprinkler system. It was as he had expected. A temperature-sensitive bead prevented the opening of the sprinkler. Any temperature above one hundred and fifty degrees would melt the bead and open the valve. Should be simple enough, Newton thought.

Newton wrapped several layers of resister wire around the bead and attached the ends to a nine-volt battery and an electronic switch. He hid the battery and switch inside a smoke detector housing.

"What are you doing?" Agent Rushford asked as she came through the door.

"Puttin' in smoke detectors," Newton replied. "Hotel's concerned about the President coming and all."

"Can't be too cautious," Rushford agreed.

"Can you pass that screwdriver?"

"Sure." Agent Rushford was pleased to note nametags on all hotel employees. That made her job easier. If she had looked closer, she would have noticed Michigan Tech issued Newton's picture ID, not the Hilton Hotel.

"Thank you," Newton said after Rushford passed him the screwdriver.

"No, thank you. It's people like you who make my job a lot easier."

If this made her happy, she should be ecstatic, Newton thought. He had two more sprinklers to go.

"How'd you do on the sprinklers?" Abigail asked when Newton returned to the room.

"O.K.," Newton replied. "Although, I did have help from one of the security agents." Abigail, Sherlock, and Moose were all smiles. "Eureka" was blinking on the computer, and Moose was holding up a magnetic key with pride. "I guess all systems are go."

Chapter Six

Undisclosed airbase, **** hours (classified)

There was no fanfare or ceremony when the jet-black, F-117 Nighthawk lifted off from a small Air Force base in an obscure corner of Nevada. No one filed a flight plan, or initiated dialogue with air traffic control. A crescent moon would not rise for several hours, making the black plane invisible to the naked eye. Once the plane rose into the air and retracted its wheels, it became invisible to radar. For all practical purposes, flight number One-Oh-Seven did not exist.

The plane climbed to fifty-two thousand feet, well above commercial flights. Since flight One-Oh-Seven was invisible to radar and had not filed a flight plan, it was imperative the plane remain above commercial traffic.

The pilot banked sharply to the left, pointing the plane's nose slightly east of due south. Then he programmed the predetermined altitude and bearing into the autopilot from memory. Since there were no written instructions on board, cover stories could be erected on the fly in case of mishap. The Nighthawk made minor course corrections in response to the new data and leveled off at fifty-three thousand feet. Two hours later, the plane crossed the Mexican border. No permission for over-flight had been obtained from the Mexican government; but then, no permission was needed. Flight One-Oh-Seven did not exist.

The pilot poured black coffee from a large thermos into a spill-resistant cup. He expected a long, boring trip and would need that caffeine edge to stay alert. It would be thirteen hours before he would hear the sound of another human voice. Three hours into the flight, the F-117 veered over the Gulf of Mexico and left Mexican air space. The pilot reprogrammed the autopilot, bringing the plane down to thirty thousand feet where a KC-130 Hercules tanker waited to top off the Nighthawk's thirsty fuel tanks.

The refueling procedure, orchestrated by hand signals from the KC-130's crew chief, took less than fifteen minutes; after which, the F-117 climbed back to fifty-three thousand feet. The Nighthawk reentered Mexican air space when it crossed the Yucatan Peninsula and then flew into Central America. Except for the lights of an occasional large city, the ground below remained invisible. Only the GPS confirmed the crossing into South America.

Two hundred miles from the drop zone, the F-117 began a slow descent, leveling off at forty thousand feet when still ten miles from the drop zone. At two miles from the target, the pilot activated the bomb bay doors. The doors slowly opened, and the F-117 became visible to radar. Somewhere down below, a man noticed a small blip on his radar screen, a blip coming out of nowhere.

The pilot lifted the plastic cover protecting a red toggle switch. He flipped the switch as the plane passed over the drop zone, ejecting the solitary payload from its belly. Flipping another toggle switch closed the bomb bay doors, and the plane was again invisible. Down below, the man behind the radar screen watched the blip disappear. He had been about to call his supervisor, but would now treat the incident as an aberration, a glitch in the system. Nothing of interest he decided as he took a sip of coffee.

After the payload had fallen forty feet, well below the turbulence of the jet's exhaust, arms and legs fanned out, increasing the wind resistance and marginally slowing the lone commando's descent through the rarified air. At one hundred and fifty miles per hour, it would take three minutes to fall the seven and a quarter miles before he would pull the ripcord on his parachute. The green "bailout" oxygen canister strapped to his left thigh provided supplemental oxygen.

At thirty thousand feet, about the height of Mount Everest, the commando checked the GPS strapped to his wrist. He was slightly off target. He had chosen the drop zone to allow for drifting as he fell through the jet stream; his parachute, once opened, was steerable, but had its limitations. He shifted his position to correct his glide.

At twenty thousand feet the city lights, which had been visible as one large glowing mass, transformed into a multitude of individual clusters. Only essential lights, such as streetlights, remained lit. The inhabitants of the city were for the most part asleep, oblivious to the man with a large wart on his nose falling through the air in the dark sky above them.

At ten thousand feet, individual lights became visible. When the ground was no more than a thousand feet below him, he pulled the ripcord, opening his chute. He checked his altimeter. He was still nine hundred and seventy-three feet above his target. Two minutes later he made a soft landing on the roof of a large office building, his black parachute collapsed around him.

A few sandwich wrappers and empty soft-drink cans suggested occasional use during daylight, but at this time in the night, the roof was deserted. The man retrieved suction cups from his pack and slipped over the edge of the building, clinging to the polished-marble with the mechanical suction devices. He maneuvered toward a window on the thirty-second floor, but arrived to find it occupied. A pigeon had constructed a nest on the window ledge and was prepared to defend it against the intruder with the grotesque snood on his beak.

The commando attached his waist harness to the suction cups, freeing his hands. Then he attached a small transparent plastic disk to the lower edge of the window just above the nest. Two microfilament wires connected the plastic disk to a miniature black box filled with electronics, batteries, and transmitter.

He looked for a place to hide the black box. Finding none, he lifted up the pigeon and placed the small box next to the two white eggs. By the time anyone discovered the box, it would have served its purpose. The black box would digitally record any speech or noise vibrating against the window and relayed them to a homeless wino sitting on a park bench below. The wino would have a large wart on his nose.

Madison, Wisconsin, 1420 hours

Agents Connie Rushford and Max Langston made a room-to-room search of the Hilton's fifth floor. They had reserved the entire floor for the President and his entourage. As agent in charge, Rushford cordoned off access to the floor and posted an agent at each entrance. No one could enter without an electronic check with a portable metal detector. Picture ID's were compared to a list of approved hotel employees.

She had assigned Man-of-War to room 508 with Al Webber in room 509 and the White House intern in room 507. The President's Press Secretary and Secret Service personal would fill other rooms on the floor. Buttercup decided at the last minute to remain in Washington, feeling preservation of the Amorous Spotted Slug needed her full attention. That was one less worry for Agent Rushford.

Rushford detested campaign tours. Control of physical structures was always limited. They could secure the fifth floor and possibly the hotel lobby, but who knew what idiot might be lurking on one of the other floors or the streets between the hotel and the auditorium. Most Presidential assassinations occurred outside the confines of the White House. Intoxicated by live audiences, Presidents were inclined toward the unexpected such as stopping a motorcade to converse with a little old lady on the street. No one can convince a President running for re-election that little old ladies now packed forty-fives.

Agent Rushford looked at her watch. Man-of-War would be arriving in forty-five minutes. Fortunately, he preferred unpretentious arrivals and would arrive without large crowds or a well-publicized motorcade from the airport to the hotel. Small crowds were nice, but no crowds were better—at least from security's viewpoint. The trip to the convention center would be a horse of a different color. She expected Man-of-War to arrive casually dressed and probably late. They would have less than an hour, to get him cleaned up, suitably dressed for the occasion, and transported to the convention center. This time it would be the traditional, slow, formal motorcade with a police escort, flashing red lights, sirens blaring, the full dog and pony show. Agents Rushford and Langston finished shaking down the last room. Nothing to do now but wait.

***

Air Force One arrived ten minutes late due to a strong headwind. Dane County Regional Airport, although not a regular commercial hub, still offered the amenities usually found in larger terminals, albeit on a smaller scale. The single concourse, with its octopus-like tentacles reaching out to assist passengers off the planes, waited patiently for Air Force One to saunter up to the open mouth of one of its tentacles. Instead, Air Force One taxied to an isolated section of the terminal, where a self-powered staircase pulled up to the plane, accompanied by the usual assortment of Secret Service agents. Several black, bulletproof limousines waited patiently not far from the base of the steps.

The President, not one for formality during travel, stepped off the plane in light blue shorts, scuffed up cowboy boots, and an old University of Michigan sweat shirt he had found lying around the White House. He assumed Jerry Ford left it. Finders keepers was one of Bart's guiding principles. He would change into something more Presidential at the hotel.

Secret Service agents sorted the disembarking passengers by rank and loaded them into waiting vehicles, while airport personnel transferred luggage from the plane to a large van. Within fifteen minutes the transfer was complete, and the caravan headed toward the hotel.

***

"Heads up," Agent Rushford whispered into the small microphone on her wrist. It was instantly relayed to the earphones of a dozen men in dark suits dispersed around the hotel lobby. "Here comes Man-of-War."

A corridor of dark suits formed between the limousine and the hotel elevator, which maintenance had programmed to go nonstop to the fifth floor. A squad of chauffeurs from the limousines carried an assortment of luggage into the hotel lobby. From that point the luggage was the hotel's responsibility, under Secret Service supervision of course.

"Where's my baby? Someone has taken my baby!" The distraught mother frantically ran up to the reception desk. "He's only two years old." Tears were flowing down the mother's face.

"Attention all agents, we have a situation in the lobby," Agent Rushford spoke into her wrist mike. "Get Man-of-War up to his room." Rushford watched as the dark suits formed a tight circle around the President, pushing him into the elevator.

In the excitement no one noticed as an extra hotel employee joined the crew caring for the luggage. Like the others, he also wore a nametag except Finlandia University had issued his nametag. Moose grabbed two suitcases, one bearing the seal of the President of the United States, and headed toward the elevators with the other employees. When the elevator stopped at the fifth floor, the other employees disembarked. No one noticed or seemed to care that Moose continued on to the sixth floor.

***

"What do you mean, my luggage is lost? How can you lose luggage on Air Force One?" Bart was not happy. He was scheduled to address the conference in twenty-five minutes. Blue shorts and a University of Michigan sweatshirt do not look very Presidential at a University of Wisconsin convention.

"My luggage is missing too," Veronica said. At least she was decently dressed and would not be the center of attention.

"Veronica, there's a gift shop in the hotel lobby." It was time for Ron Clark, White House Press Secretary, to take charge. "See if you can pick up one of those cheese hats. That will buy him points with the Wisconsin fans. If the President wears that, he can hold his cowboy hat in front of the University of Michigan logo on his sweat shirt."

"What about my shorts?" Bart asked. "Can't wear shorts to the convention."

"We'll have you surrounded by Secret Service agents. No one will see you below the waist." The Press Secretary was on a roll. "I want Veronica on stage with the President. With her looks, she'll draw some of the attention."

"We'll need to get rolling as soon as Veronica returns with the cheese hat," Al said. He could see a two-percentage-point loss in voter approval even if the Press Secretary's strategy worked.

"Do we have time to eat?" Bart asked. His stomach was beginning to growl.

"Air Force One's staff packed everyone a lunch," Al replied. "We'll have to eat on the run. This one's yours." Al passed a box to the President. Bart peered into the box, noting three celery sticks, a carrot, and a small container of cottage cheese.

"Esther's been talking to Air Force One's crew?" Bart asked.

"I'm afraid so," Al replied.

***

"I hope they aren't still looking for the lost two-year-old," Abigail said as she removed her blond wig.

"Let 'em keep looking. It'll give them something to do." Sherlock was never one to offer sympathy lavishly.

"Well, if they can't find the mother and have no picture for the milk carton, they'll lose interest," Newton said. "I'm sure they'll be more concerned with the missing luggage."

Newton adjusted some dials on a receiver that picked up radio traffic between Secret Service agents. It filtered messages through the computer's decryption software, and then broadcast it over the computer's speakers. So far the Secret Service's only concern was getting the President to the auditorium on time.

"That's not going to last," Abigail said. "We need to do our thing and get those suitcases back before they decide something sinister is about to happen."

Newton opened a box containing four unlabeled aerosol cans. "Just a light coat is all that's needed." Newton passed out the containers. "And keep it away from your own clothes unless you want to compete with Lady Godiva."

Abigail opened the suitcases filled with clothing. From the general disorder in the President's luggage, it was obvious he packed it himself. "We spray only the outer garments, no underwear." Abigail began spraying some dark-blue pants.

"Get a load of these black panties," Moose said, holding up a pair of

Veronica's underwear. "Can I keep these for my collection?"

"No, that would be stealing. Everything gets returned." Abigail experienced a moment of jealousy when she pulled out a "D" cup from Veronica's suitcase.

"We already stole a truckload of turkeys, that's grand larceny. If I take the panties it's only petty larceny."

"That would be panty larceny," Sherlock said with a chuckle. Sherlock's humor was lost on the others who were busy spraying garments.

"We return everything including the turkeys," Abigail said. "But we need to save one pair of Veronica's black panties and one of the President's white shirts. We'll return those later."

"Are you sure we can't do the underwear too?" Sherlock asked. "It looks like we'll have plenty of spray."

"Yes, I'm sure. We want to embarrass the President, not give innocent bystanders heart failure. No collateral damage."

Sherlock decided to spray the seat of the President's briefs. Sometimes you have to live in the fast lane.

"Is everyone done?" Abigail asked. There were nods in the affirmative. "Let's get everything back in the suitcases like we found it. If we put it back on the elevator, they'll assume it was just misplaced. Wipe down all metal and other smooth surfaces. No fingerprints."

*   *   *

"I thought the speech went well, considering everything," Bart said after he had returned to his room.

"You would have done better if you would have followed the speech instead of ad-libbing," his Press Secretary suggested. "That's when you get into trouble."

"How's that Ron?"

"First off, it's not the Green Bay Peckers."

"It's not?"

"They're called Packers."

"What's a Packer?"

"Also, the Golden Gophers are from Minnesota."

"What's that funny little animal then?"

"That's a Badger."

"Oh."

"And you don't make jokes about their cheese. People take their cheese seriously in Wisconsin."

"Other than that, how did I do?"

"Not too bad. I made sure the TV people didn't take any close ups."

"We do have some good news, Mr. President," Agent Rushford said. "We found the missing luggage. Apparently, someone left it in the elevator. I have to take full responsibility for the mishap. We should have been watching more closely. We're checking the luggage now for bombs and listening devices. As soon as that's done, you'll have them back."

"That's a relief," the Press Secretary said. "The President is scheduled to make an appearance this evening in the lobby. The Daughters of the American Revolution are having a reception. I was planning to cancel if the President didn't have formal attire."

"Tell them the President will be there," Bart said. "Us Texans can put on the airs, if need be."

"I think we'll have the luggage cleared by then," Rushford said.

***

"Are you a real Secret Service agent?" Abigail asked.

"Yes, I am."

"I'm Sally Bedford, reporter for the university radio station WIMP." Abigail held a microphone up to the agent. "Can I ask you a few questions for our listening audience?"

"We aren't allowed to give interviews. That's why they call us the Secret Service."

"Do you have a plan for every emergency?" Abigail asked.

"Yes, but I'm not at liberty to discuss them."

"So, if there were a fire on the fifth floor, you would have a plan?"

"If there's a fire on the fifth floor, we would use a predetermined plan."

Bingo, Abigail thought to herself. "Would it be safe to say you would evacuate the floor?"

"Yes, I'm sure we would evacuate the floor."

"What is your name?"

"Agent Bigsby."

"Agent Bigsby, I want to thank you for your time. Can you say this is Agent Bigsby in the hotel lobby, and I listen to WIMP?"

"This is Agent Bigsby in the hotel lobby, and I listen to WIMP."

"Thank you, Agent Bigsby, you have been a great help."

***

"It's almost time, Newton. I sure hope this stuff works." Abigail surveyed the electronic gadgetry with the skepticism of a non-believer.

"Oh, ye of little faith." Newton feigned his best martyr look.

"How do you know the sprinklers will turn on when we need them?" Sherlock shared Abigail's skepticism.

Liberal arts majors are so helpless, Newton thought. "You know that car door opener you have on your key chain?"

"Yeah."

"How do you know that works?"

"Because I've tried it."

"Same mechanism. If I were to stand in the stairwell and push my car door opener, the switch would turn on, electricity from the battery would run through the circuit, the thermo-resister wire wrapped around the heat-sensitive bead would warm up, and when the temperature reaches about one hundred and fifty degrees, I would get wet. Same kind of wire you find in a toaster. But since I have no desire to get wet, I have a more powerful transmitter I can use from our room. And, yes, I've tried it, and the transmitter will work at this distance."

"It's not that we doubt you, Newton, but it's all so complex."

"Ninth-grade science."

"Let's get started then," Abigail suggested.

"Let me program in some static first."

***

"Sorry it took so long, Mr. President, but we had to clear the suitcases before returning them. Can't be too cautious after that gelatin thing." Rushford was still sensitive about her previous lapse in security. She was not about to let it happen again.

"That's all right, little lady. Those things do happen."

Rushford wondered how he got any of the female vote. "The rest of the staff is already downstairs. Agent Langston and I'll escort you and Ms. Doyal down whenever you're ready."

Agent Langston, with his usual assortment of guns and knives attached to various parts of his anatomy was inspecting his 9 mm. He was feeling naked since he had to leave his Uzi in the hotel room. The Daughters of the American Revolution might frown upon such heavy armament.

"*STATIC*... This is Agent ...*STATIC*... in the lobby. ...*STATIC*... There's a fire on ...*STATIC*... floor. Evacuate the floor. ...*STATIC*..."

"You're breaking up. Please repeat." Rushford was hoping she hadn't heard right.

"This is...*STATIC*...Bigsby in the lobby. ...*STATIC*... Fire on fifth floor. ...*STATIC*... Evacuate ...*STATIC*..."

"Mr. President, we need to get out of here. There's a fire on the floor." Rushford tried to contact the other agents but received only static.

"I'll get Doyal." Langston headed next door.

"Is there really a fire?" Veronica asked when she returned with Langston.

"We're not hanging around to find out." Agent Rushford stepped into the hall to ensure the hallway was secure. The hallway was empty. "Let's go, Mr. President. We need to get down to the lobby." She would have felt better if she had contact with the other agents. They should be securing the lobby.

Langston grabbed his Uzi on the way out the door. The Daughters of the American Revolution would have to make an exception.

"I'll get the elevator," Veronica said.

"Not in a fire. We're using the stairwell." Rushford herded her charges toward the stairwell. Thank God the hotel had the foresight to install sprinklers and smoke detectors in the stairwell.

Langston, Uzi at the ready, entered the stairwell first to secure the area. "Sprinklers are on, but the smoke detectors aren't working."

"Do you smell smoke?"

"No smoke," Langston replied.

That's a good sign, Rushford thought. No smoke to trigger the alarms, but the temperature must have been over one hundred and fifty degrees to trigger the sprinklers. It wasn't hot now. The cold water must have cooled off the stairwell.

"My hair will be ruined," Veronica wailed as she entered the stairwell. "And my dress is getting wet."

"You can redo your hair, and I can assure you your dress is not water soluble." Where do they find these bimbos, Rushford wondered. "If we do get into fire, you'll be glad your clothes are wet."

All three sprinklers were spraying heavy volumes of water, which cascaded down the steps, making walking treacherous.

"Let us go first. I want you two to follow about two paces back." Rushford despised deviations from the normal plan. That was when accidents happened. She would feel better once they got the President out of the stairwell and onto the main floor where there would be additional agents to secure the area.

The sprinkler at the base of the main floor had not activated, a good sign, Rushford thought. They were probably safe. Fires spread upward, not down.

"Wait here while we check out the lobby." Agents Rushford and Langston stepped into the lobby. Ladies in formal attire were sipping on glasses of pink lemonade and eating small sandwiches impaled on large toothpicks, oblivious to any threat of fire. "You can come out now." The attention of the social elite immediately fixed on the .38-caliber revolver and Uzi submachine gun wielded by the two Secret Service agents. The point of attraction soon shifted as Bart and Veronica, draped in wet underwear, stepped into the lobby. Remnants of expensive clothing still clung to their shoulders. A five-inch diameter hole provided a southern exposure to the seat of Bart's underwear.

***

"We only have two or three minutes at best," Abigail informed the others. "It's in and out."

Moose slipped the electronic key into the lock of room 508. It opened as expected. The President's suitcase lay open on the bed.

"If you touch anything, wipe it off. No fingerprints." Abigail quickly stuffed Veronica's black panties and the President's white shirt into the suitcase. "Let's get out of here."

First Bedroom, 2235 hours

Bart tried the bedroom door. It was locked. "Honey?" Bart knocked on the door. *No response.* "Esther?" He knocked again. "Honey?"

Esther, her face covered with a thick layer of foul smelling mud, opened the door wide enough to push out a suitcase. "Here, I repacked your suitcase for you. You may need it. It's packed with underwear. It appears that's all you need to wear these days."

"I can explain," Bart lied. The truth was he had no idea what had happened. He was sure he put his pants on before he left the hotel room.

"Explain these!" Esther held up a pair of black panties. "I found them in your suitcase."

"They must be yours."

"Be a little tight on me, don't ya think? They also have 'VD' embroidered on them. What is Veronica's last name, again?"

"Doyal?"

"Bingo! Very appropriate initials, by the way."

"They told you our luggage got lost, didn't they? The panties must have gotten mixed up with my clothes when the Secret Service agents screened our baggage."

"I suppose it got mixed up with your white shirt." Esther held up exhibit "B." "Note the lipstick on the collar. And no, that's not my color." Esther pushed the suitcase out of the doorway and shut the door. Bart could hear the click of the lock.

There's always the Lincoln bedroom, Bart decided.

Chapter Seven

Oval Office, 0945 hours

Bart cinched up his pants and stepped out of the Porta-Potty. He had hoped the Presidential Seal above the door would provide a more dignified appearance to the structure, but it still looked like an outhouse. He had used outhouses many times at the ranch, and they did have their place, but that place didn't include the Oval Office. How would he greet foreign dignitaries and heads of state? If they were to ask to use the facilities, was he to say, "Right here, your highness. You better take the can of air freshener and go easy on the carbon paper. I don't know when Charlie will send up real toilet paper?"

He had received the requested air freshener after four days, and he could now open the windows. That was only because Charlie expedited the order. According to Charlie, he would have to resubmit the request for toilet paper. Apparently, TP is not an approved abbreviation on form 840-5. Bart toyed with the idea of having the IRS audit Charlie's returns, but decided against it. Charlie had the power to clean out the sewer, which outranked control of the IRS. He held all the aces. Bart could see Charlie's point. If he had made an exception for Bart, he would have to make exceptions for all future presidents.

At least the Porta-Potty was functional, fulfilling an important niche in life's daily routine. Unlike his ranch, the Oval Office offered limited trees and shrubs capable of providing biological relief; most of those that did were now dead. With the can of air freshener and the open windows, the odor was tolerable once you got used to it. It was an acquired taste. The Porta-Potty had a few drawbacks: Bart found a dark rug stain behind the Porta-Potty. They must have given him one of the leaky units.

Another disadvantage was currently strutting across Bart's desk. Bart took off his shoe and tossed it at the pigeon. It was one of his better shots, but still fell short, knocking the empty cookie jar off the desk. Bart was sure he would get the proper range with practice. The winged transgressor sought refuge in the leafless tree by the wall, but not before leaving a deposit on Bart's desk.

Bart had pronounced the nine-foot tree officially dead and put in a requisition to have the tree removed, but a pair of pigeons had set up housekeeping on one of the taller branches. All the more reason to remove the tree, Bart thought. Unfortunately, someone notified Esther who released a picture to the news media. The breeding pair of pigeons was now a national icon, at least for the Sesame Street crowd. PBS had a *name that pigeon* contest, should the two small eggs hatch into young pigeons. Bart thought they would make a better omelet. They were small, but compared to celery and carrot sticks, even small looked promising.

If it were just the Sesame Street set, Bart wouldn't have cared—they can't vote—but Esther had him on probation; and although he was no longer sleeping in the Lincoln bedroom, necessity required he keep a low profile. With a few more days of good behavior, perhaps he could renegotiate his diet—he missed his chocolate chip cookies.

Bart walked over to his open window and looked out at the South Lawn. Life was so simple out there. Tourists could go to the Visitor Pavilion on the Ellipse and find flushing toilets and hot running water. They had real toilet paper. Bart wondered if it would be a federal crime to steal toilet paper from the Visitor Pavilion.

He should be happy only two pigeons had set up housekeeping in the Oval Office. With no screen on the window, he could envision large flocks of pigeons enjoying a little R and R at his expense. Bart asked Charlie about a screen, but Charlie was not optimistic. Apparently, that was a capital expense and needed the approval of the Ways and Means

Committee. The Republicans on the committee would surely demand political concessions before approving such a request. According to Charlie, the biggest obstacle was obtaining permission from the White House Historical Society. They frowned upon changes to the White House décor.

"Enjoying the view?" Al asked as he entered the room. He had several newspapers under his arm, not a good sign.

Bart wandered back to his desk. He was beginning to hate these morning briefings. Al never had good news anymore. Today's briefing folder looked thicker than normal. Bart covered the pigeon dropping on his desk with a small potted plant and settled back in his chair. Out of sight, out of mind Bart decided. His desk now had three small plotted plants.

"O.K., hit me with the bad news. I can take it like a man," Bart lied. He wondered if he should take his aspirin now or wait ten minutes for the headache to start.

"It's not all bad news."

"It's not?"

"Well, most of it is. However, we do have some leads on the Avian Liberation League, which I'll go over later," Al said, "but we might as well get the bad news out of the way first."

Bart reached for his aspirin.

"The papers are hitting up that Madison thing." Al tossed several newspapers onto Bart's desk. The *New York Times* headline read, "President makes *brief* appearance at D.A.R."

"At least the *Washington Post* makes no mention of it," Bart said as he checked out the front page.

"Look in the Fashion Section. There's a two column article discussing whether you might have looked more presidential if you had been wearing boxer shorts instead of briefs."

"Which do you think I should wear?" Bart asked.

"According to a non-scientific phone poll conducted by the *Washington Post*, sixty-two percent thought briefs made you look more macho. Although ten percent thought the photos were computer enhanced to make you appear more endowed."

It wouldn't hurt to have the pictures touched up a bit more, Bart thought. After all, he was from Texas.

"The *Christian Science Monitor* has taken a moralistic approach," Al said. "They have an interview with Walter Brainthorpe as their lead story. We may have to take a serious look at him."

Bart shuffled the papers until he came to the *Christian Science Monitor*. "Brainthorpe questions the moral integrity of the current White House," proclaimed the headline.

"You think he wants to run for political office?" Bart asked.

"He's going around the country on the lecture circuit emphatically stating that he has no intention of running for any office and will not even consider a draft. Sure sounds like a run to me. Could make a try for congressman, maybe even senator if his popularity holds."

"Ya think he's a Republican?"

"The way he's bashing your moral character, that would be my guess."

"You said you had some good news?" Bart asked hopefully.

"Yeah, we got a break on the Avian Liberation League investigation. The FBI analyzed the clothes in your suitcase. They were impregnated with Preparation J."

"Preparation J?"

"Named after its creator, Dr. Jack Hansen. They thought it best to use the initial of his first name instead of his last name." Al flipped through his folder until he came to the Preparation J report. "According to what my staff discovered, Dr. Hansen from Michigan Tech was given a government grant to develop water soluble paper. The government wanted to use the paper for sensitive documents in foreign embassies. In the event of a terrorist takeover, the ambassador could order the papers hosed down and rendered useless. This would be faster than shredding reams of paper. Dr. Hansen didn't develop a water-soluble paper but did create a solution that can be sprayed on regular paper to make them water-soluble. We're already testing it in selected embassies."

Al paused so the President could digest the new information; high technology easily overwhelmed the President. "According to campus police, students at Michigan Tech discovered it also works on cotton and wool. This, I guess, shouldn't be surprising since many papers have a high rag content. Anyway, students are spraying their dates with what they claim to be mosquito repellant before taking them for a walk in the rain."

"Ya think you could get me a can?" Bart asked. A silly grin spread across Bart's face.

Al had seen that silly grin before, and it usually cost two percentage points in the polls. "All the Preparation J has been secured as evidence," Al lied.

"Everything keeps pointing to Michigan's Upper Peninsula: the turkey rustling, the Amorous Spotted Slug, the weapons-grade gelatin, and now this." Bart stood up to scratch a recalcitrant itch on his right buttock. The Preparation J had eaten the hairs on his buttocks, and the new growth was bristly and itchy. "I want that peninsula turned upside down. I want no expense spared. This has to be top priority in every agency. I want to put an end to this nonsense once and for all. No Yooper yahoo is going to make a fool of Bart Schroeder and get away with it," Bart said as he started pacing the floor.

"Your phone's ringing."

"What?"

"I said your phone's ringing."

"Oh." Bart sat down at his desk and reached for the phone. It would be his secretary. She screened all of his calls.

Bart: *Yes?*

Secretary: *Sorry to bother you during your briefing, but I have a very persistent lady on the phone by the name of Abigail Farnsworth. She says you would be expecting her call.*

Bart: *Abigail Farnsworth?*

"That's our bird lady," Al said.

Bart: *Put her on.*

Al retrieved a cell phone from the pocket of his hand-tailored suit and dialed security. "Security?" Al whispered. "This is Al Webber calling from the Oval Office. We need an emergency trace on the phone call to the President's phone…Right…Call me back at 555-9200."

Abigail: *Is this Bart Schroeder?*

Bart: *Yes, it is. And what can I do for you, young lady?*

Abigail: *It's what we can do for you.*

"Keep her on the phone," Al whispered. "It takes about ninety seconds to trace a call."

Bart: *Exactly what do you think you can do for me?*

Abigail: *I can help you keep your pants on. I can unplug your sewer system. I can make the Amorous Spotted Slugs disappear. And, if I'm really feeling generous, I can return your turkeys.*

"Keep her on for another thirty seconds," Al said.

Bart: *I assume all this generosity comes at a price?*

Abigail: *We want you to introduce a bill in Congress authorizing the establishment of the Upper Peninsula as the fifty-first state. We want to secede from Michigan.*

Bart: *You want to do what?*

Abigail: *You heard me. We want our own state.*

Al pointed to his watch. "Twenty more seconds."

Bart: *I would have to think about that for a while, give it some study.*

Abigail: *You're stalling. The way I see it, you need ninety seconds to trace this call, and you still have fifteen seconds left.*

Bart: *Now, why would I want to trace this call?*

Abigail: *If you wanted to know where I'm calling from, all you have to do is ask.*

Bart: *O.K., I'll bite. Where you calling from?*

Abigail: *I'm calling from the phone in your bedroom. I hope that's O.K.*

Bart: *Yes, of course you are.*

Al picked up his cell phone on the first ring.

Abigail: *I guess I should be going. You should be getting confirmation about now, and we both have lots of work to do. I'll call back later for your reply.*

Bart: *Yes, please do.*

Abigail: *As a gesture of good will, we'll even return your turkeys.* (Click)

"She hung up."

"That's O.K.," Al said, covering the receiver on his cell phone. "We got the trace. You won't believe this, but she called from your bedroom phone."

"Hello?" Al said into his phone. "We have a female intruder in the President's bedroom…Yes…Lock down the White House. No one goes in or out."

"You mean she actually is in my bedroom? How the heck did she get past security?"

Al hung up the phone. "It doesn't matter how she got in. She can't get out. The building's locked up tighter than the drawstrings on a suma wrestler's loincloth. No way she's getting away this time." Al began to hyperventilate. Bart reached into his desk drawer for Al's paper bag.

Maybe it was finally over, Bart thought. If they could catch Abigail Farnsworth, the investigation would be over and Charlie could open up the sewers. This deserves a chocolate chip cookie. Bart reached into the cookie jar, forgetting it was now empty. It would have been a good day for a cookie.

Al removed the paper bag from his mouth long enough to answer his phone. "You do?" Al listened for a moment or two. "That's great. Keep up the good work." Al hung up the phone and returned it to his coat pocket.

"That was Agent Rushford. She says she and Agent Langston caught our little prankster red-handed. Appears she's a bit deranged. Her face was covered with mud."

"Covered with mud?"

"Foul smelling stuff, Rushford said. Smelled like sulfur. Anyway, they've done a strip search, and as soon as they get more help, they'll do a cavity search. Rushford said she was pretty feisty."

Bart picked up his phone and dialed housekeeping. "This is President Schroeder, can you fix up the Lincoln bedroom. We'll need it tonight."

Chapter Eight

White House basement, 2210 hours

"How long ya think they'll keep us in the dungeon?" This was Langston's third day on dungeon duty, and it was already rattling his nerves. He preferred windows and sunlight; the White House basement offered neither. What florescent lighting was intentionally dim, designed to enhance images on the monitor screens in front of Agents Rushford and Langston.

"I'm hoping no longer than two weeks." Rushford sipped at her coffee. Caffeine was mandatory on this assignment. "The First Lady holds a grudge, but she has a short attention span. In a few days, she'll have new people at the top of her people-to-hate list."

"We were only following orders. They told us to apprehend the woman in the bedroom."

"You're thinking logically, Langston. Politics is incompatible with logic." Rushford reached for another chocolate from a box of assorted goodies. She had been eating too many of them lately, but stress will do that to a woman. As senior Secret Service agent, she had more to lose than Langston.

Dungeon duty remained an important part of White House security, but also a dead-end assignment. Nothing ever happened in the dungeon. No important decisions were made, no recognition was ever received, and no promotions were awarded. It also taxed one's sanity. Eight hours of watching video cameras and infrared sensors monitoring the White House grounds would surpass anyone's criteria for cruel and unusual punishment. Only the occasional raccoon or skunk wandering across the front lawn broke the monotony. The First Lady vigorously complained about the bright lights at night—they interfered with her REM sleep. As a result, the Secret Service only employed motion and infrared detectors after ten p.m. With the video cameras turned off, agents on dungeon duty couldn't differentiate sinister intruders from the benign raccoons. Two low-ranking Secret Service agents had to investigate all bogeys with flashlights and probing sticks guided by the dungeon's infrared monitors—a dangerous job if the bogey happened to be a skunk. A normal night produced six to eight such false alarms. If nothing more, they punctuated an otherwise boring night.

Reading on the job represented a flagrant violation of Secret Service policy, but all policies were meant to be broken. Rushford searched her purse for one of her Harlequin romance novels she used to protect her sanity. She found it nestled next to her .38-caliber revolver. She didn't know why she bothered bringing her gun to work. She would never need it in the dungeon, except to shoot Langston if were to become too obnoxious. She flipped through the pages until she arrived at the dog-eared page where she left off the night before. Propping her feet on the desk cluttered with monitors, she settled back in her chair to enjoy her book.

Everyone assumed Secret Service agents led exciting lives. Rushford would gladly trade lives with any of the characters in her romance novels. They found more romance and excitement in one day than she experienced in a year. Tonight was no exception. They had yet to produce even one furry bogey to add to the log of nightly transgressors. If they did materialize, she was confident Langston could handle the situation. He was too hyperactive to waste time reading. He preferred playing with the monitors. In his spare time, he cleaned and re-cleaned the multitude of firearms strapped to various parts of his anatomy. Any literature he did read was limited to *Soldiers of Fortune* magazines, which he thumbed through looking for additional lethal weapons to attach to the remaining parts of his body.

Washington D.C., 0300 hours

Three a.m. on a Saturday night is quiet in Washington D.C. The tourists are exhausted and recuperating in over-priced hotels, gift shops and nightclubs are closed and will not reopen until the tourists have fully recovered, and the handful of low-level government employees still on duty, were usually sequestered in obscure, back room offices. For the most part, the streets are deserted. Only an occasional vehicle, perhaps transporting a tired diplomat home after an exhaustive late-night meeting, breaks the monotony.

The old rusted-out Volkswagen bus held together by travel decals and bumper stickers was, therefore, out of place as it traveled north on 17th Street. Even more out of place was the eighteen-wheeler that followed one hundred yards behind. But no one noticed when the caravan continued north past Constitution Avenue. No one cared when they turned east on East Street, heading toward the South Lawn of the White House. Someone did care when the Volkswagen bus turned north on West Executive Avenue, heading toward the southwest gate of the White House. A Secret Service agent stepped out of the security shack to shake down the wayward tourists and head them back in the direction from which they came. The agent was twenty feet away when the bus burst into flames. He could hear people screaming inside the bus, some of them children. A pet dog was barking. With the fire too hot to approach and the fire extinguisher in the guard shack too small to be of value on a gasoline fire, the agent ran back to the shack to call in the emergency.

The eighteen-wheeler did not turn north on West Executive Avenue but continued down East Street, coming to a stop near the fence bordering the South Lawn. A car with markings similar to White House security vehicles, red lights flashing, pulled up behind the truck.

Abigail climbed down from the truck cab and walked over to the passenger side of the security vehicle. "Well, Newton, how did it go?"

"Piece of cake. The propane tank will keep the fire burning for another twenty minutes, and the tape of the screaming kids is good for ten minutes. It'll keep them busy long enough for our needs." Newton tossed the remote control device into the car's back seat. "Let's get to work."

The four Yoopers walked to the back of the trailer while emergency vehicles screamed past them, sirens blaring, all assuming the security vehicle behind the eighteen wheeler had that situation under control. They had more important matters to contend with. They had a family trapped in a burning Volkswagen bus.

Moose opened the door to the trailer, revealing twelve hundred and twenty-four unhappy White Holland turkeys. Ten minutes later the quartet had all the turkeys liberated onto the South Lawn, returning them to their rightful owner as Abigail had promised. The turkeys, relishing their newfound freedom, scattered in every direction.

White House basement, 0305 hours

"Looks like a bogey on the South Lawn," Langston adjusted a dial on the infrared monitor to enhance the image. "The heat signature is about the size of a basketball. Probably a coon or skunk."

Rushford didn't look up from her book. It was just getting juicy. Nurse Hadley had consented to have Dr. Thompson's baby, but Dr. Thompson would have to agree to a vasectomy reversal, confirmed by sperm count, before Nurse Hadley would divorce her current husband, the eminent Dr. Tugwell. The book was far more interesting than any coon or skunk trespassing on federal property. "Call Team Three and have them check it out."

Langston called Team Three on the secure communications system. A small digital device in the team leader's shirt pocket unscrambled the message before passing it on to his earpiece. Speaking into a small microphone, the leader of Team Three gave a terse reply.

"Team Three's tied up. We have a burning vehicle just outside the southwest gate with people inside. The bogeys will have to wait."

Rushford paused in her reading. She had little concern for furry animals loose on the White House lawn; still, someone needed to check them out. She did feel for the family trapped in the burning vehicle. She was not a cold, heartless person, but after the recent shenanigans, she was a bit paranoid.

"I now have three…no, wait…five bogeys on the screen," Langston said.

"They're too small for people." Rushford set her book down to study the screen. "They're spreading across the lawn. A family of coons would stay together."

"Could be people wearing infrared-absorbing fatigues. Only radiation from the head would be visible."

Langston had been reading too many commando magazines for Rushford's taste. "Call Team Three and tell them the South Lawn bogeys are top priority."

Agent Rushford monitored the screens while Langston directed the two men of Team Three toward the South Lawn. There were now ten bogeys on the screen and motion detectors were tripping all over the compound. "They have enough strength for an entire squad." Rushford grabbed the mike from Langston's hand. "Team Three, be advised you may be up against a superior force. Assume they are heavily armed."

The two agents stared at the monitors in disbelief. Hundreds of commandos were spreading out across the South Lawn and more were infiltrating every minute.

"Team Three can't deal with a force that size," Langston said, gently caressing his Uzi. "We need more firepower."

"All security units, this is Agent Rushford. The perimeter has been breached by commandos of company size or larger. All security teams are to pull back to the White House. I repeat, pull back to the White House. We'll make our stand there. And get Man-of-War and Buttercup into the bomb shelter."

Langston hung up his phone. "That was the Virginia National Guard. They'll have six Apache gunships overhead in ten minutes."

"If we can only hold out that long. As soon as all agents are inside the White House, I'm issuing an order to shoot anything that moves on the lawn. Will we be able to communicate with the Apache helicopters?"

"Are you kidding? This is the White House. We can talk to Cheyenne Mountain if we need to. We can call in a tactical nuclear strike."

"You are jesting...aren't you?" With Langston, Rushford never knew for sure.

Somewhere over Northern Virginia, 0315 hrs.

Major Crawford of the Virginia National Guard checked his altimeter. They were flying at six hundred feet. The sky was cloudless and the stars were bright, but without a moon, visibility remained low. Crawford instructed the other Apache attack helicopters to maintain running lights. A mid-air collision was far more likely than the threat from imaginary ground fire. "Keep the formation tight," Crawford told the other five pilots. "We don't want anyone wandering around in the dark."

"What the heck are we doing up here anyway?" Crawford's wingman asked over his radio. "And why the live ordnance? Someone could get hurt playing with this stuff."

"Flight OPS says the White House is under attack by commandos," Crawford replied. "Personally, I think it's another drill ordered by Homeland Security to check our response time. I just hope they don't drag out this drill. I have to fly to San Francisco in the morning." In his other life, Major Crawford was Captain Crawford, pilot for a major airline. Three years earlier, he had turned in his Air Force wings, finding the commercial pay scale more lucrative than the military's meager wages. Flying Apache helicopters for the National Guard was not as glamorous as the stealth fighter he had flown in the first Gulf War, although it did give him additional flight time.

But the Apache was more personal. With the F-117 Nighthawk, he dropped his bombs in the dead of night, sometimes as high as forty thousand feet, oblivious to what was happening on the ground below. His target was no more than a coordinate on his GPS. But the Apache, that was a get-in-your-face fighting machine. The Apache carried four rocket pods, each with nineteen Hydra 70, 2.75-inch rockets. When he unloaded all seventy-six of those babies on the target range, they tore an area the size of a football field to shreds leaving a multitude of four-foot diameter craters. Not bad for a few seconds of firepower.

If that didn't get the attention of the bad guys, he had his M 230, 30 mm cannon, which fired one-inch diameter rounds filled with high explosives at a rate of six hundred and twenty-five rounds per minute. Now that was a lot of firepower for one fighting machine, and he had six such fighting machines at his disposal. But he had to agree with his wingman. It was too much firepower to play with outside the target range. It would be safer if Homeland Security ran their drills without live ammo.

"White House control, this is Apache Six. We will be overhead with six birds in two minutes. We are awaiting instructions."

"Apache Six, this is White House control. We have militant terrorists in control of the White House grounds. All friendlies are inside the building. Place everything you got on the White House lawn."

"Say again?"

"Place all ordnance on the lawn but avoid the White House. I repeat, avoid the White House."

"Be advised, we have live ordnance."

"Hey man, that's the best kind. And the sooner the better. We don't know how much longer we can hold out."

"Apache Six leader to all birds. This drill has all the makings of a disaster, but the bureaucrats want a dog and pony show. We'll make a mock run on the White House lawn and head for home. Be advised the White House has people on the roof with Stinger surface-to-air missiles. With our luck, there will be at least one yahoo who won't know we're coming. If your threat indicator goes off, drop some flares and get the heck out of there."

Crawford checked his GPS. They should be getting close. The lights of Washington D.C. were already below him. The White House should be somewhere under his nose. He dipped the nose of his craft to get a better view.

The White House, lit only by landscape lighting and the floodlights around the fountain on the South Lawn, slowly came into view. Tracer rounds from automatic weapons sprayed out from all sides of the White

House. Some of the tracers hit rocks in the yard and ricocheted into the air, forming large, lethal arcs.

Crawford found himself holding his breath. He hadn't seen that much tracer fire since Baghdad in '91.

"Apache Six leader to all birds. This is not a drill. I repeat, this is not a drill. We will climb to one thousand feet to get above the tracer rounds. We'll hit them first with rockets. I'll take lead. Follow me in at one hundred yard intervals."

Crawford climbed to one thousand feet and leveled off. "May God have mercy on their souls," Crawford whispered when he began his run on the White House lawn. One hundred yards behind him, the next of five Apaches followed him in. He held his breath again as seventy-six rockets screamed out of their pods toward the insurgents. Crawford banked to the right when the last of the rockets left the tube, making room for the next Apache. He could see a barrage of flashes as the rockets hit the ground. Down below, hundreds of turkeys, already having a bad day, were blown skyward, some into trees, others landing in flowerbeds or pools beneath large water fountains.

"Apache Six leader to all birds. Line up on me. We'll make another run using our 30 mm cannons, this time at five hundred feet." The other birds were already lining up.

The M 230 chain gun was independently aimed, and Crawford swung the barrel back and forth, spraying the White House grounds at six hundred and twenty-five rounds per minute. Each round exploded on impact with a force greater than a cherry bomb. Shrapnel from the exploding rounds ripped into the panic-stricken birds. Any turkey unfortunate enough to receive a direct hit immediately exploded with giblets and gizzards thrown as far as twenty feet.

"White House control, this is Apache Six. We're out of ammo and heading home."

"Apache Six, this is White House control. Thanks for your help. We can handle it from here."

Oval Office 0945 hrs.

President Schroeder looked out the open window at the South Lawn. The southwest guard shack was still smoldering, having caught fire after taking a direct hit from a rocket early in the attack. Fortunately, no one was injured. A multitude of four-foot diameter craters littered what remained of the South Lawn, a testimony to the lethality of the 2.75-inch rockets. Numerous white patches lay scattered across the lawn, each representing the remains of a White Holland turkey that had paid the ultimate price and had died for its country. Later in the day, a White House press release would refer to them as collateral damage.

Large branches had been violently torn from trees with turkeys impaled on the jagged stubs. Other turkeys, caught in the crotches of knurled branches, dangled down like grotesque Christmas tree ornaments. A rocket had damaged the pump for the fountain on the South Lawn but it was still functional, pumping out water in small, inconsistent spurts. It reminded Bart of his chronic prostate problem. The water squirting from the spout was blood red as was the water in the surrounding pool. Bloated bodies, floating beak down, bobbled aimlessly in the water. Old veterans would later compare it to the beaches of Normandy.

Strange as it may sound, not all the turkeys perished during the previous night's onslaught. A good share, perhaps half, survived and were swarming around the grounds in mass confusion. One turkey was entangled in the flagpole rope and now flew at half-mast, a few feet below Old Glory. The turkey, apparently unharmed, flew around the pole tetherball style, first going clockwise and then counterclockwise to unwind.

Bart would have preferred eliminating the survivors with a small squad armed with shotguns. Unfortunately, the American Civil Freedom Union, a consortium of ultra-liberal lawyers, had demanded the government provide the surviving turkeys with all the rights and privileges accorded by the Geneva Convention. They would have to capture the remaining turkeys alive. Perhaps he would have the surviving turkeys sent to Guantanamo Bay. Out of sight, out of mind.

Down below, Agents Rushford and Langston, with butterfly nets in hand, chased survivors across the yard. With their future in the service in doubt, their supervisor selected them for the turkey-trot assignment under the assumption it was a job they couldn't screw up. Bart would have to have them make a house call. A White Holland turkey was currently strutting across his desk. Bart took off a shoe and chucked it at the intruder, but the battle-hardened veteran had survived 2.75-inch rockets and 30 mm cannon fire. A mere incoming shoe was an insult. The turkey, nevertheless, made a deposit on the desk and hopped down. The arrogant bird had either flown in or was blown through the open window during the night. Bart assumed the latter. It made him appreciate the pigeons nesting in his tree. Covering pigeon do-do only required a small flowered pot.

"You sure know how to throw a party," Al said with an attempt at levity. Al collapsed into a chair. "Just the same, I'm glad I wasn't invited." The dark circles surrounding bloodshot eyes confirmed that, even though Al had not been to the party, he had been up most of the night trying to put a positive spin on a negative situation. Under his arm was an assortment of folders and newspapers. He had done his homework.

"Ya got any idea what went on last night?" Bart asked. His eyes were also bloodshot and droopy. "Haven't seen that much lead in the air since the Bailey boys broke into Hank Henderson's chicken coop."

"Best I can figure, that Abigail Farnsworth, or whoever she is, was behind it."

"Dang that little filly. We need to have her roped and hawg tied."

"We found your turkey transporter by the fence on the South Lawn. It had 'Save the Turkeys' scribbled with lipstick on the windshield. Seems they threw the turkeys over the fence while security was trying to rescue a family in a burning vehicle."

"Think they faked the burning vehicle, you know, as a decoy?"

"Not a chance. Agents heard children screaming for a good ten minutes, even a family dog."

"We need to play that up. Maybe I can give the security agents a medal or something. Have my picture taken with them."

"You may be too busy for that." Al opened his folders.

Bart opened his bottle of aspirin. There had to be a lot of bad news in those folders. "O.K. let me have it." He took three aspirin plus a Valium he had stolen from his wife. Hopefully, she wouldn't count her pills."

"We received several formal complaints," Al said as he settled back in his chair.

He should have taken two Valium, Bart decided. He also needed a chocolate chip cookie. Why can't a President have a cookie when he needs one?

"The ambassador from the Netherlands has filed a formal complaint. They don't like your use of White Holland turkeys and are demanding a public apology."

"They think I did this on purpose?" Bart slumped lower in his chair. He needed a vacation. Maybe he should go to Camp David.

"A public apology might not be a bad idea. They could take this to the United Nations and make an international scene."

Or he could go to Hawaii, maybe get some tan.

"The Rev. Reggie Johnson wants to know why there were no black turkeys. He's thinking about organizing a march on Washington."

He would have to stop by Pearl Harbor and inspect the troops. That would make it look like official business.

"The Audubon Society is already picketing out front."

The turkey ranch is out; don't need to see more turkeys.

"Walter Brainthorpe is calling it a travesty and a flagrant misuse of the military. As you know, he's the spokesman for the Audubon Society. We need to watch that guy...Are you listening?"

"What?..." Bart vaguely remembered Al had been talking to him. "Excuse me. My phone's ringing."

Bart let the phone ring three times. He never answered the phone on the first ring. People needed to know he was real busy.

Bart: *Hello?*

"No one's there," Bart said, looking at the receiver as if he could see any noise coming out.

"I think the ringing is coming from your desk," Al said.

Bart opened a large drawer to his desk. His red phone was ringing.

He picked it up and set it on his desk. "That would be the Kremlin."

"You goin' answer it?"

Bart stared at the phone, hoping it would stop ringing—it didn't.

Bart: *Hello?*

Abigail: *I hope you don't mind me using this phone. Your wife was using the phone in the bedroom.*

Bart: *Where you calling from?*

Abigail: *The Kremlin, silly. If you trace the call, I'm sure it will confirm it.*

Bart: *What can I do for you today?*

Abigail: *Just checking to see if you got all your turkeys. There should be twelve hundred and twenty-four.*

Bart: *Young lady, you're in big trouble. The FBI is hot on your tail. You'll spend a long time in Leavenworth for this.*

Abigail: *Does that mean you're not ready to make the U.P. the fifty-first state?*

Bart: *I'd sooner sit naked on an anthill!*

Abigail: *We can arrange that.*

Bart slammed the receiver down. "How does she do that? First she calls from my bedroom, and then she calls from the Kremlin."

"I talked to the phone company," Al said. "It appears they're hacking into the phone company's computer system. They re-route the call, making it look like it originated somewhere else, totally untraceable… and they're reversing the charges. We paid for that call! The phone company can't wait to get their hands on whoever is doing it."

"Suppose they want to tar and feather her too."

"No, they want to hire her as a computer security consultant. None of their people can do what she's doing…and they have Ph.D.'s!"

"Ya think Abigail is really that smart?"

"Maybe…maybe not. This is too big for one person. We're talking major conspiracy. The Avian Liberation League is obviously a front. That fifty-first state thing could also be a front for some more sinister plan."

"How ya think they're bankrolling all this? It's got to cost a bit of money."

"Beats me. But that does remind me. Your Visa and MasterCard are both maxed out, and your account is overdrawn at the bank."

"I haven't been spending much money. I charge everything to the taxpayers. It must be Esther."

"Well, if this leaks out, it could make you appear fiscally irresponsible."

"I'll have to talk to Esther about that."

Bart returned the red phone to his desk drawer. "We need better intel. We need boots on the ground. Someone who can turn that little peninsula upside down and shake it. Who's the best undercover agent we got?"

"CIA's got a guy that's pretty good."

"What's his name?"

"Nobody knows. They refer to him as Agent X."

"What's he look like?"

"No one's seen him in years. They deposit his paycheck in an offshore bank account. The only description in his file refers to a large wart on his nose."

"But he's the best?"

"The best."

"Call Langley and get his phone number. I want him on this right away."

"He doesn't have a phone."

"He doesn't have a phone? How do they contact him?"

"Last time they put the request in a capsule with a radio transmitter and then stuffed it down the throat of a twenty-four foot anaconda. They turned the snake loose in the Amazon jungle. Agent X checked-in four hours later. We'll have Langley send out a call, and he'll contact us."

Chapter Nine

The Lincoln Memorial, 1000 hours

"This is Rob Carter for Channel 7 News here in front of the Lincoln Memorial where demonstrators are gathering for a march on the White House to show support for the Amorous Spotted Slug. As I look over the crowd, estimated at more than five hundred, I see several political heavy weights. The First Lady is here, of course, to lend her support. She has taken on the Amorous Spotted Slug as a cause célèbre. The Rev. Reggie Johnson is also here. He has just spoken to the crowd and received a warm and enthusiastic reception. This is a highly charged but peaceful crowd.

"Conspicuously absent is Walter Brainthorpe. The Committee to Save the Amorous Spotted Slug had hoped he would provide a blanket endorsement of their cause. However, a spokesman for the Brainthorpe organization released a position paper earlier this morning. It is quite lengthy, and I cannot read it to you in its entirety, but I can read some of the highlights. It says in part: *Although Walter Brainthorpe is sympathetic to the plight of the A.S.S. as well as all endangered species, he feels a workable compromise between the blind paraplegics and the A.S.S. is still feasible. It would, therefore, be premature to throw his political support to one cause over the other until we have exhausted all avenues of reconciliation.*

"That is a significant setback for the A.S.S. supporters who had hoped to have his full endorsement.

"The Rev. Reggie Johnson is heading our way...REV. JOHNSON, REV. JOHNSON, CAN WE HAVE A MOMENT OF YOUR TIME?"

Reggie Johnson smiled into the camera and adjusted his tie. "I suppose I can spare a moment or two for the media."

"I'm Rob Carter for Channel 7 News.... Can you tell our viewers what your position is in respect to the Amorous Spotted Slug?"

"Yes, Rob, I would be glad to. As an endangered species, the Amorous Spotted Slug is one of the many minority groups that are being oppressed by the masses. The current capitalistic White House, as well as the rest of corporate America, has disenfranchised minorities in their narcissistic pursuit of the almighty dollar and has forced them into economic bondage. It is time for minority groups to unite and rise up in protest against this blatant racism."

"Don't you think blind paraplegics constitute a minority group? Some of them are black."

"They're a small, nonessential minority group. Our organization only supports large minority groups."

"Thank you, Rev. Johnson. This is Rob Carter for Channel 7 News. And now I return you back to the station and Hal Mason with the Washington weather report."

Hal Mason would report to the residents of Washington that it would be partly cloudy with a high of 72 degrees, perfect protesting weather. However, at 10 a.m. with the sun low in the sky, it was still cool, making Agent Rushford wish the zipper on her black leather jacket worked. On the back of the jacket, stenciled in cheap lettering, was *Hell's Angels*, arched over a Harley-Davidson motorcycle. Under the picture of the motorcycle, again in cheap lettering, was *Road Hogs, L.A. Cal.* It was unlikely any angel from hell or elsewhere had ever worn the jacket. It was one of many articles of clothing the Secret Service maintained for undercover work. The jacket would have been O.K. if not for the stupid T-shirt, which was too short to cover her generous midriff. Her faded blue jeans were, likewise, too tight for a full-figured woman. According to her superiors, this was what demonstrators were wearing this year. Her superiors did not get out much. The picture of a black-gloved fist on the front of her T-shirt had slipped from style decades ago. The symbol of black power today was the dollar sign. It was hard work and a good education.

Rushford looked at Langston with jealousy. He only had to wear a sweatshirt, a red bandana around the forehead, and a string of beads around the neck. And he had real boots instead of sandals. A month ago she would have made a formal complaint, but after the recent turkey shoot, she felt lucky to have her job. She hated undercover work, but it was a necessary part of the Secret Service. The downside was she had no outside communications. A wire dangling down from an earplug looked out of place on a demonstrator. If she needed help, she could only count on Langston and the ".38" attached to the inside of her jacket. Amazingly, Langston didn't appear armed. She assumed he still packed sufficient hidden firepower to sustain a small revolution.

The demonstration was not officially sanctioned by the White House, hence the lack of overt Secret Service presence. The Washington D.C. police were there in force, and could help in an emergency, but it was not the same as having access to the full resources of the Secret Service.

"Buttercup is about to make her speech," Langston said.

"You cover her right flank, and I'll cover the left." Rushford looked over the crowd. Emotions were running high, but no boogeymen were in sight. "Try not to be obvious. I'd prefer the First Lady didn't know we are her undercover agents."

Langston gave a subtle nod and worked his way toward the First Lady. Most of the protesters were in their thirties or younger, many with children. Since this was a weekday morning, they obviously didn't have regular employment and probably wandered from protest to protest. In Washington, they would not have to wander far.

The uniform of the day was faded blue jeans with a multitude of holes, some patched, some not. Tops were an assortment of T-shirts or baggy sweatshirts sporting a wide variety of advertising. As cheap as their lives and clothing appeared to be, they all carried signs produced by costly commercial printers, many in four-color print. Since few of the protesters had ever seen an Amorous Spotted Slug, visual depiction of the enigmatic creature varied as much as the space invaders at Roswell.

Esther, with megaphone in hand, walked to the front of the group and waited for the noise to subside. She had chosen the rally point with care. In front of her and behind the crowd, Lincoln sat on his marble throne, looking on in obvious approval. Esther was sure, if Lincoln were alive, he would be an avid supporter of the Amorous Spotted Slug. Wasn't he the champion of the downtrodden? Five feet behind Esther was the Reflecting Pool, a rectangular, tree-lined body of water over a third of a mile long. On quiet, windless days such as this, the entire length of the Washington Monument reflected in the pool. Esther thought it made an appropriate backdrop for such a noble cause. After a few words of encouragement, she would lead the crowd along the north side of the pool to 17th Street, where they would turn north toward the White House. If her husband would not openly support their cause, they could at least rattle his cage. The elderly black man in the back carrying a large American flag would lead the procession.

When the noise subsided to a muffled roar, Esther raised the megaphone to her lips. Her voice was capable of reaching the rear of the crowd without the megaphone, but the megaphone gave her an air of authority. "I want to thank you all for supporting the Amorous Spotted Slug." Esther could feel the energy radiating from the crowd. Now it was time to whip them into a frenzy. It was time to tap that raw power and put it to use. "So far our government has ignored our pleas. Are we going to let our government turn a blind eye while the habitat of this precious endangered species is destroyed?"

"NO!" echoed a chorus from the crowd.

"Are we going to let corporate America rape our natural resources?"

"NO!"

"Are we going to let the Amorous Spotted Slug disappear from the face of the earth?"

"NO!"

"Are we going to let a few misguided blind paraplegics change our destiny?"

"YES!"

Esther stopped in mid-thought. That wasn't the correct response. The answer had come a fraction of a second before the crowd would have responded. A hush fell over the crowd. The jaws of the demonstrators drooped as they stared at each other in bewilderment. This was not how they had orchestrated the spontaneous demonstration.

Slowly, the crowd in front of Esther parted. It was like Moses parting the Red Sea. Esther looked down the newly established corridor. At the far end, Abe Lincoln sat on his marble chair. There was a determined look on his face. Just in front of him sat another man with an equally determined look on his face. Except for a pair of dark glasses that hid his non-functional eyes, the cold, emotionless face could likewise have been cast in stone. The man's large arm and chest muscles, augmented through years of pumping the wheels on his wheelchair, were in sharp contrast to his withered legs. Esther stared at the man for a moment. From the dark glasses she assumed he was blind, but she could still feel the anger behind those impotent eyes as if they could momentarily scrutinize her soul. She pushed aside the sensation. She could not let one man stand in the way of such a worthy cause. Sometimes you have to make sacrifices in life. If she had to sacrifice one blind paraplegic for the benefit of the Amorous Spotted Slug, so be it. Life was full of difficult decisions.

Esther lifted the megaphone to her lips. She had to regain control—and quickly. "We will not be stopped. Long live the A.S.S."

Esther was pleased when the crowd picked up the chant.

"LONG LIVE THE A.S.S."

The volume increased with each repetition.

"LONG LIVE THE A.S.S."

"Death to the A.S.S.!" The blind paraplegic pushed his wheelchair toward the sound of the megaphone. The elderly black man with the flag tried to stop him, but the blind paraplegic ripped the flag out of his hands and continued toward the lady with the megaphone. He picked up speed when the wheel chair reached the steps leading down from the Lincoln Memorial. Waving the American flag from side to side, the blind paraplegic bounced down the steps, heading for an unscheduled encounter with the First Lady of the United States.

Agents Rushford and Langston closed in beside the First Lady. They were trained to take a bullet for the President or First Lady, but there was nothing in the training manual about runaway wheelchairs. Agent Rushford, reaching for her gun, wondered if the American Civil Freedom Union would consider shooting an unarmed, blind paraplegic excessive force. In light of their reaction to the turkey incident, she assumed they would. She fired a warning shot over the head of the man in the wheelchair. The round went well over the heads of the protesters, taking off the tip of Lincoln's pinkie finger. Abe did not look happy.

By the time the wheelchair hit the bottom of the steps, it was traveling faster than the blind paraplegic had anticipated. He was almost thrown from his wheelchair on the last step, forcing him to lay the flagpole across his lap and secure a white-knuckle grip on his wheelchair.

Esther, like the proverbial deer in the headlights, stood her ground, unable to move. Agent Langston was the first to react. He grabbed the First Lady's left arm to pull her out of the path of the oncoming wheelchair. Agent Rushford had similar thoughts. With no time to confer with Langston, Agent Rushford pulled on the First Lady's right arm. The First Lady, held spread-eagle by her Secret Service agents, stood helplessly, a perfect target for the irate, blind paraplegic's kamikaze attack.

The wheelchair hit Esther above the knees, flipping her one hundred and eighty degrees. She landed head down in the lap of the blind paraplegic with one leg on each side of his head. She immediately crossed her legs forming a deadly headlock on her assailant.

The ten-foot flagpole, which had been lying across the blind paraplegic's lap, protruded out to the sides of the wheelchair, catching Rushford in the waist. Agent Langston, who was taller, gave out a groan that only men could appreciate.

Propelled by the momentum of the wheelchair and rider, Agents Rushford and Langston, along with the First Lady and the blind paraplegic, plunged into the Reflecting Pool. Langston surface in considerable pain and thrashed around in the water moaning about his knee. He fooled no one—he wasn't holding his knee.

Rushford's problems were more serious. She had spent $76.95 at the beauty parlor the previous morning. Her wet hair now dripped across her face in a tangled mess; and as she feared, one of her nails had broken. At least she was wearing borrowed clothes. The clothes were totally drenched, including her T-shirt. She now wished the agency hadn't persuaded her to go braless. Someone will pay for this. Where is that blind paraplegic, she wondered. She found him treading water near his wheelchair. Draped face down over the wheel chair was the First Lady, apparently unconscious. At least her head was out of the water.

The blind paraplegic reached out for any object of support, finding none. Finally, he obtained a handhold on the back of Esther's sweatpants. He gave a tug to pull himself up but only succeeded in pulling the pants down.

On shore strobe lights flashed and cameras clicked. Rob Carter of Channel 7 News interrupted a soap opera for live coverage. In his mind, he began composing his acceptance speech for the Pulitzer Prize in journalism.

Oval Office, 1500 hours

Bart hung up the phone, taking care not to tip over any of the flowerpots scattered across his desk. He had evicted the turkey, but the pigeons nesting in the dead tree remained. He was hoping the eggs would soon hatch and the young pigeons would be off on their own. He was running out of flowerpots. He had considered ensuring they would be stillbirths, until Esther threatened to notify the right-to-lifers. He didn't need them on his case, not in an election year.

He had been hoping for a round of golf, but from the urgency Al expressed on the phone, that appeared out of the question. Al didn't usually request afternoon meetings. He knew Bart reserved that time for golf.

Bart checked his supply of aspirin in preparation for the unscheduled meeting. It was times like this he needed a jar full of chocolate chip cookies. The empty glass jar sat uselessly on his desk. He might have to utilize it if he ran out of flowerpots. There appeared to be no end to the bird droppings.

"Thanks for seeing me on such short notice." Al sat down in his over-stuffed chair. The folder he carried was thin, but he brought his own paper bag. He must have been hyperventilating, not a good sign.

Al reached into his folder and extracted an eight-by-ten, colored glossy depicting a pair of portly buttocks protruding from under an American flag. He passed the picture to Bart who studied it closely.

"Yep, that's Esther. I'd recognize her anywhere."

"She was arrested earlier today."

"Arrested?"

"Along with two of our Secret Service agents."

"Don't tell me—Rushford and Langston."

"They arrested a fourth person—a blind paraplegic—but the American Civil Freedom Union bailed him out."

"What are the charges?"

"Reckless discharge of a firearm, destruction of public property, assault and battery, lewd and indecent behavior, swimming in a restricted area, resisting arrest. There are other minor charges, but you get the drift."

"I suppose we should bail them out," Bart suggested after a moment of thought.

"All of them?"

"Yeah, we'll have to bail out Esther too."

Bart looked down at the picture with an evil smile. This was his ticket to freedom. He would have all the chocolate chip cookies he wanted. No more diet. Of course he would have to show the picture to Esther periodically for reinforcement, but he would be in the driver's seat.

"It won't be as bad as it looks," Al was saying.

Bart thought it looked pretty good.

"I talked the media out of printing the picture. It took some doing. We'll have to throw some bones to Rob Carter of Channel 7 News in the future. He was disappointed. He thought it was Pulitzer Prize material. The only paper that'll print the picture is the *National Inquisition*. We'll leak a rumor that the picture was computer generated."

"Where does this blind paraplegic fit in?"

"He's a medical student at George Washington University. Wants to be a radiologist."

"But he's blind!"

"Won't make any difference. He'll make it. With the *Americans with Disabilities Act*, no one can stop him. Anyway, he says some lady paid him twenty bucks to disrupt the protest. Told him it was part of a movie they were filming."

"Abigail?"

"We found a *Save the Turkeys* bumper sticker on the back of his wheelchair."

"We need to do something about that woman. She's making us look as useless as a barmaid at a temperance meeting. What ever happened to that Agent X guy?"

"CIA sent out a notice this morning. He'll contact us in a day or two."

Al reshuffled his papers and returned them to his folder. "We should have that picture destroyed. Don't want to embarrass the First Lady."

"Heavens no, I'll take care of that personally." A silly grin returned to Bart's face as he scrutinized his newfound treasure. "We surely wouldn't want to embarrass the First Lady."

Al stood up to leave. "I'll get right on the bail situation."

"That's all right; take your time...maybe get a bite to eat. Haste makes waste. You could have Charlie downstairs help you with the forms." Bart closed his eyes when Al left the room, all the better to savor the imaginary chocolate chip cookies. They would be a welcome change from turkey. The kitchen had been serving turkey every day for the last week, turkey sausage for breakfast, turkey soup for lunch and roast turkey for dinner. He would have to phone the kitchen and have fresh cookies sent up in the morning.

Bart hung up the phone. The kitchen promised a large batch of cookies first thing in the morning. He could almost smell them in the air, or was that the Porta-Potty he smelled. Over the last week his sniffer had lost its sensitivity. Living with an outhouse can do that to a man.

Bart walked over to the window for some fresh air. Down below several bulldozers were leveling the ground. He hadn't realized rockets could create such large craters. A man in a cherry picker was removing the last of the parts-missing turkeys still hanging from the trees. It would be a long time before the White House would again have a rose garden. It was a depressing sight. Maybe dictating a memo to Veronica would cheer him up. She was more pleasant to look at than trees draped with rotting turkey carcasses.

Bart turned back toward his desk but froze in his tracks. Sitting at his desk was a man in camouflaged fatigues. His legs were crossed, and he had his mud caked combat boots propped up on Bart's desk. The stranger leaned back in Bart's chair, stifling a yawn as if he had been sitting there for some time. Bart hadn't seen him previously at the White House. He would not have forgotten anyone with a wart of such magnitude on his nose. The man had painted his face with black and green stripes but it did nothing to obscure the warty growth.

"What are you doing here?" Bart considered calling security, but the 9 mm strapped to the man's hip did not encourage confrontations. Bart assumed the short tube attached to the barrel of the gun was a silencer.

"Headquarters said you wanted to talk to me." The man opened and closed Bart's desk drawers as if out of boredom. "I'm Agent X."

"How'd you get past White House security?"

"What security?"

Bart walked to the front of his desk and sat down in a chair. It didn't seem appropriate to suggest Agent X vacate the President's chair. "We want you to investigate Abigail Farnsworth; we think her name might be an alias. The folder on the desk contains all the information we have on her." It was a thin file.

Agent X picked up the eight-by-ten glossy. "Is this her picture?"

"No, that's my wife."

Agent X studied the First Lady's buttocks for a moment. "Nice looking wife."

"Thank you." Coming from a man of his eclectic experience, Bart considered that a compliment.

Agent X returned the portrait to the desk and picked up Abigail's file. He again leaned back in the President's chair as he perused the file's contents. Bart leaned forward in his chair, his hands clasped in his lap like an applicant paying homage to the loan officer at a bank.

"You think you can help us?"

"Do piranhas eat pork?"

Bart didn't know.

"Not much to go on. The file's pretty thin." Agent X flipped through the pages. "It appears this unrest is originating from Michigan's Upper Peninsula. I'll start there."

Agent X stuffed the folder inside his shirt. "I assume you want her quietly liquidated?"

"You can do that?" Bart asked.

"Seen Jimmy Hoffa lately?"

"You liquidated Jimmy Hoffa?"

"I had to kill the last person who asked that."

"That's O.K.; I don't need to know that badly."

Bart tried to picture Abigail wearing a concrete jacket and buried under a sports stadium next to Jimmy Hoffa. It was a pleasant picture. "I suppose, it would be best if we could bring her in to stand trial."

"It's your quarter. You name the dance."

"How do we get a hold of you?"

"Ya don't."

"How'll you get a hold of us? We'd like periodic updates."

"I could carve a report on your bedpost. Maybe a message in your cereal box, or possibly a short note in a fortune cookie. You eat Chinese?" Agent X stood up and walked over to inspect the President's Porta-Potty. "Nice latrine. I like a man who stays close to nature, none of those fancy toilets. I suppose being on the second floor they wouldn't let you dig a slit trench. Kind of a shame." Agent X opened the door and checked out the writing on the wall. "Who's Kim?"

"I don't know. I've been meaning to give her a call."

"There's plenty of room on the walls. I can leave periodic reports on the bathroom wall."

Bart pulled out a small cell phone from his pocket. "Why don't you use my cell phone? The number's unlisted, so you shouldn't be getting any calls."

Agent X took the phone and stuck it in his pocket. "Mind if I use your latrine?"

"No, be my guest. Here's some fresh carbon paper."

Agent X stepped into the Porta-Potty and shut the door.

He's a little unconventional, Bart thought, but he seems to know what he's doing. Bart waited ten minutes for Agent X to come out. "Are you all right?" *No answer*. Bart knocked on the door. *No response.* He opened the door. Agent X was gone!

Chapter Ten

Clinging to the top of Michigan's Upper Peninsula like the horn on a raging rhino, the Keweenaw Peninsula extends deep into the heart of Lake Superior. The shoreline is jagged and strewn with large boulders and storm-toppled tree trunks. Half way up the Keweenaw Peninsula the land slopes steeply into a narrow valley that transects the peninsula. On the east end of the valley is Portage Lake, which the Portage River connects to the Keweenaw Bay. In the 1860's, mining companies dug a canal connecting Portage Lake to Lake Superior on the west, transforming the upper Keweenaw Peninsula into a virtual island.

The city of Houghton, home of Michigan Technological University tenaciously clings to the southern wall of the valley. Although not a large university, it produces more than its share of geeks and nerds, forcing the lone FBI agent in Marquette to squander a disproportionate amount of his time in Houghton investigating the excessive number of computer crimes. It is not as if the Michigan Tech students are inherently evil or have any diabolical desire to create cyber-havoc, they hack into government and corporate data banks for the same reason people climb mountains—because they are there.

The sister city of Hancock clings equally tenaciously to the northern slope of the valley on the other side of the Portage Canal. It, too, is a university town and home of Finlandia University. Founded in 1896 as Suomi College by Finnish immigrants who wanted a better life for their children, it is affiliated with the Evangelical Lutheran Church in America.

Finlandia students eagerly embraced liberal arts, and unlike their counterparts across the river, they read newspapers, watched political talk shows, and could, with some confidence, name the current resident of the White House. But with the beginning of the fall semester, they were more concerned with purchasing textbooks, reestablishing old friendships, and colonizing dorm rooms. It was, therefore, not surprising they paid little attention to the wino walking down Finn Street at the edge of campus. The wino walked with the gait of an old man who had weathered poorly through the years. His hunched back showed through his dirty, wine-stained trench coat. At Franklin Street, he turned left, cut across the lawn, and headed toward the Hoover Center. He wore an old, gangster-style hat pulled low over his forehead, and dragged a plastic bag filled with beer and soft drink cans behind him. He wandered from dumpster to dumpster in search of new cans to add to his growing collection. In Michigan each can was worth a dime. It was assumed by those who gave the wino any notice that his profits would not go toward fulfilling his nutritional needs.

They assumed the old man was a vagrant, a man without a home, a man without purpose. But the cold eyes peering out from under the hat shifted methodically from side to side. Little escaped his notice. If a student were to look deeply into those eyes and see the intelligence within, they would quickly recognize him for who he was, but before they could look into those eyes, they would be distracted by the hideous wart encamped upon the man's nose.

The man paused at the dumpster behind the Hoover Center, a three-story Victorian house built in 1895 that housed the President's office. With eyes still scanning his surroundings, the old man rummaged through the refuse. He plucked a can from the dumpster and added it to his bag of cans. He did it without enthusiasm; cans were not his interest. He was more interested in the pile of shredded paper. He sorted through the shreddings until he found strips that piqued his interest. The paper had been shredded sideways, parallel to the typing. Most of the strips were of no value, but some clearly revealed entire lines of print. One such strip caught his attention: *We will expect students to have "sisu" at all times. Sisu will be invaluable in overcoming all obstacles.* The man lingered at the word "sisu." He possessed a photographic memory, and he now compared sisu with the pages of Webster's unabridged dictionary, which he had previously committed to memory. Sisu was not listed! Sisu did not exist in the English language. Surely, it had to be a code name, perhaps a secret weapon. Further searching found additional references to the code word. The old man folded the paper strips, stashed them in his coat pocket, and limped toward another dumpster.

Oval Office, 1000 hours

Bart sat back in his chair with a feeling of self-assurance. The kitchen had filled his cookie jar to the brim with chocolate chip cookies still warm from the oven, and he had a brand new bottle of aspirin in his desk drawer. He was ready for anything Al might throw at him. Esther was unusually quiet, a blessing in itself. Meat and potatoes were back on the menu, and carrots and celery sticks were a thing of the past. Life just didn't get any better than that.

"Morning Bart." Al was smiling when he entered the room, and his folder didn't look too thick. Al sat down in his customary chair and crossed his legs. "We got some good news."

"So what ya got for me today?" Bart could not remember the last time his morning briefings started with good news.

"Agent X has been on assignment two days, and he's already obtaining high quality intel."

"I knew it. He's the best. This deserves a cookie." Bart reached into the jar. "Anyone who can slip past White House security and get into the Oval Office unnoticed has to be top-notch."

"Not to diminish his accomplishment," Al said, "but Rushford and Langston were working that day."

"So what kind of intel did he get for us?"

"He was able to infiltrate Finlandia University."

"Where's that? Finland?"

"Might as well be. It's in the Upper Peninsula, but it was Finnish immigrants who established the University in 1896 to promote Finnish culture. At least, that's their cover story."

"Is that bad?"

"It could be. Depends on their loyalties. Agent X says they have a whole program of Finnish Studies."

"Jumping Josephine! They're brainwashing our kids."

"Are you thinking what I'm thinking?" Al asked.

"That turkey stuff, the weaponized gelatin, preparation J, this is too big for home grown terrorists. They must have international connections. I don't think they want a fifty-first state. I think Finland wants to establish a Finnish colony in the Upper Peninsula!" Bart stood up and began pacing the floor. "We got to nip this in the bud."

"There's something else." Al opened his folder, extracting a sheet of paper stamped *Top Secret*. "Agent X says they've developed something that'll overcome any obstacle."

"We talking WMD?"

"Could be. They refer to it as S.I.S.U., obviously an acronym. Agent X didn't have much on it yet, but we have all the cryptographers at CIA working on it."

"S.I.S.U., what could that stand for?" Bart grabbed another cookie and continued to pace around the Oval office. He could think better when he was munching a cookie.

"Doesn't make any sense to me," Al said.

"That's it!"

"That's what?"

"Sense or sensory." Bart took another bit of cookie. "What if they had some sort of weapon that would alter our senses or inhibit them?"

"Sensory inhibition? I think you got something there."

Bart pulled Al's brown paper bag out of the desk drawer when Al began to hyperventilate. "But what does the S.U. stand for?"

"Wit otta ve uptin whi tick."

"I can't understand a word you say when you talk through that paper bag."

Al removed the bag from his mouth. "I said, it's got to be something high tech"

"Maybe some kind of stun gun?"

"No, that's a 'G'. It has to end in 'U'."

Bart grabbed another cookie. He had to think. "How about satellite? That could be the second 'S'."

"Unit! Satellite unit."

"Sensory Inhibiting Satellite Unit," they both said in unison.

After exchanging high-fives, they sat down. Al returned to his paper bag, and Bart grabbed another cookie. There is no better feeling than a job well done. They had deciphered the answer before the cryptographers at CIA Headquarters! "That's why the taxpayers pay us the big bucks," Bart said through a mouthful of cookie crumbs. Bart had just propped his feet up on his desk to savor the moment when the phone rang. It was coming from the desk drawer. "That's the Kremlin. They must have deciphered S.I.S.U. the same time we did." Bart pulled the phone out of the drawer.

Bart: *Hello?*

Abigail: *Hello Bart. How you doing today?*

Bart: *Abigail, you can't keep calling me on this line. This is my business phone.*

Abigail: *Sorry...I would have used your bedroom phone but your wife's been rather testy since that incident at the Lincoln Memorial.*

Bart: *That's not funny....* Bart tried to stifle a giggle.

Abigail: *I thought you would like that.... Anyway, the reason I called is to see if you are ready to help us with our fifty-first state thing.*

Bart: *O.K., I'll play along... What are you going to do with this new state? You going to be the first governor?*

Abigail: *Maybe.*

Bart: *And where will your capital be?*

Abigail: *That's easy. Bear Creek. Everyone knows that's Abigail Farnsworth's hometown.*

Bart: *Gotcha! That Abigail Farnsworth is just a legend, an alias. We're on to you. We know what you're up to.*

Abigail: *You don't say....*

Bart: *We have one of our best agents working on this, and he's closing in on you as we speak.*

Abigail: *And who might that be?*

Bart: *That's Agent X to you. Only a very few of us know his real name. And he reports directly to me. I even gave him my personal cell phone.*

Abigail: *I'm sorry you feel that way.*

Bart: *And further more...We know all about your secret S.I.S.U. Our defense industry has already come up with countermeasures. Your S.I.S.U. is useless.*

Bart slammed down the receiver. "I guess I told her."

"But you also let her know we're on to their S.I.S.U. It would have been better if we hadn't shown our hand so early. And we have no defense against it yet."

"I want them to worry a bit." Bart picked up his phone.

"Who you calling?"

"The Pentagon. We need a meeting with the Joint Chiefs of Staff. I'm going to order a preemptive strike."

"Against Michigan's Upper Peninsula?"

"You betcha!"

Marquette, Michigan, 0332 hours

The moon had set two hours earlier, but a brilliant display of northern lights compensated for the loss of moonlight. The sun had reached the peak of its eleven-year sunspot cycle, creating bursts of red, green, and white wavering rays, all pointing toward magnetic north.

The man in the kayak ignored the additional light provided by the aurora borealis. With his night-vision goggles everything looked green. Small waves lapping against the rocky islands near shore muffled the sound of his paddles striking water. Even so, his paddles made little noise as he expertly dipped them into the water of Lake Superior.

The man had a second kayak filled with an assortment of electronic gear tethered to the back of his kayak. Conspicuously absent were food and other necessities of life. The man in the kayak was not concerned. Where he was going there would be sufficient grubs, rodents and edible tubers to sustain life.

In the distance a white light blinked on and off. That would be the navigational light on the breakwater of Marquette's upper harbor. If he stayed well to the left of the light, he would land at Presque Isle, a small knob of tree-covered rock jutting into Lake Superior.

The man dressed in black saw the sandstone cliffs through his night-vision goggles long before the waves splashing against the rocks confirmed its presence. When he reached the shore, he stepped into the cold water; he could deal with temporary hypothermia.

He unloaded his electronic gear and placed it on a nearby rock. He then weighted down the kayaks with rocks and submerged them in the water. He would recover them later. He tied one end of a fifty-meter, climbing rope to his electronic gear. The other end, he tied to his waist. The sandstone cliff rose up over one hundred feet above the water's edge. Its smooth walls lacked visible handholds. Piece of cake, the man decided after he studied the wall for a moment. He chipped hand and foot holds into the sandstone with a rock pick and began to climb. Within twenty minutes, he was standing on top of the cliff pulling up his electronic equipment.

Presque Isle is a large wooded park on the northern edge of Marquette. A one-lane road runs around the park's perimeter, but visitors seldom venture into the interior. He would set up his listening post there.

After several minutes of searching, he found a secluded area that fit his needs. There was no evidence of recent activity, except for a large raccoon holed up in a hollow log. The man removed his black ski mask; he no longer needed it. The raccoon, an expert in the art of panhandling, crawled out of his hollow log in hopes of obtaining a free meal, but fled in horror when confronted with the man's disgusting nasal attachment.

White House Situation Room, 1300 hours.

The top officers from each branch of the military as well as the Chairman of the Joint Chiefs of Staff were sitting patiently around a large rectangular table when the President and his Chief of Staff arrived. The men at the table immediately stood at attention, finally sitting down only after Bart had taken his spot at the head of the table. Al sat next to Bart.

"Gentlemen, we are facing a serious crisis," Bart began. "We have unimpeachable evidence that Finland intends to take possession of Michigan's Upper Peninsula and turn it into a Finnish colony." Bart paused to allow the whispering among the generals to subside. "They already have numerous agents in place." Bart now had their undivided attention. "Gentlemen, this will not happen on my watch." All eyes focused on the President. "I am, therefore, ordering a preemptive strike to retake the land that rightfully belongs to the United States."

General Brackendorf, Chairman of the Joint Chiefs of Staff, looked around at the other military officers. This would be the first time Americans have fought on American soil since the Civil War. "What exactly do you have in mind?"

"I'm open to suggestions, but I want to see some shock and awe!"

General Brackendorf again looked around at his colleagues. "Well, any thoughts?"

After a moment of silence, an Air Force general cleared his throat. "If you want shock and awe, we could nuke the peninsula. It'll only take twenty minutes, thirty minutes tops."

"That'll work," Bart said. "They're mostly Republicans anyway."

"That would kill wild life," Al reminded the group. "Could lose the support of the animal rights groups."

"If you want to be more selective, we can use napalm," the Air Force general replied. "It's a bit tidier but could require a day and a half to do it up right."

Everyone looked at Al. "It'll also start forest fires, and there goes the tree-hugger's vote."

"Gentleman, it appears we may have to use conventional weapons and tactics." General Brackendorf stood up and walked over to a large map of Michigan, which was hanging on the wall. "What are our primary objectives?"

"I think Bear Creek is the epicenter," Bart said. "That was to be their new capital."

General Brackendorf circled Bear Creek on the map. "What else?"

"The Houghton-Hancock area is a hot spot."

General Brackendorf placed another circle on the map. "Anything else?"

"We'll need to control the port cities of Escanaba and Marquette."

"Don't forget the Soo Locks," someone else offered.

General Brackendorf added more circles to the map. He then picked up a long pointer and stood in front of the group like a teacher on the first day of class. "I suggest we activate the Michigan National Guard. They'll be down here at Camp Grayling about ninety miles below the Mackinac Bridge." The general pointed to a spot about an inch below the bridge. "We can have a column of M1A1 tanks cross the bridge to secure the Soo Locks. We'll also need air support."

"Don't we have a couple of air bases in the U.P.?" Bart asked.

We closed down both K.I. Sawyer and Kincheloe at the end of the cold war," the Air Force General replied.

"We need a carrier about here." General Brackendorf pointed to a spot in Lake Michigan just below Manistique. "I'd like to have one of our mainline carriers, but I don't think we can get one through the St. Lawrence Seaway. The locks are too small. We'll have to settle for one of those baby flat tops with Harrier Jump-Jets."

"They won't have the firepower of the mainline carriers," the admiral representing the navy said.

"We'll have to do the best we can. I think we can get a nuclear attack sub to secure Marquette Harbor—with cruise missile capability of course. We'll have a battalion of marines assault the beaches here." General Brackendorf pointed to a deserted stretch of Lake Michigan shoreline near Epoufette. We'll also need to send an amphibious unit up the Keweenaw Waterway, probably from both the east and the west. They'll secure Houghton and Hancock. Then we'll have the 82nd Airborne do a night drop over the Seney Stretch." General Brackendorf whacked the center of the U.P. with his stick. "Any questions?"

"How long will this take to prepare?" Al asked.

"Everything has to come up the St. Lawrence Seaway. I'd guess about three weeks."

"How's the public goin' to react?" someone asked.

"The public always rallies behind the President when we go to war," Bart said. "If there're any questions, we'll tell them we have hard evidence that they have Weapons of Mass Destruction. WMD always works."

"I hate to be a party pooper," Al said, "but if I remember right from my high school government class, the constitution states Congress has to approve any declaration of war."

The members of the group sat silently in dejection for a few moments. They had the perfect plan, and now a minor constitutional technicality was about to ruin it.

"We could call it a police action," Bart suggested.

"That'll work," they all agreed.

"Good, let's go for it," Bart said.

Marquette, Sunday, 0915 hours

Agent X awakened after two hours of sleep. He had trained his body to survive on two hours or less sleep per night. He had his electronic equipment assembled, linking him by satellite to CIA Headquarters in Langley, Virginia; and earphones attached to other electronic equipment monitored local TV, radio, and cellular phone transmissions. They should provide valuable insight into the political leanings of the local community.

He turned the dials on his equipment, changing the source of the feed to his earphones. He was searching for that elusive transmission that would reveal valuable secrets. He was currently listening to the audio transmission from TV 6, the local station in Marquette. He was about to turn the dial again when he heard "Finland Calling." Agent X's muscles tensed. In a few minutes TV 6 would air a program called *Finland Calling*. He needed to know whom Finland was calling—and why.

What was that? A phone. A phone was ringing. He had totally forgotten the cell phone the President had given him. He retrieved the phone from his pack. The President said it was an unlisted number. It had to be the White House calling.

Agent X: *Hello?*

Abigail: *I was hoping to catch you at this number. The President said he gave you this phone.*

Agent X: *And who might you be?*

Abigail: *I'm sorry... I'm forgetting my manners. This is Abigail Farnsworth. I thought I'd call and welcome you to the U.P.*

Agent X's photographic memory flipped through the pages of the dossier given to him by the President: *Abigail Farnsworth, legendary figure from Bear Creek, thought to be an alias of one of the terrorists.* This could be a significant breakthrough.

Agent X: *Ah, Ms. Farnsworth... And what, pray tell, leads you to presume that I am currently within the confines of the Upper Peninsula?*

Abigail: *The trail had to lead you here. This is where the action is.*

Agent X: *Well, for your information, I'm a lot closer than you think. It's just a matter of time and you're mine. I always get my man...in this case woman. And when I do, they'll lock you up so tightly you'll never get out. They'll throw away the key. But before I turn you over to the authorities, I will personally interrogate you. I have ways to make you talk...water-boarding...bamboo shoots under the fingernails. I order all my bamboo through a dealer in Bangkok.*

Abigail: *But if I catch you first, I'll chain you to a wagon wheel and whip your naked back mercilessly with my leather cat-o-nines.*

Agent X: *Would that be real leather? I've always been partial to fine leather...*

Agent X could feel his heart begin to race. He was breathing heavily. He tried to flush the thought of being flogged with fine leather from his mind.

Abigail: *Real leather? You'll find out soon enough... I hate to run, but I really should give Bart a call. Toot-a-loo.* (Click)

Agent X returned the phone to his pack. Abigail appeared to be made out of stout stuff. He liked that in a woman.

It was almost 9:30. Finland Calling would be starting soon. Agent X put on his headset and adjusted the volume. He wouldn't receive any video feed, but he would get audio. He flipped on a switch to start a recorder. With his total recall, he wouldn't need it for himself, but he would need to forward it to Langley.

Hyvät katsojat, tervetuloa seuraamaan Suomi Soittaa -lähetystä.

Finnish! The program was in the Finnish. He was fluent in forty-three languages, but Finnish wasn't one of them. A major oversight. He should have been better prepared. He had a few days before coming to the U.P. He could have learned Finnish. Maybe he was getting too old for this line of work. Fortunately, he had it taped. Langley could translate it. It was obvious he couldn't achieve all his goals from his listening post. He would have to go someplace special. He would have to pay a visit to TV 6.

Oval Office, 1000 hours

It was the beginning of a good day. Bart could feel it in his bones. Esther was not nagging him, Agent X had the terrorists on the run, the cookie jar was full. He was actually looking forward to Al's briefing. It was a good day to be President.

Al arrived on time as usual. "Morning, Bart." In addition to his folders, Al had a tape recorder tightly tucked under his arm.

Maybe he has tapes of the new radio ads. Campaign season was fast approaching. "Morning, Al."

Al placed the tape recorder on Bart's desk and took a seat. "Got this yesterday from Agent X. Go ahead, play it."

Bart pushed the play button and listened quietly to the unintelligible garble. "It's all Greek to me."

"Not even close. It's Finnish. A TV station in Marquette has been broadcasting this garbage for over forty years."

"Did you get it translated?" Bart asked.

"On the surface it appears clean, mostly music and dancing. Actually, it could be quite entertaining, but what kind of hidden messages are mixed in with that harmless chatter?"

Bart scratched his chin in a rare moment of deep thought. "Didn't the British do something like that in WWII? I think they used commercial radio broadcasts to send messages to resistance fighters in occupied Europe."

"Bingo! They could have all sorts of messages mixed in with the frivolous talk. They could be directing the entire operation right under our noses."

"And you say this is all in Finnish?"

"Not very subtle are they?" Al considered hyperventilating, but decided against it.

"That Agent X has earned his keep this week."

"Think where we'd be without him." Al breathed in slowly, trying to remain calm. In goes the good air. Out comes the bad air.

"General Brackendorf called this morning." Bart leaned over and turned off the tape recorder. "Says they got most of the details wrapped up. The Op orders should be sent out today or tomorrow."

"You know," Al said, "we can't keep this quiet much longer."

"We could tell everyone it's just routine," Bart suggested.

"That might work when the nuclear attack submarine heads up the St. Lawrence Seaway, but when people see an aircraft carrier, marine assault ships, and six or seven support vessels, they'll get suspicious."

"Think we should make an announcement?" Bart asked.

"Let's wait and see what happens. We still have a few days before any ships head up the Seaway. If we show our hand too soon, Brainthorpe will have a field day. He's developed quite a following. In the meantime, I'll try to write up a press release with a positive spin.

TV 6 Management Building, 1046 hours

"Mr. Koski, there's a gentleman here to see you."

Luke Koski, station manager, looked up from his desk. His secretary was pale and her hands were trembling. It was as if she had seen a ghost. "Send him in." The station manager rose to greet his visitor but stopped cold in his tracks. What grievous sin had this person done to deserve such a grotesque nose as that? It was the epitome of the ludicrous computer-generated graphics so frequently adorning the front pages of the *National Inquisition*. Out of politeness, Koski tried not to stare, but his eyes were drawn back to the growth. He hardly noticed the "Dept. of Agriculture" printed on the front of the man's hardhat.

"Can I help you, sir?" There's no way he could help him, the station manager decided. This man needs a good plastic surgeon. "I'm Luke Koski, station manager."

"Dr. Larson, Department of Agriculture. We're investigating a report that your station is infested with A.S.S."

"A.S.S.?"

"Amorous Spotted Slugs."

"I read about them. Someone found them in Washington D.C."

"They're rare in Washington but, unfortunately, quite common in the U.P. According to Professor Rantamaki of Finlandia University, we've taken over most of their natural habitat, which forces them into offices such as yours. Mind if I take a look around?"

"No, be my guest."

The man with the wart on the nose took a magnifying glass out of his attaché case and began his search. "They can be anywhere." He was checking under the water cooler when the phone rang. It was coming from his pocket.

"I believe that's your cell phone," the station manager said.

That was all he needed, a call from the President or worse yet, from Abigail. Agent X tried to ignore it, but it continued to ring.

"You goin' answer it?"

Agent X plucked the phone from the pocket of his trench coat.

Agent X: *Hello?*

Abigail: *Hi, Mr. X.*

Agent X: *This is not a good time to talk, dear.*

Lord have mercy on my soul. Love truly is blind, the station manager decided. He has a wife!

Abigail: *You must be at work. Kind of hard to talk freely?*

Agent X: *Yes, dear.*

Abigail: *I'll try to make this short, as I know you have lots of work to do.*

Agent X: *Please do.*

Abigail: *I just wanted to let you know I read your report. It was quite good, but you should have told me you didn't know Finnish. I could've helped you.*

She's hacked into the CIA computer. This woman should not be underestimated. Agent X made a mental note to limit use of the CIA computer.

Agent X: *Why should I not be surprised you know Finnish?*

Abigail: *It's quite understandable, Mr. X. I grew up around Finnish kids. May I call you X? Mr. X sounds so formal.*

Agent X: *Whatever.*

Abigail: *But if I refer to you as my X, people will assume our relationship is over.*

Agent X: *We have no relationship. We never had a relationship.*

"Would you prefer to talk to your wife in the privacy of my office?" the station manager asked.

Agent X covered the phone's mouthpiece. "Please. This is a private conversation."

The station manager backed away. He didn't need to get involved in this.

Abigail: *But you promised me a manicure.*

Agent X: *I did what?*

Abigail: *Remember the bamboo shoots imported from Bangkok?*

Agent X: *Can we discuss this tonight? Yes, dear, I'll bring home a loaf of bread.* (Click).

Agent X placed the phone back into his pocket. "She gets emotional at times."

The station manager tried to give an understanding look.

"Where were we? Ah, yes, I believe I was trying to find that little A.S.S." Agent X looked under the manager's desk. "None under here," he said as he attached a listening device under the desk. "Let me check your broadcasting room."

Agent X installed four more listening devices before proclaiming the inspection complete. They would transmit any conversations to his listening post on Presque Isle. "I guess we can give you a clean bill of health," the man from the Department of Agriculture said when he took his leave.

Chapter Eleven

923 feet below the North Atlantic, 1723 hours

Wally Johnson lay in his private wardroom with eyes closed. The third movement of Beethoven's piano sonata No.14 played softly in the background. He tried to imagine his fingers moving rapidly across a piano's keyboard to the polite applause of Carnegie Hall. He must be getting old; he was beginning to appreciate elevator music. Classical music had a way of relaxing his muscles and soothing his soul. Thirty more minutes of this utopia and he would be fully rejuvenated and ready to resume his command. He left instructions with his XO not to disturb him until after 1800 hours. As commanding officer of the USS Virginia, he could do that.

At 377 feet, the Virginia was longer than the Seawolf class, but slimmer and lighter. It was the first in a new class of attack submarines designed to be equally at home in shallow coastal waters as the ocean depths. With the end of the cold war, snooping around coastal waters and providing platforms for clandestine operations was becoming a high priority.

Beethoven's sonata came to a triumphant end, and the CD player switched to Mozart's piano sonata No. 11, another of Johnson's favorites. He never could understand how his junior officers tolerated hard rock. Each to his own tastes. Even with his eyes closed, Lt. Commander Johnson noted the subtle tilt in his bunk. The sub was surfacing despite his orders to maintain a depth of 900 feet. Reaching for the phone on the wall, Johnson dialed up the control room.

Johnson: *Let me talk to the XO...*

XO: *Executive Officer speaking.*

Johnson: *What's up?*

XO: *We received an alert on the E.L.F. I ordered the sub to periscope depth to receive the message.*

Johnson: *All right, carry on.*

An alert on the E.L.F. system was not an everyday event, but neither was it unusual. Electronic communications penetrated water poorly, making contact with deeply submerged submarines difficult. The navy had created an Extremely Low Frequency system called E.L.F. to notify submarines of waiting messages. Although it transmitted information too slowly for sending messages, it was perfect for calling submarines to surface to receive communications over more conventional channels.

His XO made the right decision under the circumstances, but he wished she had consulted him first. He was old school. Having women onboard made him uncomfortable, but he could have done worse than having Lt. Sara Peterson as his Executive Officer. She would call once she received the message. Johnson returned to his classical music, confidant Lt. Peterson could handle the situation, but in less than ten minutes the phone rang.

Johnson: *Johnson here.*

XO: *Sir, we authenticated and decoded the message.*

Johnson: *And?*

XO: *COMSUBANT wants us to change our area of patrol.*

Johnson: *Where to?*

XO: *Marquette Harbor... They gave us the coordinates.*

Marquette Harbor? He had been in this business twenty-two years, but had never been to Marquette Harbor... never even heard of it. Probably some rinky-dink harbor in some obscure corner of the world. Since his sub had been designed for coastal patrols, he should expect more such assignments in the future.

Johnson: *O.K, Ms. Peterson, plot a course to the new location and keep me informed.*

XO: *Sir?*

Johnson: *Yes, Ms. Peterson?*

XO: *I think you need to come up to the control room.*

Commander Johnson hung up the phone. Lt. Peterson was a confident, headstrong XO. It was unlike her to ask advice. So much for his quiet time. Johnson turned off the CD player. Chopin would have to wait until he returned.

Commander Johnson arrived at the control room to find Lt. Peterson and two petty officers leaning over the plotting table, scratching their heads.

"Don't make any sense," one of them was saying.

"So what's the big problem?" The two petty officers stepped back to give the commander some room. A bright light illuminated the plotting table from below, making the world map glow in the otherwise red light of the control room.

"Sir…" Lt. Peterson's fingers nervously toyed with a charting ruler. "We plotted the coordinates and came to this location." Lt. Peterson pointed to a spot in the center of North America.

"For Pete's sake! That's in the center of North America. Must I remind you we are the Navy, not the Army?"

"It's a spot in Lake Superior, Sir…just off Marquette, Michigan… We rechecked the coordinates… even had COMSUBANT resend their message… It came out of Norfolk, Virginia, from the Rear Admiral himself.

It was times like this that tested his patience with junior officers. "Give me the message. Must I teach you people how to plot coordinates?"

Much as he hated to admit it, when he plotted the coordinates, he arrived at a point fifty yards up the beach in Marquette Harbor. He preferred their assessment. At least the sub would be in deep water.

"Don't make any sense," the commander said, repeating what a petty officer had said moments earlier. "And you guys had COMSUBANT confirm it?" Sometimes he wondered about military intelligence.

"Yes sir, it seems to be a legitimate message."

"Did they say what we're supposed to do once we get there?"

"The instructions were to secure the harbor by whatever means necessary."

With twelve vertical launch tubes for Tomahawk cruise missiles and four tubes for the Mark 48 twenty-one inch torpedoes, Johnson assume it would not be difficult. "Well, Lt. Peterson," Johnson said, "It appears we have our orders. Please plot a course to the St. Lawrence Seaway."

Gulf of Mexico, 1932 hours

Marine Captain "Black Jack" Barton programmed the new coordinates into his Harrier Jump Jet's navigational system. The automatic pilot would guide him to his target without further commands. At 600 miles per hour, it wouldn't take long. It was times like this that Barton appreciated the integrated GPS, which took the drudgery out of navigation over open water. There weren't too many landmarks visible over the Gulf of Mexico.

The navy designed the Harrier for close air support of marines on the ground, not blue-water ocean activities, but with the end of the cold war and nothing better to do, the navy loaned the amphibious assault ship along with her menagerie of helicopters and Harrier Jump Jets to the Coast Guard to assist in the interdiction of drug smugglers.

At 844 feet, the Iwo Jima was longer than the WWII Essex class carriers, which she resembled, but it was officially designated an amphibious assault ship, not an aircraft carrier despite her flat top and assortment of aircraft. Unlike traditional carriers, the Iwo Jima had a welldeck to support air-cushioned landing craft; and if the military campaign were not going well, she had a 60-bed hospital with six operating rooms.

Barton checked his instruments. He should be approaching his destination. The Coast Guard asked him to check out a boat they deemed suspicious. The vast majority of such contacts proved to be false alarms, but it was faster and cheaper for a Harrier to check them out at 600 miles per hour than have a sluggish Coast Guard Cutter track them down. Looking below, Barton saw the sails of a large yacht. The two-masted ketch was the play toy of some wealthy corporate executive.

Barton banked around for a closer look. Dropping down to fifty feet above the three-foot waves, Barton slowed the Harrier to less than ten miles per hour just off the ketch's port side, a strange sight to someone unfamiliar with the Harrier's variable vector-thrust jet engines. Several people on deck were waving at him and taking pictures, not your typical drug smugglers. Just the same, Barton took out a pair of binoculars and made a note of the boat's registration number painted on the side. The boat was flying an American flag.

"Black Jack to USS Iwo Jima, Black Jack to Iwo Jima, come in." Barton waited for a reply.

"Iwo Jima to Black Jack, go ahead."

"The bogey is an American ketch. It appears legit." Barton transmitted the boat's registration number. They would forward the registration number to the Coast Guard for verification.

"Black Jack, we have one more boat for you to check out. It's on your way home. Are you prepared to copy coordinates?"

Barton extracted a pencil from his breast pocket. He had been hoping for a quick return to the barn for a shower and a hot meal.

"Black Jack to Iwo, I copy your transmission." Barton punched the coordinates into the onboard computer, and the Harrier responded with a slight bank to the starboard. Time to check out more mundane mariners. Fortunately, the new bogey was less than fifty miles away. He would be there in six minutes. After a quick look-see, he would be heading back for that hot meal and shower.

I must be living right, Barton decided when he found the boat in less than four minutes. This boat was a high-powered motorboat, judging from the long white wake trailing behind the boat. Barton took the Harrier out of automatic pilot and coaxed it down for a closer look. Several men with beards were waving at him. He picked up his binoculars for a closer look—they were only waving the middle finger! One of the men disappeared into the cabin and returned with an assault rifle. Even from three hundred yards, Barton could see the tell-tail flashes of automatic gunfire.

Barton banked to the left to avoid the gunfire. "Black Jack to Iwo, I have a boatload of very hostile sailors. Please advise the Coast Guard. I'll remain above the deck to assist." Most of the dope smugglers used high-powered speedboats, which were faster than the average Coast Guard Cutter. It was standard procedure to remain on scene until the long arm of the law had the offending parties under control. No boat was about to outrun a Harrier.

"Negatory, Black Jack. Return to the ship immediately."

That was not the expected response. "Iwo, say again?"

"Iwo to Black Jack, return to the ship."

"Iwo, be advised the smugglers will escape. No way the Coast Guard will catch that boat."

"That's their problem, Black Jack. We have a new assignment."

"Iwo, wait one." Barton dropped out of his holding pattern and pointed the Harrier's nose toward the speeding boat. A push of a finger sent a series of fifty caliber rounds walking across the water and over the back of the boat. The long white wake behind the boat immediately ceased.

"Iwo, the boaters have decided to wait for the Coast Guard. I believe they have engine trouble."

It was turning to dusk when Barton saw the flat deck of the USS Iwo Jima come into view. Flight control had already turned on the landing lights, but it was hardly necessary, since the deck was illuminated by one of the Caribbean's magnificent sunsets. Barton set the Harrier down on the center of the deck.

"Why the sudden call back?" Barton asked as his crew chief helped him out of the cockpit.

"The commander says we have a new assignment, but it's top secret."

"Don't give me that. There's no such thing as top secret onboard ship. Where we going?"

"Well, you didn't hear it from me, sir," the crew chief whispered, "but a guy in the commo shack said we're going to Lake Michigan."

"Lake Michigan?"

White House Situation Room, 1300 hours

Bart Schroeder settled back in his high-top swivel chair at the head of the conference table. The situation room always made him feel presidential. Bart took two cookies and passed the cookie jar around the table. No one took any cookies—that was their loss.

"Let's get started," Bart said when he had everyone's attention. "General Brackendorf, can you bring us up to date on the military situation?"

General Brackendorf slowly rose and walked over to a small podium. A map of North America hung on the wall behind him. Once behind the podium, he again paused, obviously enjoying his distinguished audience. In addition to the Chief of Staff from each branch of the military, he also had the President of the United States, his Chief of Staff, and his Press Secretary.

"Gentlemen, our military operation, which we have designated "Operation Greener Pastures" is progressing as expected. General Brackendorf paused, allowing this to sink in. "The nuclear attack submarine, USS Virginia, is already heading up the St. Lawrence Seaway." In case there were any doubts, the general whacked the map for emphasis. If his listeners were paying attention—which they weren't—they would have noticed he hit the map two states below the St. Lawrence Seaway. "It'll head up Lake Huron, through the Soo Locks at Sault Ste. Marie and into Lake Superior. It will then position itself outside Marquette Harbor." The general whacked the map again. This time his aim was better.

"The amphibious assault ship, USS Iwo Jima, will be following the USS Virginia through the St. Lawrence Seaway. As you know, the USS Iwo Jima is a small aircraft carrier with a squadron of Harrier Jump Jets that can vertically take off and land. It also has an assortment of rotary wing aircraft capable of transporting troops and equipment to shore. The Iwo Jima with 1,894 attached marines will position itself about here." General Brackendorf pointed to a spot in northern Lake Michigan along the southern shore of the Upper Peninsula. "The Iwo Jima will be our operations center and will spearhead our amphibious assault on the beaches. The other elements are on stand-by but not yet activated. We don't want to lay our cards on the table any sooner than needed."

"It seems to me," Al said, speaking for the first time, "we won't be able to keep the lid on this much longer."

"I agree with Al." Ron Clark, the President's Press Secretary cleared his throat. "We need to take this to the people before it leaks out. We need to take the initiative."

"We talkin' press conference?" Al asked.

"Prime time press conference," Ron replied. "Let the people know how serious this threat is."

"I suppose we could have the President do one without questions at the end." Al was not excited about a hostile press corps grilling the President.

"We could set up a podium on the White House lawn," Ron said. "Maybe have the Presidential helicopter in the background. He could be wearing a flight jacket, and we could tell the press corps he can't answer questions because he has to fly to Camp David for an emergency meeting on the U.P. situation."

"I like the idea," Al said. "This all assumes, of course, that the grounds crew has the White House lawn re-sodded in time."

"What'll we do with the press during the war?" one of the generals asked. "We may have to shoot some women and children. Believe it or not, we still have people in the media who can't grasp the concept of collateral damage."

"We could embed them with the invasion force," another general said. "It worked well in the second Gulf War. We control their movements and screen their reports. If we don't like their reports, we can reassign them to a logistics unit in the rear."

"Is everyone onboard with this plan?" Bart asked. There were nods of approval around the table.

The Bare Creek Gazette, 0932 hours

Karla wondered if a darker shade of red on her fingernails would clash with her platinum blond hair. It was a slow day in the office of the *Bare Creek Gazette*. With the billing finished and the phone unusually quiet, Karla sat at her desk filing her nails—a receptionist must present a proper appearance. She held her left hand up for inspection. The left index fingernail needed a bit more shaping, she decided. Engrossed in her project, Karla didn't look up when the front door opened, causing the string of small bells attached to the door to jingle.

"Can I help you?" Karla asked. Maybe she should try black fingernail polish.

"Yes, I would like to look at old issues of the Gazette, if I may."

The English was perfect but drenched in a thick Italian accent. Karla looked up from her nails to discover a massive warty growth draped in a black cassock. She tried not to stare at the fleshy stalactite drooping down from the nose, but the large wart beckoned to her. Totally mesmerized, she hardly noticed the wide-brimmed black hat or the large crucifix hanging from the man's neck by a gold chain.

"My name is Father Ginatti." Agent X scanned the room, mentally cataloguing the location of chairs and tables, mapping them into his brain. He would need to know their locations should he later need to do a black-bag job in the dark.

Karla chewed her gum for a moment of thought. "Are you a real priest?"

"The Holy See thinks so," Father Ginatti replied with his best fatherly smile. Blond had to be her natural hair color, Agent X decided.

"I'm Catholic. Even got a rosary somewhere."

"I'm glad to hear that, my child."

"Don't go to church often." Karla fought off an urge to touch the wart to see if it were real. It could be contagious, she decided. "They don't have a Catholic Church in Bear Creek."

"As long as you keep your heart pure."

"I may be a tad short at that end too." A few of her juicier indiscretions immediately came to mind. "Do you hear confessions?"

"Yes, but that is not why His Holiness sent me here."

"The Pope sent you?" Karla tried to remember who the Pope was this year.

"I've been asked to investigate the alleged miracles performed by Abigail Farnsworth. The church is considering sainthood."

"Wow." Karla had never lived in a town with its own saint.

"I was hoping the *Bare Creek Gazette* could shed some light on the subject."

"I'm new in the area. Been here about four years. You'll need to talk to my boss, Silas Kronschnabell. He's actually Silas Kronschnabell III. His Grandfather, the first Silas Kronschnabell, started the paper in the early nineteen hundreds. You think you could hear my confession sometime? Haven't been to confession for several years. All those sins add up after a while."

"Maybe someday. Is Mr. Kronschnabell available?"

"He's in the back room fixing his press. Let me introduce you."

Karla led Agent X through a double door into a large room filled with printing equipment. An elderly man in his sixties was bending over a printing press with a large wrench in his hand trying to reattaching a flywheel.

"Mr. Kronschnabell, this is Father Ginatti. He's from the Vatican. He's asking about Abigail Farnsworth."

"Hang on a minute." Silas walked over to a large switch bolted to the wall. "Let me see if this contraption works now." Silas flipped the switch, and the machine came to life. The newly attached flywheel wobbled as it spun on its axle. After a moment or two, it flew from its axle heading toward Agent X. Agent X noted the angle at separation, and estimated its velocity. The angular momentum he calculated as the vector product of the integrated sum of the position vectors of the flywheel's component particles. Using a complex variant of a Fourier series, Agent X mentally calculated the trajectory of the projectile in the time-space continuum. It would pass three inches over his head. He, therefore, did not need to duck. He knew his Ph.D. in applied mathematics from Stanford University would come in handy someday.

Silas turned off the machine. "You all right?" Silas asked, assuming the flywheel had struck the stranger in the nose. He didn't need any lawsuits. Closer inspection revealed the fleshy appendage to be of natural origin.

"It appears I am quite unharmed, thank you. In the future you may wish to increase the torque on the flywheel's setscrew by 12.4%. I believe that would be sufficient to hold it in its proper place." Agent X extended his hand. "Father Ginatti's the name."

"Silas Kronschnabell." Silas wiped his hand on a rag and shook hands. "What can I do for you?"

"I'm researching Abigail Farnsworth for the Vatican. She may be canonized if the alleged miracles can be documented."

Silas picked up a pipe from his desk and filled it with tobacco. Scratching a match against the sole of his shoe, he lit the pipe and was soon engulfed with smoke. "I don't know what you heard, but when I was a little boy, my grandfather told me about a four-year-old girl Abigail rescued from a blustering snow storm. I believe the young girl's name was Becky Hakanen. My grandfather was convinced the miracle was real."

"That would be Silas Kronschnabell the first?"

"That's him on the wall."

A large black and white portrait of a stately gentleman puffing on a pipe hung on the far wall. The smoke partially obscured his face. Agent X noted a startling resemblance between grandfather and grandson, down to the pipe's smoky haze.

"My grandmother took the picture. I've been told she was quite the photographer."

"I understand you maintain a file of old newspapers?"

"You must be referring to our morgue." Silas took another puff on his pipe and sent out a billowing cloud of smoke. "It's a gruesome title for a collection of old issues, but every newspaper has one."

"I would be honored if you would allow me access to the older files."

"Not a problem… Karla can help you." Silas led Father Ginatti back into the front room. "Karla, can you help Father Ginatti? He needs to look at the Gazette's early issues. He can use my office. I won't need it for a while. I have more work to do on the press."

"What issues did you want to see," Karla asked.

"I would like to start with December of 1923, if I may."

Karla chewed diligently on her gum for a moment while she contemplated the request and then disappeared into an adjoining room. She returned two minutes later with a stack of papers. "Sorry they're all loose. Mr. Kronschnabell talks about putting them on microfiche but never does."

"This will do fine." Agent X spread the papers across the editor's desk. It would be a long shot if he found anything.

"About that confession… You think you could hear it if I keep it down to just the most repugnant transgressions? I could give you a sort of *Cliff's Notes* version."

"This really isn't a good time." Agent X flipped through the reams of paper, converting everything to memory. Later he would digest the pertinent information and expunge the worthless trivia from his brain. He despised a cluttered mind.

"My first husband was a Buddhist. At least that's what he told me. We had to have that marriage annulled. Can you call someone an ex-husband if the marriage is annulled? He was sterile, but he didn't tell me until after we were married. Do you think that was fair? He said he had an accident on a bicycle as a child. I thought his voice sounded high pitched. Being a good Catholic, I naturally wanted kids, and there was no chance of having kids with him. Do you think I did the right thing by having the marriage annulled? Despite his injury, I thought he was O.K. in bed. He had all the right moves, you know. I guess you wouldn't know. I forgot you guys aren't into that sex thing. That must take a lot of willpower. I don't think I could…"

"Do you think I could see the issues for 1924?"

Karla returned with another stack of old papers. "My ex-husband now lives in a Buddhist monastery. He decided to devote his life to meditation. I still get Christmas cards from him. Don't you think that's ironic? I mean…a Buddhist sending out Christmas cards."

Good, her phone's ringing. Maybe that'll shut her up. Agent X let out a barely noticeable sign of relief. "Miss, I believe your phone is ringing."

Karla paused in her gum chewing for a moment of thought, finding it difficult to do both. "Nope, ain't my phone. Must be your cell phone."

Agent X retrieved the phone from his pocket. The phone let out another ring, confirming its guilt. "You're right. It is my phone. Must be the Vatican."

"Just before my ex-husband left for the monastery, we invited over some friends, sort of a going away party, you know."

Agent X: *Hello?*

"That's when I met Mike. He was an old friend of my husband."

Abigail: *I hope I didn't catch you at a bad time.*

"Mike and I hit it off right away."

Agent X covered the phone's mouthpiece. "It's Sister Abby from the Vatican."

Agent X: *I'm busy at the moment. Maybe you could give me your phone number, and I can call you back.*

"We dated about three months. Then he asked me to marry him."

Abigail: *You're being silly again... The reason I'm calling is because as soon as I hung up last time I got to thinking you would want to construct a psychological profile about me... Isn't that what you CIA agents do when you don't know what you're doing?*

"It seemed like a good idea at the time, ya know. We had the blessing of my ex-husband."

Agent X: *I know exactly what I'm doing...and I'm good at it.*

Abigail: *Let's not get testy.*

"Well, we had been married six months, and I still wasn't pregnant."

Abigail: *The Bare Creek Gazette has files of their old papers. You may want to check them out.*

"He always insisted we have sex in the dark. That was O.K. with me."

Abigail: *If you do go there, watch out for Karla, the receptionist. I think her last name is Winkelhorst, but that would depend on her current husband. She'll talk your head off.*

"One day we had sex in the daytime... That's when I saw them. A couple of surgical scars... The swine had a vasectomy before we were married, and he didn't have the courage to tell me."

Agent X: *This really isn't a good time to talk. You shouldn't call me at work.*

"I considered divorcing him right then and there."

Abigail: *That brings up another point—your antisocial behavior.*

"Once Mike completed his sex change, it was a moot point."

Abigail: *According to your CIA file, you have a hideous wart on your nose.*

Agent X: *I don't want to talk about it.*

"I didn't know if I was still legally married or what."

Abigail: *If you mother really loved you, she would've had it surgically removed.*

"I mean...Michigan doesn't recognize same sex marriages."

Agent X: *Mom did too love me.*

"Was it still a marriage or just a civil union?"

Abigail: *I know a good plastic surgeon in Marquette. She could remove it for you.*

Agent X: *She?*

Abigail: *Not all doctors are men.*

"It really didn't matter as we sort of lost interest in each other and drifted apart."

Abigail: *We can get you all fixed up, dear.*

Agent X: *And don't call me dear. We need to keep this on a professional, adversarial level.*

"You really like the lady you're talking to, don't you?"

Agent X covered the phone's mouthpiece. "Please Karla, she's a nun and I'm a priest. This is strictly a platonic relationship."

"Well, don't take it out on me. I wasn't the one who took the vow of celibacy."

Agent X: *Look Abigail, I really have to get back to work. We'll have to talk later.*

Agent X hung up the phone.

"Anything else I can get you?" Karla asked.

"You got any aspirin?"

Chapter Twelve

Oval Office, 1000 hours

"Hold it, Al."

Al waited at the Oval Office door while Bart studied the lay of the White House carpet. Little on the thick side, Bart decided. Licking his index finger, he evaluated the wind coming through the open window, finding a slight breeze from the southwest. Bart evaluated the parameters, made appropriate corrections, and then planted his feet on the Oval Office carpet. After a couple practice swings, he tapped the golf ball with his putter. The ball rolled across the carpet coming to a rest six inches to the left of the urine specimen cup the White House nurse had asked him to fill; he was due for his yearly physical. The floor must slope to the south. He would have to allow for that in the future.

"Can we proceed with the briefing?" Al asked. "We have a lot to cover."

Bart reluctantly returned to his desk. Meetings took the fun out of being President. He should limit meetings to no more than two per day. Bart washed down two extra strength aspirin with water and followed them with a cookie. "O.K., Al, I'm ready. What ya got?"

"You didn't happen to catch *Meet the Press* yesterday, did you?" Al asked.

"No, I missed that. I think *The Wizard of Oz* was on."

"They had Walter Brainthorpe on the program. He asked some very probing questions about our military deployment; specifically, why we are sending a submarine and an assault ship up the St. Lawrence Seaway."

"You think someone tipped him off?" Bart asked.

"No doubt about it. We'll have to move up the press conference."

There went his afternoon of golf. Bart had hoped to try out his new putter. Maybe he should repeal the First Amendment. The press had too much freedom.

"The press is beginning to ask questions. Brainthorpe has them stirred up." Al checked his calendar. "We could do it this afternoon, call it an emergency press conference. That'll give people the impression this came up suddenly, but we are on top of it."

"Will I still get to wear a flight jacket and stand in front of the helicopter?"

"They finished re-sodding the lawn, so that looks like a go. I'll get speechwriters working on it right away. We'll push the WMD and the imminent threat. People will rally around the flag. You'll have to keep everything vague. Give them only minimal details. No one believes anything said at a presidential press conference anyway, no matter how strong the documentation."

"They don't?" Al sure knew how to deflate a guy's ego. "Why have the press conference?"

"It sets the framework of suspicion, points the media in the right direction. News people are a strange lot. They're skeptical of even the best documented information you give them but will believe any rumor they dig up on their own."

Bart mulled this over for a moment. He thought people were listening to his speeches. "How we goin' justify a preemptive strike against the U.P. if no one's listening to us?"

"Leaks."

"Leaks?"

"High level information leaks. We do it all the time. The press'll chow down on it faster than a squadron of starving mosquitoes in a nudist colony. It's considered forbidden fruit. When we're confronted on the issue, we simply side step it, neither confirm nor deny the leak."

"Think that'll work?" Bart asked.

"Of course it will," Al said. "Especially when we get indignant about the question and appoint someone to find the source of the leak. This morning I sent Rob Carter of Channel 7 News an E-mail from the Library of Congress, totally untraceable. In a minute or two, I plan to give him a call. His caller I.D. will say White House but not where in the White House. I'll disguise my voice. I think we can make this press conference very productive."

"Will we have any graphs or pictures?" Bart liked visual aids. He could better understand what he was talking about when there were lots of pictures.

"I was hoping for satellite pictures of the U.P.," Al said. "But the pentagon is having problems with their new spy satellite. Some sort of computer glitch. They programmed it to fly over the U.P., but it flew over the St. Lawrence Seaway instead."

"I never see anything in those satellite pictures anyway." Bart checked the grip on his putter. After the press conference the helicopter would take him to Camp David. Maybe he could have them stop at the Willow Creek Country Club.

"That's the best part, no one can. Place a missile silo label on an old pine stump, and people will believe it. They'll believe anything high tech."

"Have we heard from Agent X?"

"Thought you would never ask." Al extracted some papers from his folder. *Top Secret* was stamped on the top of each page. "Agent X has been researching the origin of the Abigail Farnsworth legend. He's trying to develop a psychological profile of the individual who has been using her name."

"What did he come up with?" Bart tried a long putt toward the specimen cup at the far side of the Oval Office. The ball veered to the left, bouncing off the Porta-Potty. The floor was definitely slanted.

"The Farnsworth legend is localized to the Bear Creek area where it originated. Agent X believes our terrorist comes from that area, perhaps second or third generation. She grew up in Bear Creek, hearing the legend from grandparents. Being a young, impressionable child, she developed an idol worship and later in life took on Abigail's name."

"Ya think she really believes she's Abigail Farnsworth?" Bart asked.

"Beats me. She could be emotionally unstable. That's the type foreign powers like to recruit."

"What else did he find out about her?"

"He thinks she's single. Too much free time to be married with kids. Probably young and idealistic. She highly intelligent and well educated, maybe a college grad or perhaps still in college."

Bart walked over to retrieve his ball. "We were right, then… Bear Creek is the epicenter of this conspiracy."

"At least outside of Helsinki."

Houghton, Michigan 2330 hours

An odd assortment of papers covered the Pizza Hut's large corner table. The carcass of a pepperoni and sausage pizza sat on a separate stand, totally ignored by all except Moose who was brought up on the clean-plate-club theory. He didn't want to be responsible for starving children in foreign countries. It was almost closing time, and the Pizza Hut staff were anxious to clean up the mess. They viewed the foursome with less than amiable eyes.

"Are you sure these documents are accurate?" Abigail asked.

"The pentagon's computer never lied to me before." Newton reshuffled some of the papers, looking for one in particular. He finally found it. It was the one with the pizza stain. "The best I can figure, the United States is about to declare war on the Upper Peninsula."

"The President can't do that," Sherlock said. "That takes an act of Congress."

"Officially we haven't been at war since WWII, but we've been in Panama, Korea, Vietnam, Bosnia, and Iraq. Need I go on?" Newton asked. "They're redefined as police actions."

"Surely the President isn't dumb enough to think Finland wants to make us a colony." Sherlock sipped on his Coke while he studied some of the documents.

"Where do we go from here?" Newton asked.

"I think it's obvious… We defend the U.P." All eyes were on Abigail.

"Like in the four of us?" Sherlock believed in miracles and Divine salvation, but there was no way the four of them were going to stop several infantry divisions and an armored battalion, not to mention a nuclear attack submarine.

"Have I led you astray in the past?" Abigail asked. Her cohorts were not sure how to politely answer that question. "Look at it this way. We have copies of their game plan. Right?" There were nods of agreement.

"It's a five-point attack, and there are only four of us so we're outnumbered, but I think we can still pull it off." Abigail pulled out a map of the U.P. "We know an armored battalion from the Michigan National Guard will be coming up from Camp Grayling on I-75. They shouldn't be a problem. I have a friend who works at the Mackinac Bridge who can take care of them."

"Then we have the 82nd Airborne, which will make a night drop along the Seney Stretch." Abigail pointed to an area in the center of the U.P.

"The Seney Stretch? They can't be serious?" Sherlock asked.

"They better bring plenty of insect repellent or lots of blood," Moose mumbled through a mouthful of pizza.

"I don't think we need to worry about the 82nd Airborne," Abigail said. "We'll let nature take its course."

"What about the submarine in Marquette Harbor?" Sherlock asked. "It's armed with twelve cruise missiles. Not much is goin' stop them."

"Don't underestimate the power of the press."

"Power of the press?" Sherlock had visions of people with newspapers swatting at cruise missiles.

"Tomorrow I want you to drive to Marquette and place this ad in the *Marquette Mining Journal*." Abigail passed a note to Sherlock.

Sherlock studied the note for a moment. A smile came to his face. "Ya know, Abigail, this is so stupid it might just work."

"How we going stop the amphibious assault coming up the Portage Canal?" Newton asked. "It's going take more than a newspaper ad to stop hundreds of marines storming up from the Portage Canal."

"From what I understand," Abigail said, "they'll be approaching from both ends of the canal, and then come ashore somewhere between Michigan Tech and Finlandia University. That'll put them right where we want them."

"It will?" Moose asked.

"Once we turn the animals loose, it'll be a short, but decisive battle."

"That still leaves the Amphibious Assault Ship with a battalion of marines sitting in northern Lake Michigan just south of Epoufette," Sherlock said. "That'll be our biggest challenge. They'll have jet planes and helicopters."

"What's an Amphibious Assault Ship?" Moose asked.

"I was wondering that too," Newton said, "so I took a picture of it." Newton tossed a couple eight-by-ten glossies onto the table. "It looks like an old WWII aircraft carrier."

Abigail picked up one of the pictures. "This is a satellite photo. Where'd you get this?"

"It's two days old; but, otherwise, I think I take a decent picture."

"But how'd you take this picture?" Abigail wasn't sure she wanted to know the details.

"I borrowed a Lacrosse Intel satellite from the military."

"You borrowed a satellite?"

"I would have used a KH-12 but they don't have the SBR system like the newer Lacrosse satellites."

"What's a SBR?" Sherlock asked.

"It stands for Space-Based Radar. It penetrates cloud cover. I wasn't sure the sky would be clear over the St. Lawrence Seaway."

"You borrowed a satellite?" Abigail hoped she wasn't hearing right.

"No big deal…once you get access to the computer at NRO."

"NRO?"

"National Reconnaissance Office. It's sort of hidden within Air Force Intelligence. The hardest part was reprogramming the satellite to change its orbit. I had to use the engineering department's computer for that."

"You borrowed a satellite from the military?"

"They don't care…as long as you put it back where you found it.

They'll assume it was a computer glitch."

Abigail wondered if the project was getting out of hand; still the picture of the Amphibious Assault Ship created a better understanding of the opposition. At the moment, they had nothing to thwart a battalion of marines coming ashore on hovercraft supported by helicopters and Harrier Jump Jets. The Amphibious Assault Ship would be a formidable opponent.

"Moose, you're part Indian, aren't you?" Abigail asked.

"Seven sixteenth Indian. Why?" Moose had been hoping his Native American heritage wouldn't come into play. Traditionally, Native Americans didn't fare well whenever people played Cowboys and Indians.

"You still active in the Indian community?"

"Sort of."

"I want you to contact people in the Indian casinos. This is what I want you to do...."

Channel 7 News Room, 1545 hours

"This is Rob Carter of Channel 7 News. We interrupt our normal broadcast for some late breaking news. As many of you already know, Walter Brainthorpe dropped a bombshell Sunday on *Meet the Press* when he insinuated President Schroeder was contemplating military action without the consent of Congress.

"To help put this into perspective, I have with me today Lt. General Lucas Thornton, retired. General, can you bring us up to speed on what's happened so far?"

"I would be happy to, Rob. The information at this point is sketchy. We do know the USS Virginia, one of the nation's newest nuclear attack submarines, has been ordered into the Great Lakes. Unconfirmed rumors have it destined for Lake Superior."

"General, the only foreign nation in that area is Canada. Are you suggesting military action involving Canada?"

"Rob, at this point we really don't know. We designed the USS Virginia for coastal missions. It is also an excellent platform for inserting

Navy SEALs. We may be talking clandestine operations against terror-ists."

"We should know in a few minutes, General. President Schroeder is about to convene an emergency press conference; after which, he plans to fly to Camp David for further briefings. Is there anything particular we should be looking for in the briefing?"

"Rob, I wouldn't expect much hard information about tactics and objectives. A wise President will leave that to the generals. I would expect him to lay out the ground work and rational for the military action, whatever that may be."

"Can you hold that thought, General? We have to pause for a word from our sponsor." Rob smiled into the camera until the red light went out, signaling the end of the transmission.

"ROB, YOU HAVE A PHONE CALL," someone yelled from the back.

"WHO IS IT?"

"THE CALLER WON'T SAY, BUT THE CALLER I.D. SAYS IT'S COMING FROM THE WHITE HOUSE. DIDN'T RECOGNIZE THE VOICE, IT'S DEEP AND HUSKY."

Rob picked up the phone.

Rob: *Rob Carter here.*

White House: *I have some information for you.*

Rob: *Who is this?*

White House: *You can call me Deep Throat II.*

Rob: *What can I do for you?*

White House: *You need to know all those White House turkeys were infested with avian flu.*

Rob: *Avian flu?*

White House: *Not just avian flu, but genetically altered flu. It's more lethal and doesn't respond to any known antiviral medications.*

Rob: *How do we know this is true?*

White House: *You don't. The White House would prefer you ignore this information. They don't want that information to leak out. They fear panic in the streets, but I think the people have a right to know.* (Click).

Rob: *Hello?*

"Someone call Atlanta. I want a talking head from CDC." Rob hung up the phone. "Get me someone familiar with avian flu."

"Rob, you're back on the air in ten seconds...five, four, three..."

"This is Rob Carter, Channel 7 News. In a few moments we will have an emergency press conference with President Schroeder. Let's go to our live camera on the White House lawn. There's the podium with the Presidential Seal where we expect President Schroeder to give his briefing... In the background is the Marine helicopter... Can we get a close up of the helicopter?... Look just inside the door, General... See the golf clubs. The President must have been planning an afternoon of golf today. It demonstrates how quickly this crisis came up."

"It looks like it will be a few minutes before the press conference starts, so let's go to our affiliate station in Buffalo, New York... Bill... can you hear me?"

"Yes, Rob... As you can see behind me, it has not been a normal day here in Buffalo." A live picture of a nuclear submarine flashed across the TV monitor. "We have the nuclear attack submarine, USS Virginia, going through the locks of the Welland Canal. This has to be a first."

"Bill, any idea where they're going?"

"Nothing official, Rob, but I did have a short conversation with a sailor on the deck—actually, we had to yell back and forth—he said they were heading for Lake Superior... Again, this is unofficial."

"I hate to cut you off, Bill, but it looks like the President is coming to the podium."

Bart stepped up to the podium. He was wearing his favorite flight jacket with the Presidential Seal over the left breast pocket. A large black belt with a gaudy silver buckle held up his faded jeans. He topped off the ensemble with his traditional white Stetson and cowboy boots.

Bart paused for a moment at the podium to increase the audience's anticipation. Behind him, Old Glory waved from a pole placed just to his left. Since the ambient wind was inconsistent, Bart's Press Secretary sequestered a large fan behind a nearby bush to provide back up. A recording of the Marine Corps Band softly played *America* in front of the multitude of podium microphones to set the mood. Ron Clark had prepared well for the press conference.

"My fellow Americans." Bart paused again. Never underestimate the power of the pause. He had learned that from Paul Harvey. "It is with a heavy heart that I come before you today." Bart looked out over the White House press corps. He had their undivided attention. "I must regretfully inform you that the nation—your nation—has come under attack with chemical and biological weapons. The CIA has provided me with unimpeachable evidence that Finnish agents with assistance of Finnish-American sympathizers are attempting to forcibly annex Michigan's Upper Peninsula to Finland. In addition to routine WMD, we have information that they are close to deploying S.I.S.U., which we believe stands for Sensory Inhibitory Satellite Unit. When this becomes operational, they will be capable of incapacitating entire battalions with sensory inhibiting radiation. We are unable to release any details at this time without endangering our own intelligence operatives. Due to the serious and imminent danger this poses to our country and the free world, I have ordered a preemptive military strike to reclaim what is rightfully ours. Unfortunately, I will not have time to answer any questions, as I must now leave for Camp David, where I will meet with my military advisors to clarify our forceful and aggressive response to this tyranny. May God have mercy on us all." With his most sober facial expression, Bart held up two fingers for a victory sign and turned toward his helicopter. Time for a round of golf.

"There you have it, ladies and gentlemen." Rob looked into the camera, but the wall monitor confirmed the television viewers were still watching the President walking toward his waiting helicopter. "The President's speech was short and to the point. I timed it at fifty-two seconds, but you can't judge a speech of that magnitude with a stopwatch. We have to remember the Gettysburg Address only took a couple of minutes. We now see the President walking out to his waiting helicopter with what appears to be the weight of the world on his shoulders. It'll be some time before he gets to use those golf clubs again."

"Reactions…General, what did you think?"

"Rob, it was a very emotional speech. You could see the strain on his face. There were several pauses in the speech, as if he were choking up and finding it difficult to continue. As to the content, there was little detail. He's playing his cards close to his chest. We know WMD have been deployed against the United States, but he didn't elaborate as to type of WMD or how they were employed."

"I think I can shed some light on that, General." Rob adjusted his tie and looked into the camera. "As you know, there are no secrets in Washington. One of my personal White House sources has informed me that the turkeys that recently attacked the White House were infested with avian flu. What looked like a simple college prank may have been a deadly biological attack. Here at the Channel 7 News desk we like to have our stories confirmed by a second independent source.

"I have on the phone Dr. Jeb Gorby from the Center for Disease Control in Atlanta. We'll see if he can confirm this story." A file photo of Dr. Jeb Gorby flashed across Rob's monitor. "Dr. Gorby, this is Rob Carter, Channel 7 News in Washington. I understand you are an expert on the avian flu?"

"It would be presumptuous to refer to myself as an expert. There is still so much to learn about avian influenza, but I have studied it for several years."

"Dr. Gorby, can you tell us about the flu. Just how dangerous is it."

"Well, Mr. Carter, normally it is totally harmless, because it is confined to birds. Occasionally, the virus can mutate, and humans become susceptible. The first recorded human infection was in Hong Kong in 1997. The flu hospitalized eighteen people, and one third of them died. Since humans have had little previous exposure to the virus, it can be quite deadly."

"Dr. Gorby, if someone were to genetically engineer the virus to be resistant to our antiviral medications and vaccines, could it be used as a biological weapon?"

"I would have to say it would be quite deadly."

"Dr. Gorby, we have evidence the turkeys attacking the White House were infected with a deadly strain of avian flu. We would like your opinion...Dr. Gorby?... Are you still there?"

"...You didn't mention this was concerning an on-going criminal investigation... I think we had better end this conversation." (Click).

"This is Rob Carter of Channel 7 News. In case you just tuned in, it looks like the United States is heading toward war. We just heard from President Schroeder on the White House lawn giving what I can only describe as a very grave announcement. It appears Finland in cooperation with Finnish-American sympathizers has resorted to using WMD against the United States in an attempt to annex Michigan's Upper Peninsula.

"I am honored to have with me today Lt. General Lucas Thornton, retired. We have just talked to Dr. Jeb Gorby from the Center for Disease Control in Atlanta. He seemed a little apprehensive when we suggested the White House turkeys were infected with the deadly avian flu... Did you get that impression, General?"

"Apprehension is an understatement, Rob; but keep in mind the CDC would be investigating any such biological attack and would not be at liberty to comment on the investigation. I would like to offer a contrarian view that this is not a recent development. You don't hire a man of Brainthorpe's caliber to drive a truckload of turkeys. I believe the intelligence community had advance warning. The CIA may have placed Brainthorpe in the driver's seat, if you will, in an attempt to infiltrate the terrorist organization. It would also explain why the Secret Service pulled back to the White House as soon as they identified the turkeys. You don't go one-on-one with turkeys carrying biological weaponry. They were highly criticized at the time, but they made the right decision. You have to go with the big guns. You have to bring in the professionals. You have to call in the military."

Someone passed Rob a sheet of paper. He studied the paper for a moment, permitting General Thornton to extol the virtues of allowing the military to take on the feathered insurgents. It was a printout of an E-mail message. An engineer had penciled in the margin that the E-mail came from one of the computers at the Library of Congress.

"General, I just received a disturbing note from another one of my personal informants, this time from the legislative branch. It appears the Amorous Spotted Slugs may be carrying a deadly biological agent. Again this has yet to be confirmed, but I must add this source has never been wrong in the past."

"Rob, if that turns out to be true, it would be a particularly sinister development. As you know the A.S.S. is a nocturnal creature and is seldom seen, but can leave a slimy trail perhaps laced with anthrax or other deadly bacteria. We've identified them in a vacant lot here in Washington, but where else might they be hiding? I don't want to be an alarmist, but I think a good spray can of insecticide should be added to the duct tape in everyone's doomsday kit."

"I personally haven't had the opportunity to see one, but we do have a picture of an Amorous Spotted Slug that I downloaded from the Internet." Rob held up a picture for the camera. "They're actually rather cute, and I understand some children are keeping them as pets."

"Rob, I don't think we can be too cautious here. If anyone finds a slug that looks similar to this picture, I would immediately quarantine the room and call the authorities."

"General, does the fact that the Amorous Spotted Slug is normally found in the U.P. tell us anything?"

"I think it confirms the President hit the nail on the head. The Upper Peninsula presents a clear and present danger, and we need to rally around the President and our troops no matter what our political affiliations."

"That brings up an interesting point. According to the wire service, which is reporting reactions to the President's speech, Walter Brainthorpe has come out against military intervention. He feels we should work toward a negotiated settlement. Do you think Brainthorpe is washed up politically?"

"He is in my book. You can't give aid and comfort to the enemy and still be a good American."

"One last question, General, how easy will it be for our troops? Can we expect a quick victory?"

"That's a difficult question to answer, Rob. I'm sure the President will demand shock and awe, a military technique perfected during the second Gulf War, but it will depend on how the people of the U.P. react. Will they see our troops as liberators, or will they view the troops as occupiers? It will also depend on whether or not the Finns resort to WMD. We're assuming their S.I.S.U. program is still in the development stage. If it's operational, this could be a long and bloody conflict."

"General, can you explain to our viewers what S.I.S.U. is and what it can do?"

"Rob, it's a program we've been working on for years. The acronym stands for Sensory Inhibitory Satellite Unit. Basically, it's an orbiting satellite that's capable of sending out a beam of radiation that would alter the senses of entire battalions or divisions."

"Does Finland have the capability of launching such a satellite?"

"They don't need to. There are plenty of nations willing to launch a satellite for a fee, no questions asked."

"Thank you, General Lucas Thornton. Hopefully, we can have you back again. And that concludes our special newscast on *War on the U.P.*" Rob stared at the camera until the red light flickered off.

Chapter Thirteen

Patriotic citizens reacted quickly to the Schroeder Doctrine, as the President's speech on the lawn became known. American flags flew freely from storefronts while retired generals made the rounds of talk shows, and young men flocked to their local recruiters to fulfill their patriotic duties. At the steps of the capitol, political leaders from both parties joined hands, declaring support for the President and the brave men in uniform.

Not everyone was pleased with the Schroeder Doctrine. The ambassador from Finland vehemently denied the existence of any Finnish WMD program; but, then, no one expected them to "fess" up. A few cases of ethnic discrimination were filed with the Civil Rights Commission; although, for the most part, Finnish immigrants avoided confrontations and kept to themselves, a wise choice considering the circumstances.

Correspondents from various networks and news magazines lined up to be embedded with the invading forces. The prevailing wisdom within the news media suggested a short and decisive war. Therefore, few people packed underwear for more than two weeks.

While patriotic Americans were waving flags and attending parades sponsored by local veterans' organizations, the military quietly prepared for war. The USS Iwo Jima arrived in Lake Michigan without fanfare and began prowling along the Upper Peninsula's southern shore. Farther north, the USS Virginia traversed the Soo Locks and entered Lake Superior on its way to Marquette Harbor. Additional ships filled with logistic supplies and some of the nation's best shock troops soon followed, taking up pre-assigned positions in Lake Michigan or Lake Superior to await the fast approaching invasion date.

Similar preparations occurred on land as members of the 82nd Airborne gathered in a secure, undisclosed location. They erected a tent city along the edge of a small airfield. Energetic paratroopers trained late into the evening to maintain their finely honed combat skills. Supply tents began to fill with cases of MRE's, the military's version of the TV Dinner, minus the TV. In a more remote area of the compound, armed guards patrolled along triple strands of concertina wire that surrounded stockpiles of grenades, claymore mines, and an assortment of lethal projectiles. There is an old military dictum that good logistics never win a battle, but bad logistics can surely lose one. Military planners had no intention of losing this one.

At Camp Grayling, ninety-two miles south of the Mackinac Bridge, National Guardsmen gathered in response to mobilization orders generated by the Secretary of the Army. The weekend warriors left their civilian jobs where they worked as teachers, auto mechanics, and a variety of other jobs, to don the woodland camouflaged fatigues of their active duty counterparts.

The 147,000 acres of jack pine and scrub oak made Camp Grayling the largest military camp east of the Mississippi River and the nation's largest National Guard training site. It was also home of the 1st Battalion, 126 Armor with its fifty-eight M1A1 main battle tanks.

With sixty-three tons of steel and depleted uranium armor, the M1A1 Abrams tank was the perfect definition of an immovable object, yet its fifteen hundred horsepower turbine engine could coax it forward at forty-two miles per hour. Its 120 mm smooth bore main gun could nullify any opposing armor while its .50 cal machine gun and two 7.62mm machine guns took on lesser targets. The M1A1 was a formidable fighting machine, and fifty-eight of them were preparing to head north toward Michigan's Upper Peninsula.

White House Situation Room, 1300 hours

Bart sat helplessly at the head of the long table, playing with his half-filled cup of coffee while generals and admirals gave reports on military supply requisitions and casualty predictions. He didn't know why he had to be here. He had full confidence in his military leaders. How difficult could it be to conquer a few back-woods Finlanders? This was an election year. He needed to be out in front of the people, not sequestered in staff meetings.

"I guess we're all set," General Brackendorf advised the group. "We can launch the attack on Monday or anytime thereafter."

Everyone looked at Bart. "Monday's fine with me." Maybe they'd have it wrapped up by the weekend. The first Gulf War was over in a hundred hours. It wouldn't look bad on his political resume to have this war over in less time.

"I'll be directing the offensive from the USS Iwo Jima," General Brackendorf said. "A general needs to be near the troops he leads."

"You goin' have news media onboard the ship?" Bart asked.

"We'll have embedded media at all levels," Brackendorf replied.

Bart rubbed his chin in a rare moment of thought. The image of a rough, tough, fighting President might impress the voters. It worked well for Teddy Roosevelt. "Maybe I should go too. You don't think this will last longer than a week? I could fly out on a helicopter wearing a helmet and flight suit with a parachute strapped to my back like that Republican President."

"You'd have to fly out of Camp Grayling," Al warned. "That'll be a long trip. Long trips give you motion sickness."

"Not if I take my motion sickness pill. And I want Schroeder stenciled on the front of my helmet."

Al thought about the idea for a moment. "It might make a good photo-op at that. We could have the camera set up to catch you when you step off the helicopter. It would've been better on a jet fighter, but the Harrier Jump Jets only have one seat."

"I could stop at Camp Grayling, have my picture taken with the troops, and then fly out to the ship. That should ensure my re-election."

Camp Grayling Officer's Club, 1800 hours

Dressed in a gray jumpsuit and his Marine Corps cap, President Schroeder stepped into the Officer's dining hall. Agents Langston and Rushford, still on parole from dungeon duty, flanked his sides.

"Atten' hut!" bellowed a tall man in highly starched fatigues. Every man in the dining hall immediately came to attention. "Lt. Colonel John Winkelman commanding officer of the 1st Battalion, 126 Armor at your service, sir." Col. Winkelman threw the President a crisp salute.

Bart scratched at his right eyebrow to return the compliment. He had never mastered the fine art of saluting during his two weeks in the Marine Corps.

"I wish we had known you were coming for dinner," Col. Winkelman said apologetically, still standing at attention. "All we have is routine army chow."

"If it's good enough for the troops, it's good enough for Bart Schroeder." Bart hoped the line would garner a few extra votes. "You can relax."

"Try *at ease*," Langston whispered into the President's left ear.

"At ease." Everyone relaxed at the President's command. Those already at a table sat down and began to eat. "Now let's have some of that good ol' army chow."

"Follow me, sir."

Winkelman led the President and his two security agents toward a stack of stainless steel trays at the beginning of the service line. The trays were fresh from the dishwasher and still warm. Rushford lost her appetite when she saw the accumulation of baked-on protein in the tray's crevasses. Langston sniffed his tray. It smelled clean.

"This way, sir." Winkelman walked along the chow line where a man in a sweat-stained, T-shirt slapped dry toast onto the trays. For Bart's tray, he selected a piece of toast with minimal burnt spots—rank has its privileges.

Winkelman led his guests toward a second cook in a similar sweat-stained T-shirt—it must have been the uniform of the day. The ash at the end of the cook's well-chewed cigar appeared ready to fall at the slightest noise or vibration.

"SHAFFER, HOW MANY TIMES HAVE I TOLD YOU NOT TO SMOKE IN THE CHOW LINE!" The cigar ash fell into a pan of chipped beef in white sauce.

"Sorry, sir. I forgot." Shaffer crushed the cigar on the sole of his boot and set it on the serving counter for later use. He carved most of the ash from the main entrée with a large spoon and flung it into the sink. To curry favor with his agitated commanding officer, the cook placed an extra-large helping on the Colonel's toast.

"This is an interesting recipe." Bart looked down at the mixture of ground beef and white sauce. "What do you call it?"

"S.O.S." Shaffer replied, slopping a large portion on the President's toast.

"S.O.S.?"

"It's an old army recipe," Shaffer said. "It stands for…"

"Same Old Stuff," Col. Winkelman replied for the cook.

"Mr. President, let me introduce you to some of our officers." Col. Winkelman led the Commander in Chief to a table occupied by two officers. "This is my executive officer, Major Mortimer Moffat, and Company A's commanding officer, Captain Dan Fletcher."

Both men stood up and saluted. Bart scratched at his right eyebrow again. They returned to their seats only after Bart had taken his seat at the table. The meal was not much to look at. Bart assumed the taste improved after several weeks in the field.

Rushford and Langston sat at a nearby table where they could watch the President without being obtrusive. Rushford examined her food with a probing knife to ensure it was dead. It always amazed her what male cooks could concoct when left to their own devices. S.O.S. was a fitting name. Langston chomped down on his chow like a veteran soldier, and then went back for seconds.

After eating a small portion to avoid insulting his hosts, Bart pushed the tray aside. Maybe he would order pizza later. He noticed his hosts weren't fond of their meals either.

"Only enlisted men eat this stuff," Col. Winkelman informed the President as he pushed aside his tray. "If you got time, we can slip into the bar and order a pizza, maybe have a drink or two. We can't stay up too late since the tank convoy heads north in the morning."

The four men excused themselves and headed toward the bar. The two apprehensive Secret Service agents followed the foursome. "Let's take that round table over there in the corner," Col. Winkelman suggested. "It'll give us some privacy."

At least that reduced the perimeter to guard. Rushford thanked the Lord for small favors. The Secret Service agents commandeered an adjacent table. Rushford would have felt better if the officers weren't carrying side arms.

"Waiter, can we have four glasses and a bottle of your best champagne?" Bart could afford to be magnanimous. He would find a way to pass it on to the taxpayers. They also ordered a large pepperoni and sausage pizza. Rushford and Langston had Diet Cokes with their medium pizza.

"We should only have one drink," Col. Winkelman suggested. "We'll need to be mentally sharp when the offensive begins."

Bart poured a healthy portion into each glass. "To a swift and decisive victory." Bart held up his glass.

"I'll drink to that swift victory," Captain Fletcher said, raising his glass. "I need to get back to my pharmacy."

"Pharmacy?" Bart asked after he had taken a swallow of champagne.

"He owns a pharmacy in Dowagiac," Winkelman said.

"A temporary pharmacist is covering for me, but he's only available for two weeks." Fletcher finished off his glass.

Bart refilled the empty glasses.

"You think you have problems," Winkelman said, "I don't have a replacement." He turned to the President. "I'm the loan officer at the Dowagiac Savings and Loan. No one can get a loan until I get back, but I've doubled the number of forms. That'll keep the applicants busy until I return."

"I'll drink to that," Bart said, raising his glass. Being a courteous host, he again refilled the glasses.

"Ya know," Col. Winkelman said with a bit of slur in his speech, "by tomorrow night we'll be combat veterans."

"I hope I don't freeze up when the going gets tough." Major Moffat studied the bottom of his empty glass. "You never know how you'll react under fire."

Bart refilled Major Moffat's glass on the second try, his hand not as steady as it had been. "I didn't find combat that difficult. You do what you have to do."

Everyone looked at the Commander in Chief.

"You've been in combat?"

"Who do you think led the troops when the turkeys attacked the White House?" Bart checked the bottle of champagne. It was empty. Maybe he should order another.

How come he didn't take credit the morning after the fiasco, Rushford wondered.

"It was obvious we were vastly outnumbered," Bart said, "so I had the Secret Service pull back to the White House." Bart tried to focus on his glass. It appeared empty. They would definitely need to order another bottle.

"That was a wise move," Major Moffat decided after a moment of thought.

"Then I called in the air strike." Bart flagged down a waiter for another bottle. "You should have seen it. Those Apache gunships had those insurgent turkeys on the run in no time." Bart made a strafing gesture against the table with his hand, embellishing it with a few rat-a-tat-tat sounds.

"Give me a good tank anytime," Col. Winkelman said. "Now there's some firepower."

Bart leaned over to top off Col. Winkelman's glass from the new bottle.

"Turkeys are easy," Captain Fletcher said. "They're slow. Not a challenge like shooting ducks or geese. Ever been duck huntin'?"

"Can't say I have."

"We got to take this man duck huntin' sometime," Major Moffat advised the other two officers.

"Did ya see that big lake when you flew in to Camp Grayling?" Col.

Winkelman asked but then did not wait for a reply. "That was Lake Margarethe. I know a small cove on the lake that's chuck full of ducks and geese."

"Too bad it's dark, or we could've taken him huntin' today." Captain Fletcher took a sip of champagne to help him think. "I suppose we could see the ducks if we used a tank's thermal imager."

"You want to shoot some geese?" Col. Winkelman asked the President. "We have a tank armed and ready to go. We'll show you how an M1A1 stacks up against an Apache gunship."

"Lead on Col. Winkelman. The night's yet young." Bart grabbed the bottle and tried to extract himself from his chair. He made it with the help of Captain Fletcher.

"I don't think that's a good idea," Agent Rushford said after overhearing the conversation.

"Nonsense, my dear. We're going duck hunting...or is it goose hunting." Bart patted everyone on the head. "Duck...duck...duck." When he came to Agent Rushford, he poked his thumb into her ribs. "Goose!"

Rushford didn't find it half as funny as the President and his military buddies who were giggling like teenage girls.

"We're going on a wild goose chase, Miss Rushford." Bart leaned against his chair for support. "You don't have to come along if you don't want to. This is men's stuff." Bart looked at his three inebriated friends. "I have the Michigan National Guard to protect me."

"We can protect him, Miss," Captain Fletcher informed the Secret Service agent. "We have guns. See..." Fletcher tugged at his pistol but was unable to extract it from its holster. "We'll have him back by midnight."

Rushford looked at her watch. It was already a quarter to one. "I think Langston and I had better come along." Why did they send so few agents on this assignment, Rushford wondered.

Col. Winkelman led his three fellow duck hunters and the two nervous Secret Service agents toward the door. Outside they found a waiting Hum-V.

"This is my vehicle," Winkelman said as he tried to maneuver into the driver's seat.

"Let me drive," Langston suggested. "Officers aren't supposed to drive their own vehicles."

"He's right, you know." Col. Winkelman started to climb into the back seat but fell backward into Langston's arms. With Rushford's help, Langston stuffed everyone into the Hum-V.

"To the motor pool, driver," the Col. demanded. "It's a mile down the road and to your right."

It was close to one in the morning, and few vehicles were on the road. Except for lights from buildings where soldiers were completing final preparations for the morning assault, Camp Grayling was asleep.

Langston turned into the motor pool parking lot. A long row of M1A1 main battle tanks, squatting menacingly in front of the maintenance shops, awaited the call to battle in the morning. Since each tank was loaded with live ammunition, a squad of security guards with loaded M-16's patrolled the motor pool.

Col. Winkelman waved his ID at the sergeant of the guard. "We need to borrow one of those tanks."

The sergeant was toying with the idea of challenging the Colonel's authority, when he noticed the Commander in Chief. It had taken him seven years to make sergeant. He had no intention of starting over.

"Sir, these tanks are filled with live ammunition." The sergeant pointed to a tank in the maintenance shop. "You can use that one. It's in for maintenance but still runs well."

"We'll take this one instead," Winkelman said, pointing to the closest tank. "We'll need the ammo."

The sergeant didn't look happy. He was sure he would hear about this in the morning. He stood helplessly as the inebriated officers and the Commander in Chief swarmed over his tank.

"I'll drive," Capt. Fletcher informed the others as he climbed into the small compartment in the front. The engine was soon coughing and sputtering to life.

Major Moffat commandeered the Gunner's spot leaving the loader and commander positions to the President and Col. Winkelman. They would each have a hatch to peer out. Agents Rushford and Langston, without assigned seats, clung to the tank's exterior. It wasn't as much fun when you're sober.

The four duck hunters wore helmets with headphones for communication. The M1A1 wasn't noted for its acoustical stealthiness, and any other method of conversation was impossible. Rushford and Langston exchanged a few thoughts with sign language; but for the most part, they clung to the tank and hoped for the best—they didn't relish another three weeks of dungeon duty.

Holding up an imaginary sword in a simulated cavalry charge, Col. Winkelman commanded through his headset, "to the cove!"

The tank took off with a jolt, when Capt. Fletcher set it into gear. Captains don't normally drive tanks, but it was a short learning curve, and Fletcher soon had the machine under control, although the gate to the motor pool was now much wider.

It was a fifteen-minute drive to the cove. They made it in twenty. They drove the last mile without lights to avoid spooking their prey.

"Shhh...," Col. Winkelman whispered above the roar of the fifteen hundred horsepower engine. He held an index finger to his lips. "We don't want to scare them." That was unlikely since any ducks or geese inhabiting Camp Grayling were well acclimated to explosions, low flying jets, and the sounds of armored columns.

Captain Fletcher eased the tank to the top of a small knoll overlooking the cove. A quarter moon provided marginal visibility, enough to see the edge of the water. Darkness obscured the rest of the lake.

"See those four white spots?" Major Moffat pointed to the thermo imaging sights.

Bart looked into the imager but saw four pairs of white spots.

"Those are ducks." Moffat studied the imager for a moment. "The bigger ones may be geese. Now, we have to choose between high explosive shells and armor piercing shells. I'm going to use an armor piercing shell, because it won't damage the meat as much—we may want goose for dinner."

Moffat retrieved a shell from its armored case in the back of the turret and fed the round into the breach. "Now we align the cross hairs on the target."

Langston and Rushford were beginning to relax on top of the tank when it recoiled backwards from the blast of the 120 mm gun. Two hundred yards out in the lake, a geyser of water boiled up out of an otherwise peaceful lake. The armor-piercing round exploded several yards under the water causing little physical harm to the ducks and geese, but it did bounce them into the air along with the geyser of water. With nowhere to go in the dark, the bewildered waterfowl glided back to the water.

"That looks simple enough," Bart decided after watching the first shot. "Let me have a try."

"You shoot the main gun, and Major Moffat and I will shoot the machine guns. We'll show you the tank's full firepower."

The tank shook again when the 120 mm cannon fired a second round. This time it was accompanied by two 7.62 mm machine guns. Tracer fire arched over the water, sometimes aimed at the ducks, sometimes not.

After five minutes, the gunfire withered and finally ceased, leaving the two shell-shocked Secret Service agents to wonder if they had run out of ammunition.

"Mr. President?" Agent Rushford heard no response, although she was not certain she was capable of hearing, the way her ears were ringing.

"Mr. President?" Rushford repeated, looking down the hatch.

No response.

"Langston, you'd better check him out." That was all she needed on her record—a dead president.

Langston crawled down the hatch wishing he had brought a flashlight.

"Are they all right?" Rushford assumed the worst.

Langston popped his head out the hatch. "They've passed out."

"Thank God." Rushford mumbled a short prayer. "Is there a radio down there we can use to call for help? We'll never get this monster back. They didn't teach how to drive tanks in small arms class."

"If we call for help, we'll be in every paper by noon and international additions by evening. He has a room reserved for him above the officer's club. I say we drive the tank back to the club and tuck him in for the night."

"You can drive a tank?" Langston never ceased to amaze her.

"Between articles in *Soldiers of Fortune* and video games, I think I can manage. Help me drag this guy out of the driver's seat."

"This guy didn't look so heavy when he was sober." Rushford wished she had stayed with the Treasury Department's counterfeit division. Money is lighter, and the hours are better. With Langston's help, she secured the driver to the back of the tank; he didn't seem to mind riding coach.

Any doubts about Langston's tankmanship were dispelled when the tank smoothly backed up and started back down the road. The ride was far smoother than the previous carnival ride.

"Where do you think we should park this beast?" Rushford asked when they arrived at the officer's club. Fortunately, everything was quiet except for the tank pulling up to the parking meter.

"This tank weighs sixty tons. I say we park anywhere we want!"

With Langston carrying the shoulders and Rushford the feet, they carried the most powerful man in the nation up to his room.

A secure, undisclosed location, 0232 hours

While President Schroeder was enjoying the relaxation of a duck hunt, the 82nd Airborne Division was marching off to war. Several dozen transport planes waited along the edge of the runway while paratroopers, weighted down with over eighty pounds of combat gear, filed aboard. This was the day they had trained for. This was the day they would make history. This was the day they would make an airborne assault to defend American soil.

Actually, it was a dark night, illuminated only by a quarter moon, which invited mishap, but Major General Amos "Mad Dog" Rottweiler, commander of the 82nd Airborne, was not one to worry. That's why he had subordinates. Let them worry. He rested his hands on his pearl-handled revolvers and watched his men embark upon the planes. A pair of mirrored sunglasses covered his eyes. He felt generals looked cool with mirrored sunglasses. It made night vision difficult, but that was the price you paid for being cool.

"General, the men are all aboard and ready to go."

Mad Dog Rottweiler recognized the voice of his Command Sergeant Major. It was coming from his left. He could make out the camo-painted face of the Sergeant Major over the rim of his glasses. "Guess it's time for us to climb aboard." This would be a good day. Maybe he would get that third star. General Rottweiler extracted his corncob pipe from his shirt pocket and filled it with tobacco.

Mad Dog was a fightin' general. He would jump with his troops. He only regretted it had to be at night. There would be no photographer to immortalize the moment he stepped aboard the plane. No newsreel of the commanding general, with camo-painted face, leading his troops into harm's way. It would have looked good on the six o'clock news. He was about to ignite his bowl of pipe tobacco, but decided against it. He wasn't particularly fond of the pipe, and without the presence of TV cameras, the corncob pipe served no useful purpose. He would save it for later.

General Rottweiler followed the Sergeant Major to a waiting plane. His plane filled with headquarters staff and radiomen would lead the formation. The planes were under the control of the air force, and airmen with red flashlights began guiding planes toward the runway. If they were to fly in formation, it was imperative the planes get airborne as quickly as possible. Air traffic controllers diverted all commercial traffic from the U.P. This night sky belonged to the 82nd Airborne.

The General sat on the bench next to Col. Hansen, one of his staff officers. Paratroopers with painted faces, tight fitting helmets, and camouflaged fatigues lined both sides of the aircraft. In the red light they all looked the same.

The plane was soon airborne and flying a holding pattern while they waited for other planes to join the formation. A few minutes later the entire formation turned toward the Upper Peninsula. The pilots turned on their running lights to reduce the chances of mid-air collisions. They weren't worried about airborne attacks. Harriers from the Iwo Jima would join them shortly, providing fighter escort to the insertion point.

Finland had an air force, but even if they flew over the pole, the U.P. stretched beyond their range. The Yoopers were on their own.

General Rottweiler removed his sunglasses and looked out his window. Dozens of red lights, each representing a plane, blinked in the darkness. It was an impressive formation, probably the largest nighttime airborne assault since WW II. The name Rottweiler would be itched into the history books tonight.

"TWENTY MINUTES TO THE DROP ZONE," the plane's jumpmaster yelled at the paratroopers. The paratroopers sat quietly as if they hadn't heard. Each paratrooper had his own private thoughts and his own self-doubts. At the end of the row a young man crossed himself. It never hurt to seek the blessing of the Sky Pilot.

The bureaucrats in Washington selected the Seney Stretch, a boring twenty-five mile section of real estate between Seney on the east and Shingleton on the west, as the drop zone. The two bordering towns were connected by a section of M-28 that could have been drawn on the map with a straight edge.

The maps in Washington revealed a perfectly flat stretch of land, perfect for an airborne assault. The fact that it was in the center of the U.P. and not far from Bear Creek was another asset. The paratroopers would reassemble upon landing and make a quick march on the town. The rapid conquest of Bear Creek—part of the shock and awe—would demoralize any resistance.

What the maps in Washington didn't show were the cedar swamps, peat bogs and jack pine, perfect for deer hunters but useless for any civilized endeavor. The only significant establishment was the Seney Wildlife Refuge where the Federal Government spent endless tax dollars encouraging geese, ducks, and sandhill cranes to make use of the swamps, as if they really needed encouragement.

"FIVE MINUTES TO THE DROP ZONE." The jumpmaster seemed unusually cheerful. He didn't have to jump.

Upon command, the paratroopers stood up and attached their static lines to the overhead cable. Each man checked the man in front of him to ensure all items were buttoned down and secured. Since this was a combat jump, there were no reserve chutes. Each man had one chance.

General Rottweiler felt a blast of air as the jumpmaster opened the door on the side of the plane. Mad Dog casually strolled to the front of the line, aware that all eyes were on him—as they should be. He clipped his static line to the overhead cable in front of the others. He was a fightin' general, and he would jump first.

"ONE MINUTE TO GO." The jumpmaster watched a red light controlled by the pilot. Timing was everything. Jumping one or two minutes early or late could place the paratroopers miles from their target.

The red light turned green, and the jumpmaster yelled, "GO." But the General was already halfway out the door. The other paratroopers followed the General like lemmings leaping off a cliff into the darkness—the Yooper War had begun.

Chapter Fourteen

Bart opened his eyes and focused on the ceiling; the dark spot was moving. He couldn't remember the last time he saw a cockroach. This couldn't be the White House. If memory served him correctly, his press secretary had billeted him in a small room above the officer's club. That would explain his strange surroundings. Even stranger was the dream he had about duck hunting with an Abrams tank. It was amazing how his brain could generate such ridiculous scenarios. Must be the sign of an intelligent, creative mind.

His press secretary also arranged an early morning flight to the USS Iwo Jima where the press corps anxiously awaited his arrival. In a few hours TV cameras would saturate airwaves around the world with pictures of the Commander in Chief in flight suit, pilot's helmet, and parachute, leading American troops in defense of the nation. He had no intention of disappointing the press corps, although it would have been more enjoyable without his headache. Bart sat up in bed as a vise closed around his throbbing head. He was still wearing yesterday's clothes. That was a bad sign. Perhaps he had too much to drink the previous evening.

Was someone pounding on the door or was that his pounding headache? Bart wasn't sure. Either way, it was not a pleasant sensation. The banging continued, definitely the door. It was too early for anyone expecting him to produce a command decision. Perhaps it was room service with breakfast. Bart opened the door. It was Agent Rushford.

"Good, you're awake. Your helicopter leaves in forty-five minutes.

You need to get ready." The dark circles around her eyes matched the strain in her voice. And her wrinkled clothes gave the impression she had slept in them—assuming she had slept at all.

She looks like hell, Bart decided. She needed to cut back on her nightlife if she expected to be an effective Secret Service agent. You can't party all night and still function as a Secret Service agent in the morning. He would have to talk to her supervisor.

Forty-five minutes was not much time, hardly enough to shave, shower, and eat breakfast. He considered brushing his teeth, but decided to belch instead. His stomach was a bit queasy. Maybe he would pass on breakfast. He never did well on long flights; they gave him motion sickness. He would fare better on an empty stomach.

"Here's your breakfast." Agent Rushford laid a tray of sausage and eggs on his dresser.

Smells good, Bart decided. It looked better than the S.O.S. of the previous night. But then, how easy is it to ruin two eggs and some sausage, although they did mildly burn the toast. Maybe it would settle his stomach if he had something to eat. He would take his motion-sickness pill prior to departure. That would control any nausea. Bart devoured the food in less than ten minutes and washed it down with a cup of strong coffee. After a quick shower, he was ready to go.

The drive to the McNamara Airport took no more than fifteen minutes. The sedan provided by the Michigan National Guard wasn't as luxurious as the limos he was accustomed to; but the ride provided time to admire the scenery. Camp Grayling was the antithesis of the dry, barren land he had known in West Texas. Here there were green trees as far as the eye could see. Trees were tall and green and surrounded the blueness of Lake Margarethe. It was a pretty lake; too bad he hadn't found time to visit it.

Langston pulled the sedan up to the waiting helicopter where the usual assortment of dignitaries and news media awaited the President's arrival. A crowd of that size demanded five minutes of baby kissing and pumping flesh, maybe ten minutes if the President got windy. It was an election year after all.

"You got my motion-sickness pill?" Bart asked when he emerged from the car.

Agents Rushford and Langston each waited for the other to produce the magic pill.

"We'll have it in a minute," Rushford replied.

"You don't have the Pill?" Langston whispered into Rushford's ear.

"No, I thought you had it."

"We must have left it at the officer's club." Langston checked his pockets again.

"What'll we do now? We have to give him something."

"You got any aspirin? Any pill will do. His motion sickness is mostly in his head."

Rushford reached into her purse and produced a white pill. "Give him this."

"Mr. President," Langston said. "Here's your pill."

"Thank you." The President swallowed the pill and washed it down with the aid of a can of Pepsi someone graciously produced.

"What did we give him?" Langston asked.

"Let's just say he's not likely to get pregnant."

Invigorated by his motion-sickness pill and the two aspirin he had taken earlier, President Schroeder waded into the enthusiastic crowd for some serious jawboning. He left no baby unkissed or hand unpumped.

Rushford checked her watch. They were on a tight schedule. Ron Clark had orchestrated a ceremony covered by the major media for the President's arrival on the Iwo Jima. The President's press secretary expected such spontaneous events to begin on time.

"Mr. President, we need to go." Rushford edged between the President and the local mayor. Sometimes an agent can't be subtle.

Rushford and Langston herded the President aboard the Iwo Jima's MH-53 Sea Dragon helicopter. Normally a cargo helicopter for the United States Marine Corps, the Navy had refitted the Sea Dragon to accommodate the VIP passengers. Navy Seabees added a plush seat behind the pilots for the President and two conventional seats in the back row for the two Secret Service agents. A variety of newly-installed electronic modifications ensured the President's safety. High above, two Harrier Jump Jets waited patiently to escort the Commander in Chief to the USS Iwo Jima.

"Mr. President, we need to buckle you in." Rushford snapped his seat belt and checked his shoulder harness. This was why she never married or had kids. She didn't want to spend the prime of her life strapping kids into minivans. "Here's your helmet. It even has your name on it."

Bart checked the helmet to ensure they spelled his name correctly. It was hard to misspell Bart. The letters could've been larger. He had to consider the senior vote.

"What about my parachute? I need a parachute."

"You won't need that until you land. We'll strap it on you before we open the doors." Rushford would be surprised if the parachute even worked. Langston found it in a dusty closet at the Treasury Building. For all she knew, dirty clothes could fall out if someone pulled the rip-cord. "Do you want a plastic bag in case you get sick?"

"That won't be necessary... I took my motion-sickness pill."

Rushford and Langston strapped themselves into their seats behind the President and gave the pilot the thumbs up. A cloud of dust bellowed up around the helicopter, as it lifted off for the one-hour flight to the USS Iwo Jima.

The Secret Service had protested the President's trip to the Iwo Jima from the beginning. The Iwo Jima was too close to the front lines. In addition to the normal hazards of helicopter flight, they now had the ever-present threat of hand-held, surface-to-air missiles. Such missiles were small, and Finnish agents could extract one from the trunk of a car anywhere along the flight path. Missile wielding agents could be hiding behind any bush or tree. As a compromise, Rushford instructed the pilot to fly low and follow the contours of the ground, a technique the aging marine pilot had perfected as a cocky Vietnam chopper pilot many years ago. By the time any enemy agent locked onto the helicopter with a surface-to-air missile, the chopper would be out of sight.

Flying a helicopter was like riding a bike; the pilot had lost none of his Vietnam skills, and more than once, Rushford looked out her window to find treetops at eye level. It was like a roller-coaster ride: a slow rise up the hills and a quick return into the valleys. In her youth she had enjoyed a good roller-coaster ride. She found this experience unsettling.

"Mr. President, how you doing?" The President wasn't cheerful, but he responded with feeble O.K.

Rushford leaned toward Langston who was checking out the winch used for towing the ASQ-14 side-scan sonar unit. "Keep an eye on the President. I don't think he's doing well."

Bart looked at the trees flying past his window. This was not his typical ride to the golf course. At least he had taken his motion-sickness pill. It would've been a long trip without it. He closed his eyes. Maybe a nap would take his mind off the ups and downs…That didn't work. He could still feel the sausage arguing with the eggs.

The roller-coaster ride came to a halt once they reached Lake Michigan, but updrafts from the changing geography shook the chopper like a pit bull on a mailman's pant leg.

We're half way there, Rushford assured herself. Hopefully, he can last another thirty minutes. The President wasn't doing much talking. She would have preferred his normal, talkative, arrogant self.

Bart wasn't sure if he preferred the soft, rolling motion or the sharp, bumpy ride. Neither agreed with his stomach. That motion-sickness pill wasn't working like it had in the past, but he was halfway there. With a little luck, he would make it.

Rushford maintained a tight grip on the plastic bag. The President was holding his stomach and looking green. She wasn't feeling so well herself. It was debatable who would need the bag first. Rushford looked at Langston. He was chewing on a candy bar and reading *Soldiers of Fortune* magazine. "Langston, the President isn't doing well, and I don't think I'm going be much help. If he starts to vomit, get him out of the seat belt and shoulder harness so he can bend over. We don't want him choking on his own vomitus."

Langston nodded and took another bite from his candy bar. He would deal with that problem when it arose.

Bart looked out the window. He could see the Iwo Jima in the distance. He was going to make it. He hadn't thought so at first, but he would make it. All he had to do was swallow hard and keep his breakfast down a little bit longer. Within minutes, he would be on a large, stable ship. Maybe it would help if he loosened his collar. He reached up with both hands to unbutton the top button.

Rushford stared in horror. The President was reaching for his throat, the universal sign for choking. "Langston, the President's choking."

Langston, never one to panic, unbuckled his seat belt. "No problem, I know the Heimlich Maneuver." Langston quickly released the President's safety belt and gave the President a big bear hug.

USS Iwo Jima, 0850 hours.

"This is Rob Carter from Channel 7 News, embedded with the invasion force on the USS Iwo Jima. We are awaiting the arrival of President Schroeder who should be arriving shortly. It has been a very hectic morning as people prepare for the invasion, which, judging from the activity, may begin today. There have been rumors, unconfirmed at this point, that the 82nd Airborne has already dropped behind enemy lines during the night.

"We have with us today in our Washington studio Lt. General Lucas Thornton, retired, to help us put everything in perspective. General Thornton, have you heard anything in Washington concerning the 82nd Airborne?"

A technician at the Channel 7 station pushed a button, and the TV feed switched to General Thornton sitting at the news desk. His right hand gripped a large mug of coffee bearing the TV 7 logo. Behind him was a wall map of the Upper Peninsula.

"Rob, everyone in Washington is very tight lipped, as they should be. We have seen White House and Pentagon staffers with bags under their eyes as if they've been up all night. I think something big is about to happen if it hasn't already begun."

"Anything about the 82nd Airborne? We're hearing they had a night drop along the Seney Stretch."

"Rob, nothing at this point. That would be a bold, daring move. I'm not positive, but I don't believe there's been a nighttime airborne assault since WW II. That would make strategic sense, if they can pull it off. The Seney stretch is a critical piece of real estate." General Thornton pointed to the map on the wall while the cameraman moved in for a close up. "It is right in the center of the U.P. and close to Bear Creek, which many people feel is the epicenter of this uprising. If the 82nd can move on Bear Creek, they might just break the back of the insurgency."

"General, you described the night drop as bold and daring. Do you find this deployment risky?...assuming it's true."

"Well, Rob, if you remember your history, when the 82nd made a similar night drop on D-day, the wind scattered them over the country-side. History could repeat itself. The winds can be unpredictable in the Upper Peninsula. They do have a very capable commander in General "Mad Dog" Rottweiler."

"General?...General, I hate to interrupt but we can see the President's helicopter coming in from the east." The technician at the studio switched the video feed to a camera showing an approaching helicopter. "President Schroeder is arriving to take personal command of the invasion force. I might add he has had extensive military experience in the Marine Corps before becoming President. The helicopter is now two hundred yards off our port side. It appears they will land right in front of us. Are you seeing all this, General?"

"Yes, it appears to be an MH-53 Sea Dragon, a very dependable cargo and troop transport helicopter."

"In case you have just tuned in, this is Rob Carter embedded with the invasion force on the USS Iwo Jima. The helicopter with the Commander in Chief has just landed. We are waiting for the doors to open. The honor guard and marine band is starting to assemble. The doors are now opening...There's the President with a Secret Service agent at each elbow. They are taking all precautions. The President is wearing a flight jumpsuit with a parachute strapped to his back...He is holding his helmet in his hand...You can see "Bart" clearly on his helmet...But what is that on his jump suit?...Can we get a close up?...It appears to be...eggs and sausage!"

Michigan Tech Library, 0910 hours

Abigail was fifteen minutes late when she arrived at the library. Moose, Sherlock, and Newton were sitting at a table reading magazines. She hoped they hadn't been waiting long. "Sorry I'm late." Abigail pulled a chair up to the table. She looked at Newton. "So, what's so important? You sounded excited on the phone."

"I didn't want to say anything on the phone in case they tapped the line." Newton set aside a back issue of *Scientific American* he had been reading. "Today is the day."

"Are you sure?" Abigail knew it would happen soon, but she had been hoping for a few more days. She had a term paper due.

Newton tossed a couple eight-by-ten glossies on the table. One of them showed a road with tanks lined up like ants on the way to a picnic. "These were taken at Camp Grayling this morning."

"You borrowed a satellite again?"

"Don't worry. I've already returned it." Newton picked up the photo. "This is Howe Road. See; it's paved... Tanks aren't permitted on paved roads... The treads tear the roads to pieces. It has to be a major event to allow tanks on paved roads. This is also the main drag through Camp Grayling. They won't let those tanks block the road for long. They'll be moving out this morning."

Abigail studied the picture for a moment. "I guess we'll find out if our defensive strategy works. It looks like Bear Creek is their prime objective. I suggest we take a few days off school and head home. It'll be easier defending the U.P. from Bear Creek."

"We'll need to set up some electronic eavesdropping equipment," Newton said. "Maybe we can use the old Methodist Church. I can hang the antennas in the steeple."

Abigail set the picture back on the table. "I have to call a friend first, and then I'll head for Bear Creek. I'll meet you guys at the Methodist Church."

Peter White Library, Marquette, Michigan, 0915 hours

The librarian looked up and saw the old man walking toward her checkout counter. He was hunched over and walked slowly supported by a cane. Age had not dealt kindly with the man. She was relieved when he finally made it to her counter. "Can I help you, sir?" He looked beyond help.

"Yes, Ms. I would like to research my family tree. I've been told you have such records in this fine new library."

The librarian looked into the face of the old man and tried not to display any reaction. She hoped the large tumor on his nose was non-cancerous, but at his age, it made little difference. "The genealogy files are on the second floor. The reference desk is at the top of the stairs. The lady there will be glad to help you."

The old man turned and headed for the stairs. He paused several times to catch his breath. Why hadn't she suggested the elevator, she wondered. She considered helping him up the stairs, but the thought of being that close to his repulsive nose dissuaded her. She watched the old man painfully make his way up the open staircase to the second floor. She feared he would collapse at any time, but after what felt like an eternity, he arrived at the top. Now he was the reference librarian's problem.

"Excuse me, Ms."

The reference librarian looked up from her work. "Yes?"

"I have but a few months to live, and I need to locate any next of kin I might have. My estate is rather substantial, but I have no close relatives. I've been told you have birth and death records for the Bear Creek area."

The librarian looked at the old man's nose for a moment then averted her gaze. She hoped it would be a closed casket. No mortician could do justice to such a proboscis. "We have all the information you need on CD's. Let me get you started."

"You are so kind."

The librarian led the old man to a computer and provided him with several disks. She noted course tremors in both of his hands, causing her to question the old man's ability to operate a computer. "All the disks are labeled as to birth, death, or census records and date. Are you familiar with computers?"

"Yes, I believe I can handle it from here. Thank you."

The librarian returned to her desk after a short prayer beseeching God not to take him on her shift. She didn't need that today.

The old man's tremors quickly resolved, and Agent X's fingers stroked the keyboard like a concert musician. Abigail had to be a student at Michigan Tech or Finlandia University who was also raised in the Bear Creek area by one of the founding families. A comparison of student records from the two universities with genealogy records for Bear Creek should narrow the field to six or seven individuals. It would then be a matter of time. He had never failed on an assignment. He did not expect that to change. He had borrowed the enrollment records from the two universities during black-bag capers and committed the records to memory. Now he needed to compare them to the census records.

Engrossed with his work, Agent X didn't hear his phone until the third ring. By that time the librarian was giving him that infamous "Librarian Stare" followed by the universal librarian sign for silence—an index finger to the lips.

Agent X: *Hello?*

Abigail: *Good, I was afraid I wouldn't reach you. This isn't a bad time is it?*

Agent X: *It's never a good time.*

Abigail: *I called to let you know I made an appointment for you.*

Agent X: *Appointment?*

Abigail: *You know…with the plastic surgeon. It's a week from Thursday at one p.m. I guess you military types call it thirteen hundred hours.*

Agent X: *I didn't agree to any appointment.*

Abigail: *A little surgery is nothing to be frightened about. If you want, I'll go with you and hold your hand.*

Agent X: *I fear no one. Furthermore, you won't be around a week from Thursday. The military is launching an attack against the U.P. as we speak. It'll be over for you in a day or two unless I get to you first. If you surrender now, I can guarantee prisoner of war status with all the rights of the Geneva Convention.*

Abigail: *You're assuming we'll lose.*

Agent X: *I've seen the invasion plans. You don't have a chance against such military might.*

Abigail: *If we win, will you go with me to the plastic surgeon?*

Agent X: *If you win, not only will I go with you, but I will personally prepare a dinner of exquisite French cuisine, accompanied by the finest wine. Not to brag, but I have trained with master chefs."*

Abigail: *My mouth is already beginning to water. I really would like to talk more, but I have to boogie. We have an invasion to repulse.*

Agent X hung up his phone. He admired her spunk, but there was no way the Yoopers would win this war.

Camp Grayling, 0913 hours

Col. Winkelman stood at the front of the mess hall, hoping the two aspirin would soon take effect. From the quality of his headache, he assumed he had a good time the night before. Major Moffat and Capt. Fletcher appeared in similar pain. Winkelman called the meeting to address last minute concerns before they launched their armored attack against the Upper Peninsula. They had been preparing for the last ten days. He assumed his troops were ready.

"Listen up." Winkelman gazed at his young officers through bloodshot eyes. He hoped they were feeling better than he did. "The convoy will leave at oh nine forty-five. Capt. Fletcher will be in the lead tank. I needn't remind you this is not a drill. We don't expect much resistance, but if captured, we don't want to reveal compromising information. Advise your troops to carry only their dog tags. No wallets with credit cards, pictures of girlfriends or home addresses. Do I make myself clear?" Seeing no signs of dissension, Winkelman put on his helmet. "Let's roll."

By nine forty-five, the fifty-eight M1A1 Abrams tanks of the 1st Battalion, 126th Armor Regiment were lined up along Howe Road like a row of squatting bullfrogs—compact, low to the ground, but coiled and ready to spring. Capt. Fletcher sat impatiently in the commander's seat of the lead tank, his head protruding from the turret as he strained for a better view. The headset attached to his helmet provided instant-access to the battalion commander as well as the other tanks in Co. A.

"It's nine forty-five. Let's move out," Fletcher heard the battalion commander relay over the radio. The fifty-eight Abrams tanks plus support vehicles coughed to life and began waddling down the road. Although the tanks are capable of forty miles per hour, thirty is a more realistic convoy speed, making the trip to the Straits of Mackinac a three-hour drive.

The convoy paraded east through the town of Grayling where patriotic citizens waved flags and shouted words of encouragement. A cameraman from the local TV station was there to record the event for the six o'clock news. The large number of "closed" signs in the storefronts confirmed that the entire town had turned out to send the boys off to the war.

At the intersection with I-75, the convoy turned north. Fortunately, I-75 was a divided highway, which allowed faster traffic to pass. The morning traffic was heavy and a multitude of cars and commercial trucks, all in a hurry to get somewhere, raced past the convoy. Some of the passengers waved; a few old veterans saluted; no one passed without straining their necks for a better look. Four teenagers in a convertible were less patriotic. They pulled alongside the lead tank and proceeded to give Capt. Fletcher the finger. When Capt. Fletcher rotated the turret and poked the 120 mm cannon into the car's back seat, the driver stepped on the gas, not wishing to make any further political statements.

White Fish Bay, 0950 hours

Wally Johnson looked out over White Fish Bay. It was a pleasant and peaceful view. He had been in the navy over twenty years, but had not seen much water. In the submarine service, he was always surrounded by water. He always knew the water was there. But he never saw it. He never felt the ocean spray against his face. He never saw the seagulls flying overhead or experienced the reds and yellows of a spectacular sunset. He never pulled watch under an endless stream of stars on a cloudless night. It was moments like this that made him envious of surface ship officers.

"Commander, what are we supposed to be looking for?"

Lt. Commander Wally Johnson looked up at one of the two lookouts he had posted on the sail of the USS. Virginia. An expensive pair of navy-issue binoculars hung from the seaman's neck. The seaman was obviously uncomfortable with this new assignment—lookouts are not the norm for a nuclear attack submarine.

"Enjoy the view. Look at the girls on the beach. Watch the seagulls flying overhead. See if the fishermen are catching any fish. Someday you'll wake up an old man, having missed all those opportunities."

The lookout wondered if the Skipper had been too long at sea. Just the same, this was better duty than being stuck below deck.

"Enjoying the view, Commander?"

Johnson moved over to make room on the bridge for Lt. Sara Peterson, his XO. "Should be enough view up here for all of us."

"Sir?..."

"Yes?"

"Do you have any idea what we're doing?... I mean...we're in a nuclear submarine that just traversed the Soo Locks. Out there is Lake Superior, the largest freshwater lake in the world. Fresh water! We have to redo all our protocols just to compensate for the buoyancy differences."

"Ms. Peterson, if I knew the answer to that, I'd be an admiral. I suggest you do what I'm doing. Sit back and enjoy the cruise. But don't take Lake Superior for granted. We're passing over the gravesite of twenty-nine men who went down on the Edmond Fitzgerald."

"What are our orders?" Marquette is a little over a hundred miles away. We'll be there by afternoon."

"As soon as the water gets deeper, I suggest we dive and at least act like a submarine. It'll give us practice maneuvering in fresh water. When we get to Marquette, we surface and take control of the harbor using whatever force necessary."

"Aye, Aye, Sir." Lt. Peterson returned below deck to prepare for the conquest of Marquette Harbor. A hundred and twenty-five miles ahead of the USS Virginia, other navy ships loaded with marines prepared for a similar assault on Houghton and Hancock, home of Michigan Tech and Finlandia University. The Yooper war was rapidly progressing toward its climax.

Chapter Fifteen

Headquarters, 82nd Airborne, 1022 hours

Major General Amos "Mad Dog" Rottweiler adjusted his mirrored sunglasses. A general needed to be cool despite the hardships of combat. The coolness was offset by the torn shirt and trousers. The left sleeve of his shirt was missing, and scratches covered his arm. They were the result of Mad Dog's unfortunate encounter with a belligerent spruce tree on his descent. Just for spite, he would have the tree cut down once he assembled his troops. You don't do that to Mad Dog Rottweiler and get away with it.

The Command Sergeant Major missed the trees but discovered one of the Seney Stretch's many swamps and was now huddling around a makeshift campfire trying to thaw out. The Upper Peninsula mornings can be cool for those wearing wet clothing. He was roasting a pair of soggy socks on a tag elder branch. A steady flow of white steam confirmed the effectiveness of the operation.

The only other surviving member of the headquarters group was the radioman who was diligently monitoring reports from various segments of the 82nd Airborne. He had managed to avoid both trees and swamps.

General Rottweiler spread a map on the ground. According to his GPS, he should be about here. He placed an "X" on the spot. They were not far from Bear Creek. He would assemble his troops and immediately march on the town. The town would be his by evening. "Have you contacted all the units?" Rottweiler asked with the impatience of a general.

"I reached a few, sir, but it's mostly garbled." The radioman fiddled with his dials. "It appears the wind scattered men all over God's creation. Most of them are beyond the range of our radio."

That was not what Mad Dog wanted to hear. He considered shooting the messenger but decided against it. He currently had two people in his command, and he would need both of them. "What about the ones you did contact? Are they regrouping?"

"That appears to be a problem too. They can't distinguish members of the 82nd from the native Yoopers. They don't know who's who."

The General reconsidered shooting the messenger. "How hard can that be? Members of the 82nd are dressed in camouflaged fatigues and have their faces covered with green paint."

"That's the problem, sir. This is bow-hunting season. Everybody is wearing camouflaged fatigues and paint on their faces. Yoopers are hanging from tree stands and hiding behind every bush. I think they have us out numbered."

The General swatted at a mosquito molesting his exposed arm. "Damn Yoopers!" This was only a minor setback, but Mad Dog did not like setbacks. "Keep on the radio, son. I want to know every change in our status before it changes... What's that horrid smell?" The General looked over at his Sergeant Major—the white steam from the socks had changed to black smoke.

***

Beagle one, this is sawbones eight three, come in." PFC Stan Richards listened for a reply but was not surprised when no reply was forthcoming from his radio. He had been trying most of the night without results. The wind must have blown him too far from battalion headquarters.

He hadn't seen anyone from his unit since he jumped. He had a compass, but without a map, he could be walking away from his unit. With land this flat, he wasn't sure a map would be of value. The best he could do was wander around and periodically try the radio. With a bit of luck, he might make contact. "Beagle one, this is sawbones eight three, come in."

As a medic with company A, he didn't normally carry a radio. The company commander gave him the honor in retaliation for declaring his regular radioman unfit for duty because of a broken leg. The commander remained convinced the radioman was malingering despite X-rays confirming the fracture.

Richards looked around, trying to decide which direction to go. For all he knew, he could be walking in circles. The land was flat and what few depressions did exist, Mother Nature converted to swamps. Jack pine and the occasional white pine covered the rest of the land. Thorny bushes filled any gaps in the coverage.

Richards took the path of least resistance and headed for a tall white pine. "This is sawbones eight three, is anyone out there?" As usual, there was no response. He was beginning to wonder if his batteries were dead. It wouldn't be the first time the military had screwed up.

Richards removed his pack and radio at the base of the white pine and sat down to do some serious thinking. Wandering around the woods was getting him nowhere. At least the ground here was dry, and he had the white pine as a backrest. Eventually, he would need food and water, but for now he had a full canteen and two MRE's in the cargo pockets of his pants. He open one of the MRE's and extracted a candy bar. He could think better while eating.

With nothing better to do, he keyed the mike on the radio. "Just in case anyone is listening, this is sawbones eight three." Richards set the mike on the ground to enjoy his candy bar.

"It's nice to hear another voice."

Did he hear right? Richards grabbed the mike. "This is PFC Richards from Company A. Which company are you with?"

"Company C."

"Anyone else with you?" Richards asked.

"Nope, just me. You wouldn't have an extra candy bar, would you? That one looks pretty good."

How did he know about the candy bar, Richards wondered. "Where are you?"

"Up here."

Richards look up into the tree. A fellow paratrooper dangled from his camouflaged parachute twelve feet above the ground. With his painted face and camouflaged fatigues, he blended in with the tree.

"What ya doing up there?"

"The buckle on my harness is jammed, and I dropped my bayonet, so I can't cut myself loose. Been sort of hanging around most of the night."

"You're lucky. It's dry up there. I spent the night wandering through swamps."

"My name's Corporal Higgins, John Higgins."

"Stan Richards."

"About that candy bar, my MRE's are in my backpack. I can't get to them."

"Right, sure." Richards tossed a candy bar up to Corporal Higgins.

"Thank you… I was getting hungry."

"I suppose your predicament has its drawbacks," Richards said after a moment of thought.

"You don't know the worst of it. I can pee from up here, but that's about it."

"You will let me know?"

"Let you know?"

"I mean…if you have to pee…being down below and everything."

"Sure, that would only be common courtesy."

With no better plan of action, Richards sat at the base of the tree to discuss women, sports, women, politics, and women. He found Corporal Higgins quite knowledgeable about sports and politics, but he didn't understand women either.

"I think someone's coming," Corporal Higgins said from his superior location. Moments later two men in camouflaged uniforms and green painted faces stepped into the clearing. Each one carried a compound bow and had a quiver of arrows strapped to his back.

"Ya see dat twelve point buck, eh?" one of them asked Richards.

"Looky, Toivo. Dare's another one up in dat tree," the second one said. "Yoose guys have goot tree stand."

Richard stood up. "My names PFC Stan Richards...and this is Corporal John Higgins." Richards pointed to the man in the tree.

"Da name's Eino Luokkala and dis is my no goot brodder-in-law Toivo."

"What unit you with?" Richards asked.

"Unit? We's from Camp Destitute."

"We...Corporal Higgins and I...got separated from our units. We were wondering if we could go back to Camp Destitute with you?"

"Ya, we play poker and drink beer."

"The problem is that my friend, here," Richards gestured toward Higgins. "He can't get down from the tree."

"My no goot brodder-in-law, Toivo, can fix dat."

Without further discussion Toivo took an arrow from his quiver. The blades of the broadhead were constructed of high-carbon steel and honed to a razor's edge. A single shot severed the strap above Higgins's left shoulder, sending him swinging back and forth from the strap above his right shoulder. A second arrow also found its mark, and Higgins plummeted to the ground.

Corporal Higgins hit hard, leading Richards to wonder if Higgins would be his first casualty. Grabbing his aid bag, Richards ran over to the crumpled paratrooper, but Higgins had fallen on a soft carpet of pine needles. Other than being shaken up, he seemed to be no worse for the wear.

"Yoose guys follow us." Eino headed down a path.

"I hope someone has a fire going back at your camp." Richards felt his boots slosh with each step. "I've been wading through swamps all night. Got a bit of a chill."

"We put yoose guys in sauna. Dat'll warm yoose up."

Richards and Higgins fell back slightly, and Richards whispered into Higgins's ear. "Where do you think these guys came from? There're not from A company."

"I think there're from a special unit...like snipers. Did you see how they shoot those bows? Probably a special commando unit."

"They sure talk funny."

"Maybe so, but if we follow them back to their base camp, we may find someone who knows where our units are."

Iwo Jima, 1000 hours

"How ya feeling?" Al asked.

Bart sat up in bed to check his equilibrium, finding it adequate. The quartermaster had provided a clean jumpsuit with a U.S. Navy patch over the left pocket instead of the Presidential Seal; it would have to do. "I think that shot the doctor gave me helped."

"If you're up to it, General Brackendorf is giving a briefing in the conference room. Looks like everything is going better than we expected." Al was smiling.

Bart stood up and poked at his abdomen to ensure all the innards were in their appropriate places. "Let's go. I'm feeling better than a three-armed masseuse."

"First, I need to show you something on the bridge." Al led Bart up two flights of stairs, through a doorway, and onto a balcony overlooking the flight deck. "We've been landing marines on the beach for the past hour."

Bart looked toward the shore. A steady stream of hovercraft skimmed to and from the beach, ferrying marines ashore. Cargo helicopters bringing supplies hovered above them like a swarm of bees.

"Here, try the binoculars." Al handed the President a pair of government issued binoculars.

Even with the binoculars, the shore looked small from the distance of four miles, and the men on shore looked like ants. But there were hundreds of them.

"Any casualties?" Bart asked. Casualties wouldn't look good in an election year.

"That's the best part. The Yoopers are greeting the troops with gifts and flowers. The Yooper War may be over in less than twenty-four hours."

"Twenty-four hours, hot diggity damn. This will ensure my reelection… If the beach is secure, ya think I could have my picture taken wading ashore like MacArthur?"

"I suppose that could be arranged, but we need to get down to the General's briefing. It should start in a couple of minutes."

The military staff were already assembled and sitting at the table in the makeshift command room when the President and his Chief of Staff arrived. Behind the table, sailors monitored computer screens and radio equipment. One of the two shore patrolman guarding the door yelled "atten' hut" upon the President's arrival. The generals and admirals came to attention.

"At ease." Bart was getting good at the military jargon. The senior officers remained at attention until Bart had taken his seat.

"Gentleman," General Brackendorf remained standing. "We are witnessing one of the most decisive military campaigns in U. S. history." The General paused to allow the significance to sink in. "In years to come, West Point strategists will be lauding the brilliance of our tactics. It appears our shock and awe has totally demoralized the opposition. I think it's safe to say we can have this mopped up by evening."

"When can I go on the air and proclaim the war over?" Bart asked. "Maybe we could hang a banner proclaiming 'Mission Accomplished' from the ships superstructure."

"I wouldn't rule out the six o'clock news." General Brackendorf was envisioning a glorious political career upon retirement from the military. This was one general who had no intention of just fading away. He could easily be President Schroeder's replacement.

"As most of you know," the General continued, "our troops are being greeted at the shore with gifts and flowers. We've also received word from the troops in the Houghton-Hancock area. They are meeting no resistance. They have taken over Michigan Tech and Finlandia University and are now proceeding toward Greek Row."

"What about the 82nd Airborne?" Al asked. "Any word from them?"

"Not yet, but knowing Mad Dog Rottweiler, we may not hear from him until he reports in from downtown Bear Creek. The USS Virginia expects to arrive in Marquette harbor this afternoon, and the commander of the 1st Battalion of the 126 Armor reported twenty minutes ago that they are approaching the Mackinac Bridge and expect to be on Upper Peninsula soil in less than an hour. All our units are ahead of schedule."

"We need to get my speech writers working on this," Bart said. "Maybe I could give the speech after the cameras document my walking through the water toward the beach."

General Brackendorf looked at his watch. "I suggest we meet back here in two hours for another update."

I-75, 1010 hours

"Hold up a minute, driver." Capt. Fletcher raised his binoculars to his eyes. Before him was the five-mile span between Michigan's two peninsulas, connected by the western hemisphere's longest suspension bridge.

Fletcher switched his radio to the battalion frequency. "Col. Winkelman, Fletcher here. You sure that bridge will support a sixty-three ton tank?"

"I think so... Let me know if it doesn't."

Fletcher stared at his mike. *Let him know if it doesn't?* Did the Colonel think the tank's radio would carry through three hundred feet of water? "Sir, that's not very reassuring when you're riding in the lead tank."

"Sorry, Fletch. That's the best I can do. I'm hoping the Pentagon knows what they're doing."

Fletcher didn't find that reassuring either. "Not that I distrust Pentagon analysts, but I'm going to space my tanks fifty yards apart. Fletcher out." Fletcher switched the radio frequency back to Co. A. "This is Captain Fletcher. We're heading across the bridge. Keep the tanks fifty yards apart. I hope you guys can swim." Capt. Fletcher placed the mike back in its holder, offered a silent prayer, and crossed himself. "O.K., driver let's go. Take it slow and easy."

The tank chugged along at ten miles per hour. At that rate, Fletcher figured they'd be across in half an hour. Nothing like prolonging the anxiety.

The bridge was an impressive structure with twin towers rising five hundred feet above the water. The eighty-six hundred feet of suspended bridge dangled from a pair of two-foot diameter cables, all built by the lowest bidder.

Capt. Fletcher began holding his breath as he crossed the bridge but discovered that was impractical for a thirty-minute transit. The bridge vibrated under the tank's weight, and Fletcher soon regretted the heavy meal he had eaten for breakfast. At least it wasn't windy. Somewhere he had read the center span could sway thirty-five feet in a strong wind. That gave him visions of his sixty-three ton tank swinging like a pregnant walrus in a hammock.

The first tower came and went without mishap followed by the second tower. In the distance, he could see the tollbooths at the north end of the bridge. Beyond the tollbooths sat their objective—the Upper Peninsula.

"Capt. Fletcher to Col. Winkelman."

"Col. Winkelman here."

"Looks like we're goin' make it. The tollbooth is right ahead of us."

"Fletch, see if you can find an open field past the tollbooth. We'll regroup there and determine our next move."

"Roger,…Fletcher out."

This was going too smoothly, Winkelman decided; but then, how does one stop a convoy of M1A1 tanks. They were almost on Upper Peninsula soil, and it wasn't even noon. If the other units were faring equally well, perhaps the conflict would be over before the 1st of the 26th arrived. That wouldn't be bad. He could return to his bank, and Fletcher could get back to his pharmacy. Yes, it was just as well they didn't have problems.

"Col. Winkelman, we have a problem."

"Yes, Fletch, what is it?"

"Colonel, can you come up to the tollbooth? You're not going to believe this."

Whatever the problem was, was interfering with forward movement. The convoy had come to a halt. Can't have tanks parked on the bridge, Winkelman decided. "Driver, pull the tank into the left lane.

I need to get to the head of the column." Fortunately, the Mackinac Bridge had four lanes, and the driver was able to ease into the left lane. Winkelman wasn't sure if it was his imagination, but the bridge seemed to sag every time he passed another tank.

Winkelman was almost across the bridge when he met Fletcher walking toward him. Winkelman stopped the tank long enough for Fletcher to climb up on the turret.

"So, what's the hold up, Fletch? Why we stopped?"

"The lady at the tollbooth won't let us through."

"Is that all?" Never send a captain to do a colonel's work, Winkelman thought. "Driver, head over to the tollbooth."

The driver pulled over to the tollbooth on the far right. It was the only lane wide enough for a tank. A wooden tollgate prevented further advance.

"Is that little Johnny Winkelman?" the lady in the tollbooth asked.

"Mrs. Vanderlaan!... Hey, Fletch... This is my third-grade teacher, Mrs. Vanderlaan."

"Sit up straight in that tank, young man...and spit out that gum!"

"Yes, Mrs. Vanderlaan." Winkelman spat out his gum and tried to sit a little straighter. "This is Capt. Fletcher... We're in the National Guard."

"Mr. Fletcher and I have already met. If he had been in my class, he would have grown up with better manners."

"Mrs. Vanderlaan, we're on a military mission and need to get through... It's a matter of national security."

"Pay the toll and I'll let you boys go about your game."

"How much will that be?"

"Well, Johnny, if it costs three dollars per axle and you have fifty-eight tanks and twelve Hum-V's, and each tank has seven axles and each Hum-V has two axles, how much do you think it would be?"

Winkelman pulled a small calculator from his shirt pocket.

"No calculators!"

"No calculators?"

"You should be able to do this in your head. First break it down into parts... How many tank axles do you have?"

"Well, Mrs. Vanderlaan, if there are seven axles per tank and I have fifty-eight tanks, that would be seven times fifty-eight. Seven times eight is fifty-six, carry the five. Seven times five is... What difference does it make; we didn't bring any money or credit cards. We don't do that in case we get captured."

"Johnny, you never did like story problems."

"Why don't you just add it all up and give me the bill. I'll send you a check in the mail."

"Johnny, remember when those bullies stole your milk money?"

"Yes, Mrs. Vanderlaan, you wouldn't give me the milk without the money. You said it would build character."

"The concept hasn't changed over the years. Neither a lender nor borrower be."

"But I won't be able to complete my mission."

"You'll have to settle for an incomplete, just like that volcano project you never turned in."

"The dog really did eat that project... If I turn in the volcano project, can I get that incomplete off my record?"

"Yes, but I'll have to knock it down a full grade for being twenty-two years late... Now if you'll please move the tank over to the side. You're blocking traffic."

"Driver, can you park the tank over by the water's edge? I got to think this out."

The driver parked the tank as ordered. Colonel Winkelman climbed out of the turret and sat on the edge of the tank with his feet dangling over the side.

Capt. Fletcher sat down beside him. "What's Little Johnny goin' do now?"

"Must Little Johnny remind the Captain that the mortgage on his pharmacy comes due in two weeks, and he will have to come to Little Johnny to have it refinanced?"

"Sorry, sir. I guess I got carried away... If it makes you feel any better, I didn't like story problems either.

Bear Creek, 1032 hours

Abigail clicked off her cellular phone. "Hey, guys, that was Mrs. Vanderlaan at the Mackinac Bridge. " She says she stopped the tanks in their tracks. No heavy metal for the U.P."

"One battle, but hardly the war." Sherlock, always the realist, was not ready to raise the victory flag. "We still have a way to go."

Abigail sat down at a table with a map of the Upper Peninsula taped to its center. They had commandeered the local United Methodist Church basement with the blessing of the pastor. It was a weekday and not otherwise in use. Newton's computer station filled most of one corner, and several coaxial cables connected sophisticated electronic gadgets borrowed from the electrical engineering department to antennas in the church steeple. Only Newton appreciated their value. They had already blown two fuses causing a confrontation with Moose whose edibles in the portable refrigerator were placed in harm's way.

Abigail studied the map. Sherlock was right. They had a long way to go. She placed a toy car upside down at the bridge. At least they didn't have to worry about tanks.

"Moose, have you heard from your contacts at the universities?" Abigail waited a moment for a reply. Moose's mouth was filled with a ham and cheese sandwich.

"I spoke to them a half hour ago. They said the marines had taken Houghton and Hancock, and they're heading toward Greek Row."

"That's to be expected. We planned to sacrifice the universities. We'll make our stand at Greek Row." Abigail studied the insert on the map depicting downtown Houghton. "I just hope our defense at Greek Row holds… Any news from the other fronts?"

"I intercepted a transmission from the USS Virginia," Newton said. "They'll be in Marquette Harbor in less than two hours."

"That advertisement I placed in the *Mining Journal* better work," Sherlock said, "or the city of Marquette is toast."

"Never underestimate the power of the printed word." Abigail wished she believed half of what she preached. She wouldn't admit it publicly, but it had her worried. "How about the marines that landed near Epoufette?"

"We had people meet them at the shore with gifts and flowers," Moose said. "They seemed appreciative."

"I guess all we can do is wait."

Seney Stretch, 1035 hours

General Amos "Mad Dog" Rottweiler used the last of the Scotch tape. His fatigues had ripped during his encounter with the tree, and the tears were increasing in size. Hopefully, the Sergeant Major's Scotch tape would prevent further destruction. Even with mirrored sunglasses, it is hard to look cool in a torn uniform. There was nothing he could do about the missing right sleeve, but he would proudly wear the rest of his uniform, tattered that it might be.

"General, sir?"

"Yes, Sergeant Major, what is it?"

"Sir, I'm afraid we have bad news… We made radio contact with some of our men."

"That's bad news? That's what we've been waiting for. Now we can assemble our men and march on Bear Creek."

"Sir, the radioman said the contact was with PFC Richards and Corporal Higgins. They have been taken prisoner by the enemy but were able to radio in a brief report."

"And what was the nature of this report?"

"It…It isn't pretty, sir," the Sergeant Major said with a quiver in his voice.

"Pull yourself together, Sergeant Major. We're U.S. Soldiers!"

"Sir, they were tortured!"

"Tortured?"

"They stripped them naked and locked them in a cedar box. Then they pumped it full of steam until our men could hardly breathe. After they became totally dehydrated, they were taken out and drenched in ice water. The Yoopers laughed at them and apologized for not having a snow bank to throw them into!"

"The savages!"

"That's not all, sir. After they threw ice water on them, the Yoopers beat their backs with birch boughs."

"Mark my words, Sergeant Major; they'll pay for this. I'm bringing them up on war crimes when this is over. No one treats Mad Dog Rottweiler's men like that and gets away with it... Any word from other units?"

"The radioman says he's getting garbled messages but nothing he can understand. He thinks the other units were scattered too far apart by the wind."

"Well, gather up what men we have. We're marching on Bear Creek. We can't wait for the entire division to arrive."

"But sir, with the radioman and me, we only have two enlisted men. How are we going to take Bear Creek?"

"Leadership, my boy. You two are being led by General Amos 'Mad Dog' Rottweiler!"

Iwo Jima, 1200 hours

Bart flipped through the pages of the Playboy magazine he had found in the officer's head. Hopefully, the briefing wouldn't take long. It was almost lunchtime and the mess steward had promised a batch of chocolate chip cookies.

The seamen in the briefing room were unusually busy, talking into headsets and adjusting monitor screens. One of them handed General Brackendorf a message. Brackendorf read the message and then discussed its contents with several of his senior officers. They were not pleased.

Brackendorf placed the memo in a folder marked top secret and waited for the other officers to take their seats. "Gentleman, Operation Greener Pastures is still on schedule, and I fully expect to wrap it up in twenty-four hours. We've had a few minor glitches, but we didn't expect this to be problem free."

"How minor are the glitches?" Al asked, well aware that minor glitches meant sizable drops in approval ratings.

"The 1st Battalion of the 126th Armor Regiment is running a little behind schedule."

"How little and how far behind?"

"They can't get past the tollbooth."

"The tollbooth? They were stopped by a tollbooth?"

The General's self-assurance began to falter. "The way I understand it, the lady in the tollbooth is the battalion commander's former third-grade teacher, and she won't let them through unless they pay the toll."

"Why don't they just pay the toll?" Al asked.

"They left their money and credit cards at Camp Grayling. It's a standard precaution in case someone is captured. They don't want any identifying documents on their person."

"What is a third-grade teacher doing in a tollbooth?" Bart closed his Playboy magazine. "This is fall. She should be back in school."

"Remember that education bill you vetoed last spring?" Al asked.

"Oh." Bart stuffed the magazine inside his shirt for later reading.

"This is ridiculous." Al began hyperventilating. "The battalion commander is sitting in an M1A1 tank. Why doesn't he just crash through the gate?"

"I believe he considered that, but his school teacher threatened to tell his mother. It's as if he's lost all common sense."

Bart and Al looked at each other. S.I.S.U.!

"General, is it possible Finland has an operational Sensory Inhibiting Satellite Unit?"

The suggestion caught the General by surprise. He adjusted his tie and wiped some sweat from his brow with a handkerchief. "We know Finland hasn't launched any satellites, but another nation could have placed one in orbit for them. A lot of nations are putting up satellites these days."

"I don't think we should read too much into this," one of the Air Force generals said.

"Let me remind you," General Brackendorf said, trying to insert a positive note, "the rest of the campaign is proceeding as scheduled. The marines we landed on the beach are moving inland after receiving an enthusiastic reception. Our assault forces have taken over Michigan Tech and Finlandia University without resistance and are moving into

Greek Row. It's been an hour since we last heard from them, but I can assure you, Greek Row is now under our control.

"What's Greek Row?" Bart asked.

"That's where all the fraternity houses are located," Al said.

"Gentleman, that's all I have for now. I suggest we return at 1400 hours for another briefing. I'll have my people check into that S.I.S.U. thing.

Bart raised his hand.

"That's two o'clock," Al said, anticipating the President's question.

Chapter Sixteen

Seney Stretch, 1330 hours

Light from the campfire danced across the General's reflective sunglasses as he sat motionless in front of the fire. If the General hadn't been roasting a venison steak, the Sergeant Major would have assumed he was asleep.

The Sergeant Major removed his boots and messaged his feet. He had a generous crop of friction blisters sprouting up under his damp socks. He hoped his socks would dry if he held his feet near the fire. The aroma from the venison steak at the end of his roasting stick momentarily diverted his attention. He had forgotten what a forced march could do to one's appetite. His mouth began to water. Venison was better fare than the MRE's they were issued.

"Sergeant Major, I been thinking." The General proclaimed his steak done and took a bite. "We should give the citizens of Bear Creek an opportunity to surrender. Much as I'd like a good fight, it's the only humane thing to do."

"Sir, our deployment here in the Seney Stretch may not be progressing as smoothly as it would appear on first impression."

"Nonsense, Sergeant Major, it couldn't be better. Here we are sitting around a campfire eating fresh venison steaks like a couple of Boy Scouts; and if I read the map correctly, Bear Creek is only five miles away. We should be there in two, three hours tops. After we take the town, we can commandeer the local hotel for our headquarters and have a hot bath... By the way, where did we get the venison?"

"The radioman got it. He thought as long as everyone was deer hunting he would give it a try. He bagged a ten pointer."

"The meat's a little tough, but still better than MRE's," the General said. "Remind me to give the lad a commendation when this is over... Where is the boy? He's supposed to keep us in touch with the rest of the unit."

"He was arrested, sir."

"Arrested?"

"By the game warden. Apparently, in Michigan you aren't allowed to use grenades during bow season."

"What about the radio? That's our link to the other units." The General swatted at a mosquito lunching on his bare arm. The tape on his uniform had not survived the forced march through the dense undergrowth, and now both shirtsleeves were ripped off, much to the delight of numerous hungry mosquitoes.

"The game warden confiscated the radio too... That's what I mean, sir. There are only two of us left, and we have no communication with the rest of the battalion. We have nothing left to fight with. When General Wainwright was out of food and ammunition at Corregidor, he surrendered. There was no dishonor in it. They awarded him the Medal of Honor."

"Surrender? General Amos 'Mad Dog' Rottweiler never surrenders. Must I remind you we have both food and ammunition? As long as you have your M-16 and I have my trusty pearl-handled revolvers, we will fight to the finish!"

"It was just a thought, sir."

"I have no intention of spending the duration of the war locked naked in a cedar box—with or without steam. Get your boots on... We have five miles to go."

USS Virginia, 1345 hours

"Sir, you wanted to be notified when we reached Marquette Harbor."

"We there already?" With the phone still pinned to his ear, Lt. Commander Wally Johnson switched off his CD player. It was time he earned his pay.

"No, sir, but we will be in five minutes." Lt. Sara Peterson hesitated for a moment. "Any change in orders?"

"No, Ms. Peterson… I guess we play this one by ear. Bring it up to periscope depth. Might as well have a look around to see what we're up against. I'll be there in three minutes." Johnson hung up the phone. This whole mission was giving him bad vibes. He wished his orders had been more specific. He still wasn't sure what he was doing in Marquette Harbor.

The Virginia had leveled off at periscope depth when Johnson arrived in the control room, and Lt. Peterson was doing a 360 on the periscope.

"Anything exciting?" Johnson asked.

"It looks peaceful, sir." Lt. Peterson stepped back to allow the ship's commander access to the periscope.

Johnson adjusted the periscope upward. He had a good ten inches in height advantage over his XO. She was also nearsighted. Johnson refocused the lens bringing Marquette's lower harbor into view. A 360-degree sweep revealed no significant traffic. Other than a couple of sailboats, there was none. Once he was assured no collisions were imminent, he began a detailed, systematic evaluation of the harbor.

A long concrete break wall extended out from the north side of the harbor, terminating in an automated navigational beacon. On the south shore a freighter was docked at a pier and off-loading coal. Johnson assumed the structure next to it was a power plant. A column of white smoke bellowed out from its chimney. Nothing menacing there… A small marina occupied the center of the harbor. To the left of the marina, an iron ore loading dock jutted into the harbor. The trestle leading up to the loading dock was missing; the structure was obviously no longer used.

"Down periscope."

Lt. Peterson gave the Commander her best what-do-we-do-next look. "Well? Sir."

"Looks pretty harmless." Johnson looked at his watch. It was 1350 hours. "Shall we take the boat to the surface and see what happens?"

"Aye, aye, sir." Lt. Peterson relayed the orders to the seamen in the control room, and the ship began to surface.

"Ship's on the surface," the helmsman sang out moments later.

"Ms. Peterson, will you please go up and stand watch...and take two seamen with binoculars. I'll be up as soon as I check with communications... I want to see if we received any new instructions."

Lt. Peterson volunteered two seamen, and the three of them climbed up the ladder, disappearing through the hatchway that led to the bridge on the conning tower. A loud clank echoed through the control room when they sealed the hatch behind them.

Johnson picked up the phone. They sent him halfway around the world to an American harbor in an inland lake to secure an obviously secure harbor by any means necessary. One would think COMSUB-ANT could have been more generous in providing details. The mission's birth probably developed over cocktails in the senior officer's lounge at the Pentagon.

A quick check with communications provided no further guidance. No messages from Norfolk. He was on his own. He had winged it before. He could do it again. Securing a harbor in the heart of America shouldn't be hard.

"Excuse me, sir," one of the seamen said. "The XO is requesting your presence on the bridge."

"Tell her I'll be right there." He was heading that direction anyway—after he stopped in the kitchen for a cup of coffee. He would pick up an extra cup for his XO. That would pacify her and make up for being late. Why did he have to pacify her, he wondered. He was the commander of the ship. Twenty-three years of married life will do that to a man, he decided.

"What's up?" Johnson asked upon his arrival on the bridge. He passed the hot coffee to his XO who accepted it without comment, as if she had been expecting it. He was pleased to note the sun was shining and the weather warm, no need for a jacket.

"See for yourself." Lt. Peterson passed a pair of binoculars to the Commander. "I don't know what to make of it."

Commander Johnson raised the binoculars to his eyes. Before him was an immense armada composed of anything and everything that could float—all heading in his direction. A menagerie of powerboats, rowboats, kayaks, sailboats, and personal watercraft were flowing out of the marina. One person in a wetsuit was paddling out on a surfboard.

"I'm not sure what to make of it either, but I suggest we breakout side arms for all the officers and the two lookouts."

"Aye, aye, sir." Lt. Peterson disappeared below and returned moments later with an armful of forty-fives and web belts. "Here's your weapon, sir." She passed weapons to the two lookouts who accepted them with minimal enthusiasm.

Johnson strapped on his weapon. "Hopefully, we won't need these."

"I don't see anyone with guns, sir. Just lots of people in boats, including women and children…and a few dogs." Lt. Peterson lowered her binoculars. "They look like people on a family outing."

Commander Johnson scratched his head, hoping to stimulate the gray matter into a plan of action. "Heck if I know what to do."

"Sir, maybe I should go down to the deck and greet them…sort of see what they want."

Lt. Peterson's plan seemed as good as anything he could offer, Johnson decided. "Take the two armed seaman with you…and be careful."

Lt. Peterson climbed down to the submarine's aft deck. The two armed seamen followed like a pair of reluctant puppy dogs.

The faster powerboats and personal watercraft were first to reach the USS Virginia and swarmed around the submarine like deerflies circling the head of a sweaty hiker. Some of the more courageous boaters began docking up to the rear deck of the submarine. They were waving coupons cut from the *Marquette Mining Journal*.

"Sir." Lt. Peterson said upon returning to the conning tower's bridge. "I found out what this is all about." Peterson handed a coupon to the Commander.

"They all have these?" he asked. Lt. Peterson held up a fistful of coupons. Commander Johnson looked at the coupon with an apprehensive eye.

Free tour and submarine ride on the USS Virginia, the U.S. Navy's newest nuclear attack submarine. The USS Virginia will not dock in the harbor. Individuals must provide transportation to the submarine. Bring coupon. Fireworks at dusk.

"There must be hundreds of them, sir. What'll we do?"

Lt. Commander Johnson stared at the coupon while he waited for his adrenaline to settle. "I suppose we'll have to put on a dog and pony show...but someone in Norfolk will hear about this when we return."

"Yes, sir."

"I want the crew in starched uniforms and clean shaven faces in twenty minutes. Secure all classified material. We'll give them a short ride around the harbor at slow speed...and on the surface. Give them a tour, but no one goes near the reactor."

"But sir, with this many people, it'll take all day."

"Is that a problem, Ms. Peterson? You got a hot date tonight?"

"Sorry, sir. I'll make the arrangements right away."

Commander Johnson watched his XO disappear down the hatch. He shouldn't have snapped at her. It wasn't her fault. Although, he did feel better now that he had done it. On the aft deck people were setting up lawn chairs and starting charcoal grills. It would be a long day.

Bear Creek, 1405 hours

Debris from the well-endowed pizza that had provided sustenance to the entire Yooper defense council covered the table. Moose had his eye on the remaining two pieces, and everyone knew better than come between Moose and an edible object. The map of the Upper Peninsula taped to the table was stained with pizza sauce, a victim of collateral damage.

The Yooper command center wasn't as elaborate as its counterpart on the Iwo Jima, but its members were just as dedicated. The Yoopers had the home turf advantage. Whether that would be enough Abigail expected to know within the next two hours.

They had set defensive measures in motion, and the Bear Creek foursome were now passive observers incapable of affecting the outcome. With fingers crossed, they monitored the battlefield hoping for the best. Newton, scrutinized encrypted messages from the aggressors with his electronic listening devices, while Sherlock and Abigail contacted informants by phone, looking for any tidbits of information. With nothing better to do, Moose ate the last two slices of pizza.

"What's so amusing?" Abigail asked.

Newton, with earphones clamped to his ears, was chuckling. "I'm picking up transmissions from the Mackinac Bridge. The 1st Battalion, 126th Armor Regiment has given up and is heading back to Camp Grayling. They don't sound like happy campers."

"One down, four to go. I think this deserves a toast." Abigail held up her can of diet root beer and clunked it against three other assorted soft drink cans. Of the five assault groups, the armored battalion had worried her the most. "Never underestimate the influence of an elementary school teacher."

"Let's not get carried away." Abigail took another sip of root beer. "We only won a battle; we need to win the war. Moose, call your friends at the Indian casinos again. We need another update…and, Sherlock, find out what's happening at Greek Row."

Moose and Sherlock pulled out cell phones and began dialing numbers. If they were to repulse the invasion, they needed to win all the battles. Moose hung up his phone and made a few notes on his clipboard. "I called five of the casinos. They report only limited action. I think it's too early to make an assessment."

Sherlock had better news. "According to my sources, the marines took Michigan Tech and Finlandia University, but…we stopped them cold at Greek Row!"

"Let's hear it for the Greeks." Four soft drink cans were again raised in salute.

USS Iwo Jima, 1400 hours

General Brackendorf is a little surly this afternoon, Bart decided. You would think a general at the doorstep of victory would be in a better mood. Bart took a sip of coffee and set the cup on the table. Much as he enjoyed the war, he was looking forward to evening when he could proclaim victory and put this matter behind him; the White House made better chocolate cookies.

General Brackendorf finished his conversation with the petty officer at the communications desk and stepped up to the small podium. His cheerfulness of the morning was gone, and he sagged at the shoulders. "Gentleman, it appears we had another setback. The marines that assaulted the Houghton-Hancock area," Brackendorf pointed to the Keweenaw Peninsula on the map, "have marched through the towns and have taken over the universities. Then they marched on Greek Row."

"That's a setback?" Al asked. "Sounds pretty good to me."

Brackendorf ignored Al's optimistic assessment. It was obvious he was not the bearer of good news. "Unfortunately, the fraternities were having toga parties…with keggers…and free beer." The general's voice began to quiver. "The marines never had a chance! I regret to say the marines are no longer a significant fighting force."

"How accurate is the information?" Al asked.

"We received two phone calls from marines at Finlandia University requesting early outs so they could attend school. Finlandia University offered them scholarships. Three marines called from Michigan Tech requesting information about G.I. educational grants. The calls are still coming in."

"S.I.S.U.?" Al asked.

"It's a possibility we can no longer ignore."

"What about the other units?"

General Brackendorf lifted his shoulders, trying to look more confident—it didn't work. "We're working in an intelligence vacuum. We haven't heard from General Rottweiler since he jumped last night. The marines we put ashore moved inland without resistance and should have linked up with General Rottweiler by now."

"Have we heard from the USS Virginia?" Bart asked. This was getting depressing.

"Good question, Mr. President." General Brackendorf paused, trying to think of a good spin to put on the answer. "We can't communicate with the submarine when it's submerged. We can instruct the sub to surface for a message, but we prefer to avoid micromanagement. We usually wait for them to contact us."

"What you're saying is we haven't heard from them either?" Al asked.

"No, sir." General Brackendorf looked at his staff for support. "I suppose we could send a Harrier jet to Marquette on a recon mission."

Seney Stretch, 1420 hours

Major General Amos "Mad Dog" Rottweiler pushed aside some tag elders as he plowed his way through the brush. The tag elders snapped back like carriage whips, hitting the Sergeant Major who followed a few paces behind the General. The tag elders weren't as bad as the wild raspberries and a multitude of other thorny shrubs that reached out and tore at their clothing. The General's shirt, already torn from his encounter with the tree, had to be discarded as a total loss. The General took the loss particularly hard since it was the two stars on his shirt collar that proclaimed his rank. The pearled handled revolvers and the mirrored sunglasses should make his rank obvious to the astute observer, he rationalized.

"Sir?"

"Yes, Sergeant Major?"

"I hate to appear ungrateful for all the army has given me…three dehydrated meals a day…a sixty-hour workweek…a first-class sleeping bag, and an occasional cold shower; but don't you think the army sometimes asks too much from us?"

"And your point is, Sergeant Major?" The General swatted at a mosquito that was taking advantage of his bare chest. Some insects had no respect for rank.

"Well, sir, I been thinking we have done our best…under the circumstances." The Sergeant Major cleared his throat. "The army can't expect us to do the impossible."

"Are you suggesting we surrender again?"

"The army couldn't fault us for it, sir. We have nothing left to give. In a prison camp we could provide resistance... like they did in that old TV series."

"How much resistance can we provide from a steam-filled cedar box? Must I remind you we would also be naked! Definitely not appropriate attire for a general. The barbarians might even take away my mirrored sunglasses. No, we will never surrender. We will fight to the finish. We will fight to the last soldier. And in the end, we will be victorious."

"I hope you're right, sir. But I don't see how the two of us can overpower Bear Creek, even though it is a small town."

"That does make it difficult. I had planned on a larger force." The General mulled over the situation for a moment. "We'll have to stick to the basics. First we'll surround them."

"Surround them, sir?"

"Right. You'll come in from the north with your M-16 on full automatic. I'll come in from the south with both my pistols blazing. It's the classic technique of shock-and-awe."

The Sergeant Major was already beginning to feel the shock. "If you say so, sir."

"Let's pick up the pace. I want to secure Bear Creek before dark."

Marquette Harbor, 1430 hours

The afternoon was unusually warm for early autumn, and for those individuals resigned to watching leaves turn red or geese fly south, the invitation to ride in a nuclear powered submarine came as a pleasant surprise. The School Superintendent declared a holiday, sending children home early. Mothers packed picnic baskets while fathers commandeered boats and any other floatable objects for the trip to the submarine.

The excitement was not lost on Hans and Ingrid Rantamaki or their five-year-old daughter, Virginia. Hans tried to call in sick, but was unable to reach his boss at the real estate office—his boss had called in sick. Ingrid packed a lunch of tuna fish sandwiches, potato chips, and soft drinks into a small cooler, while Hans tied the family's inflatable boat to the top of the car. Since Virginia couldn't swim, her overly protective mother strapped her into a life jacket. The life vest was a least one size too large and rode up on Virginia's neck like a cervical collar. Much as she tried, Virginia was unable to mover her head.

"Why do I have to wear this thing?"

"Because you can't swim."

"Why do I need to swim?"

"Because we're going on a big boat."

"Why are we going on a big boat?"

"So we can take a tour and see the inside of the boat."

"Why do we…"

"Can we get on with this?" Hans looked at his watch. It was two-thirty. "We're already late. I'm sure there'll be a big line."

"I'm working as fast as I can." Ingrid rechecked the straps on Virginia's life jacket to ensure they were snug.

"I need my Dolly." Virginia ran to her bedroom and returned with a large Raggedy Ann doll.

"We can't take Dolly." Ingrid grabbed the cooler and headed toward the door.

"I'm not going without my Dolly. Dolly wants to see the boat too."

"We don't have room for Dolly."

"Can we get on with this?" Hans asked. His patience was wearing thin. "We're late as it is."

"Well, I won't be responsible if Dolly gets wet. Virginia will have to survive without Dolly while Dolly's drying out."

With nothing more than a small electric motor to push the inflatable boat, the Rantamaki family arrived late, finding the USS Virginia already infested with Yoopers. A diverse assortment of humanity covered the submarine's fore and aft decks. Freshly caught lake trout sizzled over charcoal grills, sunbathers on beach towels absorbed a few rays, and senior citizens in lawn chairs discussed the declining moral values of the younger generation.

The submarine had been making small circles around the harbor at five knots, but this was reduced to three knots at the request of fishermen who found the higher speed too fast for trolling. It was still fast enough for kites on an otherwise windless day. Several exotic kites danced aimlessly from the boat's stern.

Overworked deck hands helped the tourists debarked from their small boats and directed them toward the back of the submarine where the tour began. A steady stream of visitors disappeared down a hatch on the aft deck only to reappear at a hatch on the fore deck after the fifteen-minute tour.

Hans found a vacant spot alongside the submarine and threw a line to a waiting deck hand.

"Welcome to the USS Virginia." The deck hand secured the line and offered to help them out of the inflatable boat. "The tour begins at the rear of the boat."

Hans passed Virginia to the deck hand. She clung tightly to Raggedy Ann, having won the family argument. Being an only child, she expected to win such arguments.

"How old are you?" the deck hand asked.

"Five." Virginia held up five fingers as proof.

"Well, I hope you enjoy the tour. The line begins over there." The deck hand pointed to a mob of people at the rear of the boat.

***

Lt. Commander Wally Johnson lay in his private wardroom with his eyes closed. He had taken two aspirin in hopes it would assuage his throbbing headache. As yet, he had no relief. Chopin was playing in the background. Maybe that would help him relax. Annapolis had not trained him for a tour guide.

But this was good experience for his XO, he rationalized. Putting Lt. Peterson in charge gave her valuable command experience. Some day she would command her own submarine. This would provide the confidence needed for such a command. He had no doubt she could handle any problems that might arise.

Johnson heard a knock on his door. He waited, hoping it would go away—it didn't.

"Yes," Commander Johnson said when he opened the door. It was Lt. Peterson. Her normally perfect hair was messed up, and her shirt partially pulled out from her trousers.

"Sir, how much longer is this going to go on?... I mean, there's no end. They just keep coming."

"Is that a problem?"

"Sir, we have charcoal grills on the deck, which is a fire hazard; we stopped twice because fishermen trolling from the back of the sub got their lines caught in the propeller; below deck we have kids running wild in the hallways; we're finding them hidden in closets and torpedo tubes; and we caught several teenagers doing cannon balls off the conning tower. Someone could get hurt."

Johnson looked at his watch. "It's almost fifteen hundred. It'll be dark soon. We'll give it a few more hours; then we'll find an excuse to quit. You can manage a few more hours, can't you?"

"Yes, sir."

"And do something about your hair and that uniform. You're representing the United States Navy."

"Yes, sir. I had a little problem."

"A problem?"

"Yes, sir. I was on deck, and one of the visitors tried to kiss me. He said he used to be a marine, but never kissed a sailor before."

"What'd you do?"

"I gave him a judo chop and pushed him overboard...told him his tour was over."

"In that case I believe we can overlook your personal appearance."

Lt. Peterson lingered in the doorway.

"Is there something else, Ms. Peterson?"

"Yes, sir. I've noticed items missing from my room."

"Exactly what is missing?"

"Personal items, sir."

"Ms. Peterson, we are both adults. Just what in particular is missing?"

"The top to my yellow bikini."

"I'm sure it'll turn up. After this is over, I'll have the men shake down the boat. It'll give them something to do. That'll be all, Ms. Peterson."

"Yes, sir."

***

Marine Captain "Black" Jack Barton looked out the cockpit window of his Harrier Jump Jet. At the moment all he could see were tree-covered hills. The leaves were just starting to turn. Fall comes early in the Upper Peninsula. According to his navigational instruments, Lake Superior and Marquette Harbor should be minutes away.

His mission was implausible: find an American submarine in the vicinity of Marquette Harbor. If it were running submerged, which is what submarines do, there would be no chance of finding it. Granted, Lake Superior water was crystal clear, but if the submarine were more than thirty feet down, it would be undetectable.

According to his GPS, Marquette Harbor should be coming up on his right. Barton tipped his wing to get a better view of the land below him.

"Black Jack to USS Iwo Jima, Black Jack to Iwo Jima, come in."

"Iwo Jima to Black Jack, go ahead."

"Marquette Harbor is in sight. I'm going down to check out the harbor, and then I'll search the surrounding area."

"Roger that, Black Jack."

"Black Jack, out."

Captain Barton eased back on the thrust, allowing the Harrier to coast toward the harbor. He was at ten thousand feet—too high to see anything. He coaxed the jet down to five thousand feet and began a slow circle around the harbor. A small ship, possibly the submarine, cruised at slow speed near the mouth of the harbor. Barton reduced his altitude for a better look.

"Black Jack to Iwo Jima."

This is Iwo Jima, go ahead, Black Jack."

"I found the sub. It's on the surface in Marquette Harbor. From the length of its wake, I'd say it's moving under its own power at three to five knots."

"Anything else, Black Jack?"

"Yes, the entire harbor is filled with small craft."

"How about the sub? Does it look OK?"

"Its decks are covered with people. It looks like civilians."

"Are they friendly? Does it look like the ship has seen any action?"

"Wait one, Iwo Jima."

Captain Barton brought the Harrier down to two hundred feet, making sure the jet wash did not damage any of the small craft below him. "Iwo Jima, this is Black Jack. The ship appears undamaged... There's a yellow bikini top flying from the periscope." Barton picked up his binoculars. "It looks like a D-cup. Yep, I'd say they've seen some action."

***

Lt. Commander Wally Johnson covered his head with a pillow. One more hour and it would be over. He turned up the volume on Tchaikovsky's 1812 Overture hoping to drown out the noise in the hallway. The cannon fire in the overture was unusually loud...and it shouldn't come in the first movement. The banging continued—obviously the door. Johnson opened the door to find Lt. Peterson holding a soggy Raggedy Ann doll.

"Sir, we have a problem."

As if he didn't know. "Aren't you a little old for dolls?"

"We have a missing girl, either kidnapped or fallen overboard. We found her doll in the water." Lt. Peterson held up the soggy doll. "Her parents are beside themselves."

"What's her name?"

"Virginia Rantamaki."

Commander Johnson turned off his CD player. People had no respect for classical music. "Get all civilians off the sub. Only a skeleton crew stays below deck. I want everyone else topside with side arms. We'll commandeer some of the powerboats, two armed seamen per boat. We'll search those boats one by one. If she's kidnapped, we'll find her. If she fell overboard...well, we can't do everything."

Chapter Seventeen

Bare Creek Gazette, 1510 hours

Silas Kronschnabell increased the torque on the flywheel's setscrew by an additional 12.4%, hoping the priest's assessment was correct. Just the same, he fortified his position before starting the press. He didn't need any long-term disability. Silas pulled down on the power switch from his hiding spot behind a cart filled with rags. The press creaked, groaned, and then sputtered into a full roar. It sounded healthy. Silas peeked out from behind the rag cart but didn't see any flying parts, always a good sign. The priest knew his machinery. Paper from the large roll at the back of the machine was weaving through a series of rollers that fed it into the press. At the front of the press, freshly printed sports sections were stacking up. He was back in business. Silas programmed the press for five hundred copies.

It would take most of an hour to print the sports section, plenty of time to finish his weekly editorial. Silas gave the press another once over and retired to his office. Previously, he had considered writing an exposé on the Department of Natural Resource's decision to develop snowmobile trails through residential areas in flagrant disregard for the personal safety and wishes of local residents, a subject in which Silas had strong feelings. No one should have to endure convoys of noisy snowmobiles racing past their bedrooms at sixty miles per hour day and night. It was little wonder so many Yoopers wished to secede from Michigan.

He had also considered taking the federal government to task for closing K. I. Sawyer Air Force Base, pulling millions of defense dollars out of the local economy. Now, if he correctly understood the wire service reports, the Department of Defense was conducting military exercises in the U.P., but they weren't spending any money in the area. They were importing provisions from other states. The Upper Peninsula would receive no benefit from the exercise other than additional litter on the beaches.

Silas booted up his computer, still unsure which editorial to write. Eventually, he would write editorials on both subjects. Perhaps he should postpone the snowmobile issue until winter.

"Excuse me, Mr. Kronschnabell." Karla was standing in the doorway chewing gum.

"Don't you ever knock?" Sometimes he wondered why he kept her around. Being his wife's favorite niece was a point in her favor.

"Sorry, the door was open. It seemed silly to knock." Karla examined her green fingernails. She could have seriously damaged a nail knocking on the door.

"What can I do for you?"

"Got a guy out front who wants to talk to you. He's kind of weird."

"Weird?" He was surprised Karla would recognize weird.

"Yeah, he's wearing combat boots, yellow polka-dot boxer shorts, mirrored sunglasses, and nothing else… He's carrying a white flag."

"What's he want?"

"Something about a mad dog."

Chief Cuwadin's Cozy Casino, 1515 hours

"Can I get a refill on my drink?" Major Gallagher leaned his M-16 against the bar. For reasons of safety, he had removed the magazine prior to his first drink. He didn't need any collateral damage on his military record. The paper work alone would be gruesome.

The bartender refilled the Major's glass. Good tippers got priority service. "Need more peanuts or pretzels?"

"No, thanks. I'm fine." Major Gallagher paid for the beer, leaving a generous tip. He needed to call headquarters. He would finish his beer first; the extra beer should make the call more palatable.

Gallagher downed his beer and wiped the foam from his lips with his sleeve. "Bar keep, you got a phone I can borrow?"

The bartender retrieved a phone from behind the bar. "Dial nine to get an outside line."

"This will be long distance, but I'll reverse the charges."

The bartender wasn't concerned. His boss paid the phone bill.

Major Gallagher dialed the number and thumbed his nails against the bar until a man identifying himself as Seaman Herrington answered the phone. Herrington was reluctant to accept the collect call and only did so after Gallagher threatened him with great bodily harm. Even at a distance, majors can be intimidating. Herrington connected Gallagher to General Brackendorf.

Iwo Jima, 1530 hours

The growing concern among the senior officers was not openly discussed, but there were no secrets aboard a small ship, and the doubts about Operation Greener Pastures spread through the ranks. The enthusiasm that had once been so prevalent began to dwindle. Men performing routine assignments now did so without fervor. Tempers flared and harsh words were frequently exchanged.

Depression was the pervasive mood throughout the control room where petty officers sat apathetically in front of their monitors, convinced their input no longer mattered. President Bart Schroeder was sitting at the conference table with his head in his hands, nursing a headache. It had not been a good day. He was the leader of the most powerful military in the world. Yet, eight hours into the campaign, half his forces were decimated. Evidence was beginning to accumulate that Finland did have a functional Sensory Inhibitory Satellite Unit. With a fully functional S.I.S.U., Finland could become the next super power. They could have a Finnish colony on America's northern border. It was enough to give any president a headache.

General Brackendorf was examining recent recon photos with his magnifying lens. Finally, he reshuffled some papers and stood up. "I suppose it's time we get this briefing underway." A weak smile belied an otherwise grim face. "I have some good news," General Bracken-dorf said, trying to put a positive spin on his briefing. "Even though we've had a few minor setbacks, our primary objective should be in sight. As you all know," General Brackendorf tapped his pointer at the center of an Upper Peninsula map, "Bear Creek is the epicenter of this uprising. We take Bear Creek, and the ball game's over."

"Can you explain again how we take Bear Creek?" Maybe there was still some hope. Bart was always the optimist.

"Yes, Mr. President. If you remember, we dropped General Rottwei-ler and his 82nd Airborne Division here on the Seney Stretch, just west of Bear Creek. They'll be attacking Bear Creek from the West. We also sent an augmented marine battalion ashore from the Iwo Jima. They're proceeding north and should have already linked up with Rottweiler's group. General Rottweiler, who will be in charge of the combined task force, plans to have the marines attack from the south. There's no way the little town of Bear Creek can counter such a force. Victory will be ours I can assure you."

"Have we heard anything from either force…anything positive we can feed the news media?" Al asked. They had reporters imbedded with the marines at Michigan Tech as well as with the armor battalion at the Mackinac Bridge. Al feared their reports could give voters the wrong impression.

"We haven't heard anything yet. We're assuming they're too busy, but I'm expecting a report any time." Brackendorf paused to sip his coffee. He wished he were half as optimistic as his rhetoric.

"General Brackendorf? I have a Major on the line two." A petty of-ficer offered a phone connected to a long cord. "He's quite insistent."

General Brackendorf: *Brackendorf, here.*

Major Gallagher: *General Brackendorf? This is Major Gallagher.*

General Brackendorf: *Who?*

Major Gallagher: *Major Gallagher…from the marines you put ashore at Epoufette.*

General Brackendorf: *Great guns! Are we glad to hear from you.*

Brackendorf covered the phone's mouthpiece. "It's the executive officer of the marine battalion we put ashore. I told you we would hear from them soon. I'll switch him to the speaker phone."

General Brackendorf: *Have you linked up with General Rottweiler yet?*

Major Gallagher: *Not exactly.*

General Brackendorf: *Where are you?*

Major Gallagher: *At the Chief Cuwadin's Cozy Casino in Sault Ste. Marie.*

General Brackendorf: *Sault Ste. Marie?*

General Brackendorf looked for Sault Ste. Marie on the map. It was in the northeast corner of the Upper Peninsula, at the entrance to Lake Superior.

Major Gallagher: *Yes, sir. Remember those Yoopers who met us at the shore with gifts?*

General Brackendorf: *Yeah.*

Major Gallagher: *They gave everyone casino tokens. As long as we had the tokens we figured it wouldn't hurt to try our luck at the casino.*

General Brackendorf: *You mean the entire battalion is at Sault Ste. Marie?*

Major Gallagher: *Not exactly.*

General Brackendorf: *You're testing my patience, Major.*

Major Gallagher: *I believe there's about ten of us here, sir.*

General Brackendorf: *Ten? Where's the battalion commander?*

Major Gallagher: *Well, sir, it seems each casino has their own tokens, and the tokens they gave us were not all from the same casino. Do you have any idea how many Indian casinos they have in the U.P.? The battalion is scattered all over the Upper Peninsula.*

General Brackendorf: *Your radio, Major. What about your radio! Can't you contact the other units with your radio?*

Major Gallagher: *Sorry, sir. Freeman lost the radio at the crap table...Sir, I was wondering. As long as I'm already here, would it be O.K. to hang around a bit longer? Faith Hill is giving a live concert tonight. They hired some of the boys as security guards.*

General Brackendorf hung up his phone. "I can't believe it. They were one of our best battalions, battle-hardened marines."

"S.I.S.U.?" Al asked.

"I don't know how else to explain it."

"What about the airborne unit? Any chance they could have been neutralized by S.I.S.U.?"

General Brackendorf shrugged his shoulders. "We need to consider that possibility."

"We still have that nuclear submarine…What is it? USS North Dakota?" Bart asked. "They have cruise missiles and everything. Fire off one of those babies, and they'll get everyone's attention."

"That's the USS Virginia." General Brackendorf decided it best not to mention how much attention the submarine already had. "We had Capt. Barton do a fly-by. He confirmed that the Virginia made it to Marquette."

"He said the Virginia was on the surface. We should be able to contact her by radio," one of the admirals suggested.

General Brackendorf turned to one of the petty officers. "Hook us up to the Virginia, and run it through the speaker phone."

"Aye, aye, sir." The petty officer changed frequencies on his radio. "Iwo Jima calling USS Virginia, Iwo Jima calling USS Virginia, come in."

Small voice: *Hello?*

"I'll take it from here, son." General Brackendorf set the speakerphone directly in front of him.

General Brackendorf: *Is this the USS Virginia?*

Small voice: *Yes, this is Virginia.*

"Is that a woman?" Bart asked. "I didn't know we had women on submarines."

"It's a pilot project. We have four or five submarines with female officers," Al explained. "They seem to be doing an adequate job."

General Brackendorf: *Do you have the situation under control?*

Small voice: *I don't know.*

General Brackendorf: *Have you taken any casualties?*

Small voice: *I don't know.*

General Brackendorf: *Is the Commander there?*

Small voice: *No.*

General Brackendorf: *How about the Executive Officer, is he there?*

Small voice: *No.*

General Brackendorf: *For Pete's sake, is anyone there?*

Small voice: *No. They're all looking for me. We're playing hide-n-seek.*

General Brackendorf: *Hide-n-seek?*

Small voice: *I shouldn't talk to you. Mommy doesn't like it when I talk to strangers.*

General Brackendorf: *Wait! Don't hang up.*

Small voice: *I have to go. Some one's coming. I need to hide.* (Click.)

Bart stared at the speakerphone in disbelief. "Is she really in charge of a nuclear submarine?"

"It sounded like she's regressed into childhood," Al observed. "It doesn't sound like anyone is in charge."

"S.I.S.U.?" Bart asked, hoping someone would provide an alternative explanation for what they heard.

No one offered a rebuttal. Everyone sat at the briefing table with blank stares. Finally, General Brackendorf rose to his feet. "Mr. President." Brackendorf paused while he tried to regain his composure. "Mr. President, it appears we are no match for their S.I.S.U. I am, therefore, recommending we recall our troops before it's too late."

"You mean surrender? Admit defeat?" Bart asked.

"Sir, not all problems can be resolved on the battlefield. Sometimes you have to resort to diplomacy."

"I think the General's right," Al said. "We can't continue… We'll provide a positive spin, of course. We can say you recalled the military to avoid unnecessary civilian bloodshed."

Bart felt a sudden craving for a chocolate chip cookie. He felt like taking a platter of chocolate chip cookies back to his room and getting wasted. "O.K., give the order." The President of the United States stood up and walked out of the briefing room.

Bear Creek, 2015 hours

"Well, that confirms it," Newton said as he removed his headphones. "All units are being recalled. We won."

It had been a long day. The four battle-weary veterans won the war, but no one had energy for a victory dance. The victory had not come without sacrifice. They had lost several days of school. Grades would suffer.

"Did we really win?" Sherlock asked. "We're no closer to becoming the fifty-first state. Everyone's convinced it was a Finnish plot."

Abigail sat down to rest her weary feet. Time for a cold one, she decided, grabbing a diet root beer from the ice chest. She took a sip and allowed her muscles to relax. "I think we won some of our objectives. The President has been placed on notice that we're a force to be reckoned with. That will give us more political clout in the future. People can at least find us on the map. They know there's more to Michigan than that mitten thing. Unless my guess is wrong, we can expect some political changes in the coming months."

Moose could care less about political clout. It was 8:15, and they hadn't eaten dinner. To make matters worse, the ice chest was conspicuously void of gastronomical goodies. He might have to run out for a pizza or some hamburgers and fries, not what he would call a victory feast.

"Hey, guys. I'm running out for a pizza. Pepperoni and sausage O.K.?" There were nodes of approval.

Moose headed toward the parking lot. His colleagues may be good at electronics and political ventures, but they totally overlooked the most basic of logistics: food. Everyone has his own priorities, he decided.

Moose returned moments later. "Hey, guys, you won't believe what's in the parking lot."

"Why bother to tell us if we won't believe it anyway?" Sherlock asked.

"No, you have to see it."

Abigail hadn't seen Moose this excited since he won a free ticket to an all-you-can-eat pig roast. "I'm not sure my feet can carry me up the stairs."

Moose wouldn't accept no for an answer. "Sherlock, Newton, let's go." Moose pulled Abigail out of her chair.

Abigail, Sherlock, and Newton dutifully followed Moose up the stairs and out the side door. The sun had set, and it took a moment or two for the quartet's eyes to adjust to the darkness.

A large circular table covered with a white linen tablecloth graced the center of the parking lot. Four white candles perfectly spaced around four long-stemmed red roses in a crystal vase provided illumination. A tall, muscular man in a black tuxedo stood off to the side. A white linen towel draped over his left forearm.

"And you would be Abigail, I presume," the man said.

Even in the dim light, Abigail could see the hideous wart dangling from his nose. The rest of his facial features were perfectly symmetrical. If it weren't for the wart, he would be a handsome man. "And you must be Agent X."

"I believe I promised a meal of the finest French cuisine if you were to win."

"I believe you did."

"I am a man of my word... And let me congratulate you on achieving the impossible."

"Thank you."

"I hope you don't mind, but I took the liberty of arranging place settings for four. If my research is correct, there should be four of you." Agent X pulled back a chair to assist Abigail to her place at the table. Moose, Sherlock and Newton managed their chairs without help. Moose found the large plate and multiple forks promising. This had to be better than hamburgers and fries.

"We will begin with a *Gigondas,* which is a robust, fleshy red wine from *vallée du Rhône.*" Agent X produced a chilled bottle bearing a French label. He carefully removed the cork and passed it to Abigail. "Note the sweet bouquet."

Raising the cork to her nose, Abigail closed her eyes to fully appreciate the fragrance. Satisfied, she passed the cork to Moose who sniffed at it a couple of times, licked it, and then passed it on to the others.

Agent X wrapped the bottle in linen and carefully poured wine into the crystal goblets. "The wine nicely complements the main course of *Noisettes D'agneau Caramelise a L'ail.*"

"What's that?" Newton asked.

"Lamb médaillons with garlic," Abigail replied. "If Tech would teach something other than math and science, you might pick up some culture."

"For an appetizer we have *Salade de Fruits Frais*, followed by *Potage de Poireaux et Pommes de Terre*, and for desert, *Tarte Fine Aux Pommes.*"

Newton gave Abigail a helpless look.

"That would be a fresh fruit salad followed by leak and potato soup, and a thin apple pie for desert."

Abigail turned to Agent X. "It's very gracious of you to provide this elegant French dinner, but I believe you also agreed to some minor plastic surgery in Marquette? We might be able to find some financial assistance."

"My dear, a promise is a promise. As for financial assistance, I have enough money in offshore accounts to buy Marquette. But let us not dwell on such mundane thoughts. I would like to offer a toast. A toast to hardworking, freedom-loving people everywhere." Agent X lifted up a goblet of wine. "I offer a toast to *sisu.*"

Epilogue

South Lawn of the White House, January 20

"O.K., folks, if you would please follow me. The White House tour will begin shortly. My name is Connie Rushford, and I'll be your tour guide... Just step this way please... Before we enter the White House grounds, we need to clear security." Ex-Agent Rushford paused to give several stragglers time to catch up with the group. "If you would please walk through the metal detector, we can get started. Give any hand-bags with keys or coins to Max Langston. He's the tall gentleman by the metal detector. He'll briefly check your hand bags, remove your loose change, and drive away with your car." No one laughed. Rush-ford could see it was going to be one of those days. "Just a little joke, folks. Actually he doesn't take the car."

"Oh, Miss." One of the tourists waved to get Rushford's attention. "Can you tell us when the President will be sworn in?"

Rushford looked at her watch. "It'll be another ten minutes. It's tak-ing place in the Rose Garden, which is our next stop. I'm told it will be a short ceremony. We won't see much of the Rose Garden until after the President leaves. The Secret Service agents will make sure we keep our distance. The Rose Garden is really quite pretty in the summer when the roses are in bloom."

"Mommy, I have to go potty." A young boy tugged at his mother's arms.

"Not now, Johnny. We'll miss the inauguration."

Rushford looked at the boy, who had his legs crossed and was doing the customary I-got-to-go-potty dance. "I think we have time for a short pit stop. There's a restroom right over there." Rushford pointed to the Visitor's Pavilion.

"You get to take him," the mother informed her husband. "He's your son."

Father and son returned five minutes later, the son now more relaxed.

"Has everyone gone through the metal detector?" Rushford asked. Everyone nodded in the affirmative except for the father and son, who were being scanned by Ex-Agent Langston.

"I guess we're ready." Rushford led her group toward the Rose Garden. "Off to our right is the East Wing, which houses the offices for the President's military aides. If we were to go to war, the President would conduct military activities from the situation room deep underground."

"Miss, is that where President Schroeder conducted the war against Upper Michigan?" one of the tourists asked.

"That was just a military exercise testing our ability to defend the homeland. I don't know how the media got the silly notion it was an actual war. The President conducted the operation from a small ship off the southern shore of Michigan's Upper Peninsula. If it had been a real war, I'm sure the Secret Service would have demanded he conduct it from his underground situation room where he would be safer."

To keep the inauguration simple, the President-elect had opted for a small ceremony in the Rose Garden. There was no snow on the ground, but it was still winter and only the evergreens flaunted any color. Folding chairs had been set up for approximately two hundred dignitaries. Behind the chairs, a yellow do-not-cross ribbon guarded by Secret Service agents separated the dignitaries from the common folk.

"We have to stay behind the yellow ribbon," Rushford informed her group. Other tour groups had already arrived, and a crowd was beginning to gather. People jockeyed for position. The ceremony would take place on a raised platform, but visibility would still be a problem for any vertically challenged individuals in the back row.

"I want to see,' Johnny informed his parents.

"There's nothing to see," Mom replied. "They haven't started yet."

"I want to see." Johnny had no intention of being placated. As an only-child, he expected to get his way.

To avoid the tantrum of an only-child, Dad raised Johnny to his shoulders. "Can you see now?" Hearing no reply, Dad assumed the affirmative. The ceremony was carried live by all the major networks including Washington's own Channel 7 News, which had graciously provided speakers for those in the rear. The Marine Band was entertaining the audience with patriotic music.

"This is Rob Carter of Channel 7 News taking you live to the White House Rose Garden, where the President-elect is about to take his oath of office. Although the sun is shining, it is still chilly."

The Marine Band, deciding they couldn't compete with Channel 7 News, finished their current piece and sat down to warm their bare hands.

"Mommy, I can't see the President."

"It's almost ten. They should start anytime now."

"In case you just tuned in, this is Rob Carter live at the Rose Garden, where we expect the President-elect to appear momentarily... The Chief Justice is now taking the stage... He will be administering the oath of office. And here comes the President-elect." Rob waited for the applause to die down. "He's not a very tall man, five feet two inches I've been told. According to a press release, the Bible they will be using belonged to the President-elect's grandfather, who was a small-town Methodist pastor back in the early 1920's. They are about to start so I'll switch over to the podium mike and let you hear the exchange between the Chief Justice and the future President of the United States.

"Mommy, which one is the President?"

"The short, fat one, dear."

"Will you raise your right hand and place your left hand on the Bible." The Chief Justice held out the Bible. "And repeat after me... I, state your name, do solemnly swear."

The President-elect placed his left hand on the Bible. "I, Walter Brainthorpe, do solemnly swear."

"That I will faithfully execute the office of President of the United States."

"That I will faithfully execute the office of President of the United States," Brainthorpe repeated.

"And will to the best of my ability."

"And will to the best of my ability."

"Preserve, protect, and defend the Constitution of the United States."

"Preserve, protect, and defend the Constitution of the United States."

"Ladies and Gentleman, I give you the President of the United States."

"Do we know him?" Johnny asked. "Is he from Pasadena?"

"No, he comes from a small town in Upper Michigan. It's called—Bear Creek."